Critical acclaim for Zoë Fairbairns' novel

STAND WE AT LAST

"A splendid saga...rich and absorbing."
Glamour

"Passionate, beautifully written, deeply moving."
Publishers Weekly

"A wonderful story...realistic, eminently readable."
The Guardian (London)

"A beautifully written story...A considerable achievement."
Philadelphia Inquirer

Other Avon And Bard Books by
Zoë Fairbairns

BENEFITS
STAND WE AT LAST

HERE TODAY

Zoë Fairbairns

AVON
PUBLISHERS OF BARD, CAMELOT, DISCUS AND FLARE BOOKS

First published in Great Britain 1984
by Methuen London Ltd.

Grateful acknowledgment is made to Mark Bunyan for
permission to quote from his song "Only Me." Copyright ©
1978 by Mark Bunyan. All Rights Reserved.

AVON BOOKS
A division of
The Hearst Corporation
1790 Broadway
New York, New York 10019

Copyright © 1984 by Zoë Fairbairns
Published by arrangement with the Author.
Library of Congress Catalog Card Number: 84-91188
ISBN: 0-380-89497-1

The Methuen London Ltd. edition contains the following British
Library Cataloguing in Publication Data:

Fairbairns, Zoë
  Here today.
  I. Title.
  823'.914[F]   PR056.A48

First Avon Printing, December, 1984

Printed in the U.S.A.

WFH 10 9 8 7 6 5 4 3 2 1

All characters and events in *Here Today* are imaginary. The same applies to companies and offices. If, despite careful checking, I have inadvertently used the name of a real person or business, I hope this unfortunate coincidence won't make anybody cross, embarrassed or litigious.

I was fortunate to have been writer in residence at three very different but equally supportive institutions while writing *Here Today*: Elmfield School, Bromley; Rock Hills School, Anerley and Deakin University in Australia. Thanks to them for their generosity and advice; and particular thanks to Elsbeth Lindner and John Petherbridge for their ideas, encouragement, patience, support, perceptiveness and tact.

Zoë Fairbairns

Contents

PART ONE

1 Temp of the Year   11
2 Taramasalata   17
3 Clients of Ours for Years   24
4 Do It Yourself   32
5 Voice of Calm   42
6 Madly Urgent   56
7 Original Sin   65
8 Appetite for Stars   74
9 All I Dreamed Of You Touching Me   82
10 So Nice To Me This Morning   89
11 User Friendly   95
12 Against the Cuts   106
13 The Recovery Section   115
14 A Good Time For Giving Up   125

PART TWO

15 HooRay Holidays   135
16 Jellyfish   142
17 It's My Job   149
18 Gypsy Dancing   154
19 Dead Stars   162
20 It Doesn't Matter What You Do   170

PART THREE

21 I Didn't Think So   177
22 Working It Off   185

23	My Fault	193
24	Temp of the Year	202
25	A Bit Big	208
26	Samantha	217
27	Catherine	225
28	Antonia	231

PART ONE

CHAPTER ONE

Temp of the Year

The entrance to Here Today_was a dark doorway off a Soho street, a tunnel with a frayed brown carpet. To the left there was a sex shop with a window full of plastic flesh, frilly underclothes and weapons. To the right a huge doner kebab revolved slowly in the window of a Greek takeaway, browning and dripping alongside a low heat.

Antonia was rehearsing what she would say while she waited for the lift.

It's just not good enough, Mrs Hook.

Would she dare?

Anyone would think I was still at school and you were the headmistress, sending for me like that.

Mrs Hook had always reminded her of a headmistress. That was what came of going to Here Today straight from school. Six years ago.

The lift didn't come. She walked up the stairs, passing the different firms that shared the building.

Oh Sir Jasper Books.

Campaign Against Harmful Additives in Tinned Goods.

Thames & Severn Enterprises.

Here Today Agency. Office Staff, All Grades.

'I've got an appointment to see Mrs Hook at three.'

The receptionist, whom Antonia had never seen before, put away her *Girl About Town* and said, 'Antonia Lyons?'

Antonia nodded and scowled. She was expected. Not just by Mrs Hook, by the whole office. By this newcomer to the firm whom she didn't even know but who said smugly, 'She sent for you, didn't she?'

'Did she?' Antonia unzipped her black trench coat and hung it with the coats of the permanent staff. Underneath she was wearing a blue, grey and pink fair isle jumper and a short grey skirt. 'She might have.' She took out a comb and tidied her hair which was light blonde and cut in a chin-length page boy. 'I was wanting to see her anyway. It's all right, I know my way.' She slung her bag over her shoulder and sauntered through the swing doors into the general office. It was crowded and noisy, though less so than Antonia remembered it.

'Avril from Here Today calling to check your requirements.'

'Such a nice girl coming for interview, Mr Harris.'

'*Didn't she?* Well, we'll send someone else.'

Everyone was on the phone, receivers nestled under their chins so that their hands were free to mark newspaper advertisements with red felt-tips at the same time. 'Looking for a copy typist, sir?'

Here and there despondent applicants perched on the edges of chairs, waiting. The staff seemed to have no time to talk to them. Each time a phone was put down it rang again. It seemed always to be someone looking for work.

'Nothing at the moment, Laura. Sorry, Laura.'

'Would you like to come in and register?'

'Try again tomorrow, Anne.'

It was five to three. Antonia looked round for someone who might be free to chat. Mrs Hook's PA, Maggie, was finishing a call. 'Nothing just now, Janet, sorry, Janet, *by-ee!*' Maggie had a deeply sincere voice and hard little eyes. Her glossy curls bounced as she beamed up at Antonia. Antonia might have been the last person she was expecting to see. 'Hel-*lo!*' Antonia nodded, lit a cigarette and offered Maggie one. Maggie declined, she'd given up again. 'How are you doing, Antonia?' she asked innocently.

'Starving, thanks. How come I'm not getting any work any more?'

'Quiet time.'

'Do me a favour.' Antonia wanted to stop herself – she hadn't meant to challenge Maggie. Just have a cigarette and a chat till it was time to go in to Mrs Hook. She knew Maggie didn't like her but she also knew that no one got the big freeze treatment at Here Today without Mrs Hook's agreement. Still, she might as well go ahead and find out what she could, now that she'd

12

started this. 'I'm her temp of the year, remember? That means I'm supposed to have first refusal on anything that comes in if I'm not working. Otherwise I might go somewhere else.'

Maggie raised her eyebrows. 'Maybe *that's* what she wants to talk about.'

'You know, don't you? You know what she wants.'

Maggie's phone rang. It was two minutes to three. Antonia smoked furiously while Maggie enthused: 'Oh Julie, I'm so glad you called. I've got just the thing for you.'

'Julie your favourite now, then?' Antonia snarled when Maggie had finished dictating an address.

'*I* don't have favourites.'

'What sort of mood's she in, Maggie?'

'The usual. You know.'

Antonia finished her cigarette. 'She's so two-faced. One minute she's all over you and you're temp of the year. Then she's treating you like something stuck to the bottom of her shoe. And you never know what you've done wrong half the time.'

'Have some juice,' said Mrs Hook. She waved at a tray with clean wine glasses on top of the tiny fridge which Antonia knew contained bags of raw vegetables and a carton of orange. Mrs Hook was in her fifties. She was very slim and had smooth skin. Her silver-grey hair hung like a straight veil across her brow and tapered boyishly at the back of her neck. She always wore black for the office, and silver or platinum jewellery. A notice on the wall (surrounded by photographs of her relatives and certificates of her achievements in the Personnel world) said, THANK YOU FOR NOT SMOKING IN MY HOME.

Antonia poured herself some orange. She craved hot coffee but it was not on offer. She wondered if she would like to look like Mrs Hook when she was fifty. Sometimes that fake youthfulness gave her the creeps, but it was quite an achievement. She poured herself a second glass.

'Steady on. That's got to last me all day.'

'Sorry – ' Antonia tried to pour it back through the opening in the carton, and made a mess on the tray.

'No, no, go on, have all you want. And come over here and have a look at this.' Antonia stood at Mrs Hook's shoulder; not a dot of dust or dandruff, not a single stray hair sullied the black wool. The picture she wanted Antonia to look at was of an electronic office, softly lit by unseen lamps. Elegant girls sat at word-processor keyboards, watching text come up on screens.

'Looks like a spaceship,' said Antonia. Mrs Hook chuckled and Antonia relaxed a little. 'I hate those things.'

'As well you might, dear, as well you might.' Mrs Hook turned her head and stared up accusingly at Antonia, as if shocked at her presumption in standing so close. 'Go and sit down, please. I've had some rather disappointing news about you.'

Antonia felt as if she had been hit. *Who told you?* The blood in her head screamed for nicotine. *Why do you have to know everything?* As she walked round to the other side of the desk she was imagining Mrs Hook fat, coughing and covered with spots.

But she might not know. She might be talking about something else. Antonia hung her head, letting her hair fall forward. When she looked up again her face was far back in the pale nest of hair. She felt safer because she knew she looked vulnerable, like a girl behind a veil.

Mrs Hook was having a real go at her. She kept saying 'my temp of the year!' She hadn't said what it was all about yet, but it wasn't what Antonia had feared. How could it be? How would Mrs Hook know?

' – asked Maggie to draw up a list of my six top temps. The reliable ones. The ones employers ask for by name. Naturally I expected to see your name on the list.'

Antonia reached surreptitious fingers into her bag and felt the cellophane of her cigarette packet for comfort. 'Maggie's never liked me.'

'Yes, I think she may be a little jealous of you, Antonia, you've always been such a favourite of mine. So I checked your time sheets, just to be sure. Goodness me. I couldn't believe my eyes. This can't be little Antonia Lyons, I thought. This can't be my temp of the year, letting me down like this.'

All right, all right, I'll tell you something. 'Mrs Hook, I've been ill.' *Could say that.*

'Late here! Left early there! Maggie didn't want to tell me – '

'I bet she didn't.'

' – but I forced it out of her. Inaccurate work! Surliness – '

'Mrs Hook, I've been – '

'Of course, it's no more than people expect from some temps. But my temps are not *some temps*. Here Today Means What We Say. Here Today. On time. In the office. Here *today*, now, in body and in spirit, paying attention and getting on with the job. I told Maggie to demote you from priority status.'

' – ill.'

'You've said that twice. Are you planning to tell me what was the matter with you? No? Why expect me to be sympathetic, then? Was it a nervous breakdown? It usually is, when people say they've been *ill* in cryptic tones like that.' Antonia shook her head. 'I'm so glad,' said Mrs Hook with a nervous, confidential laugh. 'I never know what to say when people have nervous breakdowns. What does it mean? How do you distinguish a nervous breakdown from just being a bit . . . I don't know.' Her tone became impatient, bored. 'I always think of people going all juddery – like a car that won't start – and dropping things.'

'It wasn't a nervous breakdown, Mrs Hook.'

'What, then? If it had been a nervous breakdown I'd have been sympathetic, but now it's beginning to look like sloppiness.' Her voice had reached a peak of irritation. Now it became gentle. 'The party's over, Antonia.' She smiled sadly, a single wrinkle appearing above each eyebrow. She pointed at one of the word processors in the picture. 'One of these can do the work of five Antonias.'

'If you're firing me,' said Antonia levelly, 'you could've said so on the phone.'

'How *dare* you? Fire you? As if I'd fire my temp of the year without giving her one last chance. I suppose it doesn't matter to you whether you work or not, with your husband to support you, and never mind if you spoil things for everybody else.'

There it was. A chance remark but spot on. 'I haven't got my husband to support me.'

'Pardon?'

'Paul's leaving me. He's moving out this afternoon.'

'Antonia,' said Mrs Hook after several seconds in which she seemed actually to lose composure, 'why don't you smoke one of your cigarettes?' And she brought forth an ashtray from a drawer.

The shock of this calmed Antonia as much as the cigarette did. Mrs Hook said she was sorry to hear the news and went on to express her lack of any intention to probe into what was none of her business. Then she paused expectantly. Antonia just smoked. Mrs Hook seemed to consider her duty done in the way of offering condolence, and returned to business. It might be a timely moment for a new career opening. She planned to set up Here Tomorrow, a word-processing temp service. She would send her best temps on a course and develop them into a crack team. Antonia could be a member of that team provided that, between now and the course, she proved herself worthy of the investment. Talk of word processors sped up the rate at which Antonia was smoking the cigarette. She had seen and heard a lot about them and didn't like any of it. The last bit of ash fell from the filter tip. Antonia's hand dived into her bag for another cigarette but Mrs Hook had whisked away the ashtray and was wiping it. 'Don't push it, Antonia.' Then Maggie was summoned. Maggie had probably been listening on the intercom if the truth were known but she came in looking bright and innocent till her piggy little eyes nearly came out on stalks at the smell of tobacco . . . Maggie was told that Antonia must be guaranteed work for the next four weeks; Maggie must monitor this work, asking employers for reports on Antonia's work and conduct. To crown it all, Mrs Hook dismissed the two of them with the words, 'Come back in a month, please, Antonia. And we'll see if you've improved.'

'What is this?' Antonia screamed. 'The doctor's, or the KGB?'

Maggie took charge and hustled her out of the room, trying to calm her down. 'It's just her way. You shouldn't let her upset you.'

'I'm not upset,' said Antonia, weeping.

'She really likes you, you know. *Nobody* gets four weeks' guaranteed work these days. And were you *smoking* in there?'

'You don't have to be nice to me,' said Antonia. 'I know you hate me.'

'Don't be daft,' said Maggie.

CHAPTER TWO

Taramasalata

She came up out of Balham station and started along the street. It was supposed to be spring but the evening was raw and it had started to rain. She remembered the peculiar taste of cigarette smoke in the clean air of Mrs Hook's office. She could still feel dried tears on her cheeks. She wondered if she had really told Mrs Hook what she could do with her word-processing course.

All the shops were closing and there wasn't any food at home. Home. The empty flat. What would he have taken and what would he have left? 'I suppose you expect me to do your packing!' she'd flared, terrified that he might say no, which he did. Calm after the savagery and anguish of the weekend that had just passed, he'd said, 'I think it'll be easier for both of us if you go out while I pack.' Managed on his own, had he? She'd see. One thing he wouldn't have thought to do was go shopping, even though he knew as well as she did that everything had run out. They'd gone hungry together yesterday, picking at odds and ends after fighting all day Saturday instead of going shopping together as usual. He enjoyed their Saturday shopping trips as much as she did but he reckoned anything that didn't get bought on Saturday, bought itself.

Mr Ali was closing down for the night. As he pulled the metal shutters down over his windows they showered him with accumulated rain. Someone had written PAKIS OUT in red spray paint on his wall.

Antonia said, 'I'd like to know where they shop when they get home late. Give me a cloth and some turps and I'll clean that off for you.'

17

He smiled: 'They will write it again if you do. Please hurry with your shopping, my wife is waiting to close.'

Mrs Ali, wearing cardigan and boots, waited while Antonia picked up a packet of fish fingers, a tin of sliced peaches, a small Hovis, apples and Coca Cola. At the counter she chose some magazines and sweets and asked if they had any taramasalata because she suddenly fancied some.

'It is with the refrigerated goods if there is any left.'

There was none. She paid for her purchases and went back into the street. She hesitated by a call box, went in and dialled her own number. It rang and rang. Coming out she tried the door of an off-license, but it wasn't open yet for some reason.

Lights glowed behind the doors of the other flats as she made her way to her own. Someone was cooking a fragrant stew, someone else was listening to 'The Archers'. She felt for her keys. The flat was dark and quiet but she knocked once before opening the door.

'Hello, Paul. I'm home.'

The central heating ticked. She sighed, closed the front door behind her, went to the bathroom and hung her raincoat to drip into the bath.

Half the steel rail gleamed where his towel had been, and his dressing-gown was gone from the hook on the door. Her own hung with drooping shoulders. His shaving shelf was empty except for a little smear of shaving cream which it wouldn't have hurt him to wipe up. He had managed to pour some bleach down the lavatory though. She put her teeth-cleaning things on the shelf and spread her own towel to cover the space on the rail. There was a dead fly in the wash basin. She stripped to her underclothes, avoiding the mirror, and put on her dressing-gown.

She sluiced the fly away and washed her face and hands, then applied moisturizer and hand cream. She wanted to hang up her jumper and skirt but she wouldn't go into the bedroom yet.

A phone bill had arrived and been picked up. PAID LAST WEEK, Paul had written. There was a postcard from friends in New York and a free newspaper which Antonia threw away.

The kitchen would be easiest, he hadn't exactly left his mark there. She was surprised to find he'd taken three of their six coffee mugs, some cutlery, glasses and plates. His mother wasn't going to expect him to provide his own things, was she? Then she remembered they were wedding presents.

The fridge was nearly empty: she couldn't miss seeing the single paper bag from the delicatessen. She took it out, tried to unbend the staple that sealed it, lost patience and tore the paper. Inside was a pot of taramasalata, pink and fragrant. She stared at it and put it down and picked it up and clasped her hands round it and unclasped them and the phone rang. She listened with interest. How did he know to ring at precisely the moment she found the taramasalata? He must be watching the block. He was certainly keen enough to get through. On and on he rang. The phone was in the bedroom by the bed. She had to sit on the bed to answer it. As she sat on the duvet, the air between its feathers puffed up all round her like a nest. The door of his wardrobe swung open in the draught. It was empty. She kicked it shut. How like Paul to go to all that trouble. To make it look as if he really meant to leave her. She'd thought he would stay away for a month at least, to frighten her and punish her. And now here he was ringing her up on the first evening. She'd be nice to him, but a bit cool.

'Antonia? It's Pat. Antonia?'

Antonia coughed and looked round for her cigarettes which were in the kitchen. 'Pat! I just got your postcard, I thought you were in America.'

Pat squealed. 'You *only just* got it? We've been back for *days*. Can you and Paul come round?'

'Tonight? Paul's away but I'd love to.'

'Well, I didn't mean tonight necessarily.' said Pat. 'Some time when you're both free, okay? Give me a call.' Pat waited expectantly and Antonia said, 'Did you have a nice time?' and Pat said, 'Yes, *great*,' and talked for five minutes and in the middle of it Antonia went and got her cigarettes and Pat was still talking when she came back.

The sitting-room radiators were tepid and the room was chilly. Antonia closed the curtains and turned on a bar of the electric fire. He'd taken the stereo, he'd have been in two minds about that, the fuss he made if she so much as moved a speaker when she was dusting. He'd taken his records, carefully weeding them out. He might as well have taken hers as well; what did he think she was going to do, sit and look at them? She took a few out of the cabinet, what wouldn't she give now to put on the cans and listen to the Bee Gees very loud and smoke a cigarette. She'd watch television later, he hadn't taken that: it was rented.

He'd taken all his books and files, including his file of articles on herpes.

How had she missed all the fuss? There were articles from her own magazines, but she hadn't seen them. Didn't *want* to see them, Paul had said, bit near the bone when you're screwing around –

Near the bone. Ha ha very funny when the articles said the virus lurked in your spine when it wasn't out gobbling your flesh into great sores where it hurt most and the best you could hope for was that it would be happy in your spine and wouldn't come out too often to do it again, which it could at any time.

'I was *not screwing around!*'

'*One man* is screwing around if you're a married woman and that man isn't your husband!' He had a way of putting things. To be fair, he hadn't gone on at her while she was really ill. He'd looked after her, secretly doing his research and saving it all up for last weekend, though even last weekend he'd had moments of being kind. 'Do you think I don't wish it wasn't true?' The taramasalata, that would have been another of his kind moments too: it would have dawned on him that she would be hungry and would appreciate something special. Not that he'd thought to get olives or bread or salad to go with it, but still. A little treat for her. A gesture to show they were still friends. 'We're not enemies, Antonia. But you're my wife. How can I live with you without wanting you? But whenever I want you now I get this great *disgust* –' And fear. He wouldn't say that, though she couldn't see why not. He'd seen what she'd gone through, any sensible person would be afraid. There were precautions you could take, but – 'Why should I risk it? Why the bloody hell should I? Married people shouldn't have to worry about these things! Whoever he was I hope you damn well enjoyed it because it's going to have to last you a long time!' Five years, the articles said, to develop a cure. Or possibly ten. He had a way of knowing things. He was an information officer for a local authority. 'What do you do?' 'I'm an information officer.' 'Does that mean you know everything?' 'No, it just means we know where to look it up.'

Her hair was still wet. She dried it with her hair dryer, sitting in front of the fire and watching a film about a bank robbery. She smoked. After a while she returned to the kitchen and fried two fish fingers, eating an apple as she cooked. She heard gunshots and screaming from the sitting-room and ran back to see what was happening in the film. When she looked at her fish fingers again they were turning black so she tipped them into the flip-top bin. She ate taramasalata for her supper, straight out of the pot with a spoon, with slices of brown bread and Flora. She decided to save her last cigarette to smoke while she watched the news, but when the news came on she found she had already smoked it.

The Iron Duke was packed. She got change from the bar and fed it into the cigarette machine, coin after coin, and a packet of Silk Cut fell out. A man behind her said, 'Bad for yer 'ealth, love.' and she came back quick as a flash with, 'You're a long time dead,' but when she turned round with her cigarettes she couldn't identify who had spoken, she couldn't tell if they'd heard her reply. She liked to give as good as she got.

She had to push through a tight packed crowd of men to get to the door. They looked like a rugby club, all brawny and wearing the same tie. She said, 'Excuse me,' and they said, 'Excuse her, go on, excuse the lady,' and, 'Why, what's she done?' and Antonia smiled and hung her head and looked up at them through her eyelashes and her fringe and they let her through.

Six girls were sitting at a table near the door. Antonia recognized someone she'd once temped with.

'What are *you* doing here?'

'Only came in for a packet of fags. What are *you* doing here?'

'We're having a girls' night out. Judy – that's Judy, Judy, meet Antonia – Judy's getting married tomorrow and we all came down here to give her a sendoff. D'you live round here or something?'

There was a pile of money in the middle of the table. One of the girls scooped it up and took orders for another round of drinks. She asked Antonia what she'd like.

'No, it's a private party,' said Antonia. 'I won't butt in.'

Kathy said, 'See, Judy, what did I tell you about getting married? Antonia's married and she's not even allowed to stay

21

and have a few drinks.' Everyone laughed and Antonia joined in a little. They chorused, 'Don't go,' and, 'Stay, we're teaching Judy the facts of life,' and one of them began, 'Any friend of Kathy's –' and another interrupted, ' – needs all the friends she can get,' and they fell about laughing, eyes bright in the warmth of the pub, and one of the rugby players said, 'Keep it down, girls,' and Antonia sat and asked for a lager and lime because the girls liked her and wanted her to stay. She couldn't even contribute to the kitty, she'd only brought money for cigarettes, but she passed these round and the girls said it was all right, this was their last drink, they had to get Judy home to build up her strength for tomorrow.

They stayed till closing time. Out in the cold street they said, 'How do we get home from here?'

'Yeah, Judy, you made us come down here, how do we get back to civilization?'

Judy winked at Antonia. 'Better call a rickshaw, hadn't they?'

'You could all come back to my place,' said Antonia, 'and have coffee and call a minicab.' She wanted to take their brightness and warmth home with her. But they said they'd better get a tube. 'Sharing a minicab's cheaper sometimes,' she said, but they worked out that it wouldn't be because they were all going to different places.

She hadn't wrapped the burned fish fingers before putting them in the bin and now the smell filled the flat. She took out the bin liner, sealed it with a bit of wire and went to take it to the dustbins outside. A second before the front door slammed, she put out her hand to stop it and went back into the flat to collect her keys.

The night was quiet apart from the occasional dripping of the gutters. Cats ran from her approach as she hurried towards the shadowy area where the dustbins stood. She had never seen them at night. She took the lid off her and Paul's bin, the newest, and found that one of the other residents had used it. Vegetable peelings, wet newspaper and dirty tissues lurked at the bottom. Antonia was furious. Everyone was supposed to have their own bin. She threw in her carefully sealed bag and her keys went too. She heard them plop into the mess at the bottom of the bin. She pulled out the bag but she couldn't see

22

the keys. She rolled up her sleeve and felt around, finding them. Holding them in front of her and scarcely breathing, she ran back to the flat. She dropped the keys into a bowl of Dettol, then turned on the hot tap and ran water over her hand until the flesh turned pink and she couldn't stand it any more.

Looking for her lighter to smoke a last cigarette, she found an envelope in her bag that she had not noticed before. It was a letter of introduction to a firm in Covent Garden, Anderson & Lee, plc. Here Today must have given her a job.

CHAPTER THREE

Clients of Ours for Years

Shortly before nine the following morning a small queue formed at the unstaffed reception desk of Anderson & Lee. As the clock flipped through 0901, 0902, 0903, the woman three from the front took out the time sheet that her agency, which was called Bright Girls of Mayfair, had given her, and ostentatiously wrote '9 am' as her starting time. Then she opened her *Guardian* at the foreign news page and read with an air of great absorption. People who kept you waiting didn't always like you to read, she had observed. She always read if she was queueing to pay in supermarkets, and she had once reached into her bag for a book while lying in the dentist's chair because the dentist had been called away to the telephone. 'If you're quite ready?' he'd said when he came back, taking the book out of her hands.

She was thirty and she wasn't really a temp, she was a teacher who had just been made redundant. She had wondered whether she ought to do something about her clothes if she was going to pass herself off as a temp, though she didn't want to spend the money. Then she'd found a copy of *Options* on a train and read that classics were all right this year, classics apparently being expensive versions of the sort of thing she had preferred to wear to teach in anyway because nothing a teacher wore would satisfy teenage students, you might as well let them dismiss you as a frump and get on with it. Today she had on an old tartan kilt, a cream Arran sweater and a suede jacket. She was five foot ten and always wore flat shoes. None of the other women in the queue (she assumed they were all temps) was particularly well dressed either. Couldn't afford it, probably. Except for the little blonde one at the front who was the type Catherine used to envy when she was her age and (she told herself) cared about such things. Not that there was anything remarkable about the belted black raincoat and matching pink scarf and leg warmers, they just looked cheerful and appealing. She was the type who would look lovely in anything.

At last a security man arrived and devoted a great deal of time to arranging things on his desk and doing up his bootlace. He responded to the young woman's polite 'Good morning' with an unnecessarily churlish 'What's good about it?'

'*I've* arrived. What more do you want?'

'And who are you when you're at home?'

'Antonia Lyons. Here Today.'

'And gorn tomorrer?'

'Thanks. One point to me.'

'Eh?'

'Every time someone says "gone tomorrow" we get a point. Whoever gets the most points in a year gets a free holiday for two in the South of France. Want to come?' The youth looked nonplussed. Catherine was enjoying herself. One of the things she liked about London was the spunky wit of its working people. She wondered whether the blonde woman was always this sharp or if it was put on and if so why. If she'd been with Here Today long she probably found 'gone tomorrow' jokes every bit as tedious as Catherine found the inevitable response when she, in different circumstances, revealed her origins. Even the interviewer at Bright Girls of Mayfair, glancing down her c.v., had announced, 'I have relatives in Rhodesia myself. I wonder if you know them.' Catherine had replied as she always did: 'It's called Zimbabwe now,' and the interviewer had said, 'I don't blame you for getting out.'

Bright Girls of Mayfair's logo, draped across its time sheets and its ungrammatical letters of introduction – 'Introducing Miss Catherine Lambert whom we trust will be of satisfaction' – was a dewy-eyed, bowler-hatted nymph. Who on earth was supposed to identify with that? At last week's job she'd introduced herself with the words 'I'm a bright girl of Mayfair', but she didn't propose to try that on this wise guy, even supposing she did ever reach the head of the queue. The agency was in Moorgate, for heaven's sake. Not that it didn't strive to

25

make up in pretentiousness for what it lacked in geography. Thick pile carpets. Fake antique desks. And while the interviewers asked loaded questions about your skills ('Fifty words per minute shall we say?') they made notes under headings like 'appearance' and 'speaking voice'. What other kind of voice was there? Singing voice? On a scale of one to ten Catherine had been awarded five for appearance and nine for speaking voice. She was both exasperated and delighted. Her voice was supremely phony. She practised BBC English each night with the World Service news. She thought she sounded awful but at least when she met left-wingers they no longer accused her of being South African.

Antonia Lyons' voice could be the voice of thousands of office girls from homes in London or its lower-middle-class suburbs, halfway between BBC and what Catherine's parents' expatriate English friends would have called Gorblimey, mingled with a touch of mid-Atlantic picked up from disc-jockeys. Beneath her wisecracking she seemed eager to please. But she hissed her s's sharply when, the youth having picked up his phone and begun, 'I've got a Miss Lyons here – ', she interrupted: 'Mrs'. Catherine was surprised.

'*Mrs* Lyons. From Here Today.' He paused. 'Yes ha ha that's what I said and got a flea in my ear. Right. Will do. You're in Legal, Mrs Lyons.'

'Which way's Legal?'

'There's lots of ways that's legal, Mrs Lyons,' he said, deadpan. Then his grin spread like a sunrise. 'Depends how you like it.'

Antonia's shoulders froze. She accepted the youth's directions in tense silence. As she headed towards the lift Catherine saw her profile. It had the small-featured delicate prettiness Catherine had expected but the cheeks were flushed, the mouth tight, the eyes angry. Good, thought Catherine. Antonia Lyons is making her protest.

Catherine was sent up to Legal too, but she was not in the same room as Antonia who was with the typists. Catherine was in filing. Her companions were three middle-aged women and a teenage girl. Catherine took her place beside them, facing a row of shoulder-high filing cabinets. Various documents were spread out on top of the cabinets like playing cards. Over by the window a man with a bald head had the B drawer on his lap, and was going through the files and calling out names, which were in random order apart from the fact that they all began with B. Every time he called a name, Catherine and the others had to look quickly through the papers on top of the filing cabinets, which were also randomly arranged, and see if they had the name to match.

'Beeston Electronics, anyone? Bowen, Mrs J? Boots the Chemists?'

'Bingo!' said one of the women, handing over a document wound in red ribbon. This was obviously an old joke. 'No, not Bingo,' said the bald man. 'Mrs J Bowen. *Thank* you. Banstead? Billison, Byers, Blair, Buxton.'

Catherine couldn't contain her impatience. 'Wouldn't it be better if we sorted them into alphabetical order first?'

'No time for that,' breezed Mr Parks, returning the B drawer to its slot in the cabinet and starting on the Cs. 'Crampton, Cooksbridge, Crewe Carryout . . .'

'Crewe Carryout!' exclaimed the teenager.

'Nice to see you're alive, Sheila.'

'It's a wonder, Mr Parks, the diet I'm on. All I've had in the last twenty-four hours is a tablespoon of olive oil and a carrot.'

Catherine found all this very interesting, sociologically. Sheila reminded her of one of her students. Not one of them, all of them. What would they be doing now, last year's leavers? The same as Sheila. If they were lucky.

'I'll take you up the canteen,' said Sheila at lunchtime. Catherine agreed, though what she really fancied was a solitary hour on a bench in Covent Garden with a bag of crumbs for the pigeons.

Sheila fetched a plate of shepherd's pie for Catherine and another for herself. She chattered endlessly. 'Want to know what I did at the weekend? Friday night – stayed in. Saturday night – stayed in. Sunday night – went down the pub with my mate, she's crying her eyes out because she thinks this bloke she goes round with's going to pack her in.' Catherine took small mouthfuls and recoiled from the flavour of powdered potato. 'Then this other bloke gets chatting to us and he asks for her phone number and do you know what? She gives it to him.'

In the afternoon Mr Parks started getting in a state and phoning round for help. 'We've got a panic on in filing. Got any girls to spare?'

A number arrived, Antonia Lyons among them. Mr Parks asked her if she minded giving a hand with the filing, being as she was a typist. Antonia smiled politely. 'It's all in a day's work for a Here Today temp.'

Catherine was disappointed in her.

At a quarter to five everyone started taking turns to go to the toilet for a long time. At five they put on their coats. Antonia worked on, spreading a new pile of documents over the tops of the filing cabinets. She seemed to be in some kind of gloomy dream. When someone pointed out the time, she said, 'I thought it was five-thirty we finished.'

'Glutton for punishment,' crowed Mr Parks.

'I could do some overtime.'

'Can't leave temps to work unsupervised, unfortunately. It's more than my job's worth.'

'You mean I might put my feet up and not do any work?'

'Rules is rules, no offence meant.'

'None taken.'

Mr Parks put his coat on, winding a tartan scarf round his neck and spreading the ends to keep his throat warm. He had dust all over his trousers. Catherine's sweater was grubby too, stupid to wear cream, but Antonia's frilly white blouse seemed spotless. 'Night night, girls, see you tomorrow.'

Catherine fetched her own coat; Antonia was still sorting papers. She said defensively, 'It'd be much quicker if they were in alphabetical order.'

'*Wouldn't* it? Why don't you tell them? Parks didn't take any notice of me, but coming from two of us –'

'No fear, I'm keeping my nose clean.'

'But it's a *good* idea.'

'Yeh, but don't you find they hate it when you come in as a temp and on your first day you start telling them they're doing it all wrong, even if they are?'

'*Particularly* if they are, I would have thought,' said Catherine. 'Actually, I'm not really a temp. I'm a teacher.'

'Oh.'

'Look, it's five past five, you really ought to stop. And I've got to go to Bright Girls to pick up last week's money.'

'To where?'

28

'Awful, isn't it?'

'Here Today pays the same week. I hate to leave a job half done, why don't you give me a hand while we're talking?'

'No, I've got to go.' It was hard to get away. Antonia's neatly-manicured fingers sorted busily as she explained about an ultimatum her agency had given her about her work. Catherine listened with increasing outrage. 'So you're expected to do four weeks of unpaid overtime to prove you're suitable to learn a machine that's going to exploit you even more effectively!'

'I don't see it like that.'

'How, then?'

'I like temping.'

Tired and angry at the futility of the day's work, Catherine hurried towards Bright Girls. She supposed there were reasons why a woman might prefer to temp. Particularly if all office jobs were as bad as this one. And if Antonia Lyons was married, the insecurity might not be a problem. Still, she disturbed Catherine. There was something forlorn and distant about her, something pathetic about the firmness with which she declared, 'I like temping,' as if someone had argued. Was she still working? Ridiculous to suppose she would get any credit for it even if she were. Catherine toyed with the idea of ringing up that agency herself – Here Today? – and reporting what a diligent worker Antonia Lyons was. And getting her on to a word-processing course? That was what she wanted. Catherine sighed and scolded herself for rationalizing. It wasn't that simple. Antonia had other reasons for staying in the office. Catherine had seen it but refused to acknowledge it; she had seen it dozens of times at school: a child, usually but not always a girl, hanging around after four, spring-cleaning her locker with an air of great purpose or offering to carry books but really wanting company and not wanting to go home. Catherine had loved to be the one they would talk to. She had refused to be Antonia's confidante because she had had enough of Anderson & Lee for one day and she wanted to get her money. She didn't even have urgent need of the money – they'd have posted it to her. She just didn't like to have tasks hanging around, she didn't like untidiness in her life.

'Temporary Staff are requested to check their money before signing for it as –'

– as we sure as hell won't give you another penny once your name's in the book.

'BGM jobs are open to all applicants, irrespective of race, colour, sex or creed –' That 'or creed' was a dead giveaway: who in London in the 1980s discriminated on the basis of creed? Who asked about creed, who even had one? But it oiled the cliché nicely.

Catherine's money was 5p short. She was about to sign for it when a little calculation occurred to her. Say BGM had five hundred temps. If each of them was 5p short and thought it too petty to say anything, it would be a nice little tax-free bonus for somebody. She gave the clerk a look that said, 'You're rumbled,' and counted her money again.

While she was doing this the phone rang.

It was Mrs I-have-relatives-in-Rhodesia Harmsworth who answered it. She listened for a moment, then assumed an expression of bored exasperation. She put her hand over the mouthpiece. 'It's Samantha Yardley,' she said. All round the office, lips curled.

'Oh Samantha, dear, how are you?' Another pause; another hand over the mouthpiece. 'Guess what? Samantha doesn't like working at Forlex. She wants to be sent somewhere else.'

'Surprise surprise.'

'So what else is new?'

'She says she's walked out,' said Mrs Harmsworth.

Someone who appeared to be in charge said, 'We can't have that. She's done it once too often. Tell her we can't help her.'

'Samantha, dear. You can't expect us to just – there's lots of girls only too willing to – now don't start crying. I can't hear what you're saying if you cry, dear. Oh. Oh. Well don't tell me, dear. That's a matter for the police.' She glared into the phone with an expression that suggested Samantha had rung off. She did so herself. 'If it's true.'

Curiosity bristled on the faces of all the staff. But they wouldn't ask. Catherine fumbled her money with an expression of great calculation. Mrs Harmsworth couldn't contain herself any longer.

'Says she was raped. I told her straight. Tell the police. Don't tell me.'

'At *Forlex?*'

'They've been clients of ours for years.'

'She should be so lucky.'

'Are you all right?' the wages clerk asked Catherine.

'I'm short.'

'How much?'

'5p.'

The clerk took a 5p coin out of her handbag and presented it ceremoniously. 'Okay now?' With no further excuse to remain, Catherine went home. She had a lot to do this evening: three sets of minutes to write up from the various groups she belonged to – her women's group, Teachers Against the Tories and Amnesty International.

CHAPTER FOUR

Do It Yourself

Catherine ate cheese for supper and settled down to her minutes. But she couldn't concentrate. Stray phrases drifted into her mind, phrases that might give her some clues as to what kind of person Samantha Yardley might be.

It could be an aristocratic name. *Lady Samantha Yardley is to marry Prince Edward.* On the other hand, she'd had girls in her classes called Samantha. *Stop that, Samantha Yardley, and pay attention.* Or a famous name. *A new film starring Samantha Yardley, an exciting new novel by . . . Samantha Yardley, you have been convicted of a serious offence. The body has been identified as that of Samantha Yardley, of no fixed address.* Address. Now there was an idea. Catherine reached for the S–Z phone book. There were about sixty Yardleys in various parts of London, not counting the cosmetics firm.

Could she? Why not? The minutes could wait and this might be urgent. She decided on a casual approach. She would ask for Samantha, not Miss or Mrs Yardley. Then if her mother or flatmate or even husband answered, Catherine would just sound like a friend. If she hit on Samantha herself she could quickly explain: *You don't know me and I don't want to interfere but –* It wouldn't take that long to phone sixty people; there would be no need for a long interchange once it was clear she'd got the wrong place. She'd start with the As and work systematically down the list. No reason to attach special hope to the S. Yardleys, for what were the chances of a temp having a telephone registered in her own name? *You're a temp,* she retorted to herself, *and you've got one. All right, split hairs. Straight to the S. Yardleys.*

But neither the S. Yardleys nor any of the other Yardleys was able to help. 'Who?' they barked. Each Yardley sounded more irritable than the last, and Catherine had the uncanny feeling that she was getting through again and again to the same household. Either that or they were all one family and telephoned warnings to each other, which would explain the occasional engaged tone, or the more frequent no reply. She imagined groups of Yardleys, sinister and criminalized, or clucking with genteel indignation, gloating at the ringing phone: *here she is again*, they said. Once, excitingly, someone said, 'She's still in hospital.' 'I know,' said Catherine, thinking fast. 'We want to send her some flowers and we've lost the address.' They directed her and her flowers to a maternity ward.

It wasn't nearly as quick a job as she'd hoped, and when the replies started to get really angry she glanced at her watch. It was long past eleven. No minutes done but she decided to call it a day. She opened up the folding sofa that was her bed, filled a hot water bottle, made a pot of tea and took a quick shower while she waited for the tea to draw. With relief and disgust she watched the dirt of a day in central London flow off her and down the drain. She had Anderson & Lee to look forward to in the morning.

Little specks of spit and blood spattered the mirror as Antonia, getting ready for bed, drove a taut string of dental floss up and down between her teeth, grinding it into her gums. From a foil packet she pressed out a tablet of disclosing dye to show up plaque. She chewed it, swilling the dye round with water. When she bared her teeth again the whole inside of her mouth was as red as a vampire's. She squeezed toothpaste on to her brush and scrubbed till her mouth overflowed with pink foam.

She rolled her tongue into a tube, tilted her head back, jerked it forward and spat the mixture of blood and dye and saliva and toothpaste at her reflection in the mirror. Then she spread it on the walls, rubbing it into the white wallpaper with her hands.

When she got up the following morning it looked as if a murder had been done.

She scrubbed at the red marks and a corner of wallpaper started to come away. She grabbed at it and pulled. Fragments of plaster fell to the floor, the whole place was coming down.

She couldn't leave it like this. She couldn't come home to this. She wondered if Paul had taken his do-it-yourself things. She checked the cupboard; everything was intact.

She was late for work. She was in no state for work; she was shocked and frightened at what she had done; what if she started pulling down walls there? It would serve Anderson & Lee right. It would serve them right if she didn't go in today. They'd hired her as a shorthand typist and put her on that stupid back-to-front filing with that awful old man and that snobbish head prefect type to whom she had nearly told everything. She'd wanted to, it was the sort of thing you could only tell a stranger, but only if they didn't know your name and there was no chance of seeing them again. She hadn't said a word, thank God; but she felt embarrassed at the idea of seeing Catherine again, who might even have guessed.

A shorthand typist, damn it. Not a filing clerk. Not a word-processor operator. Why did everyone keep wanting to change her? At school they'd said shorthand and typing was all you needed, she'd worked hard at it, it was the only thing she could remember working hard at, typing especially, it was lovely having a machine she could learn how to control. Once they were learning how to change ribbons and Antonia had changed hers without needing to be shown, it was obvious how to do it, you just had to look.

She went out and bought wallpaper stripper and two tins of cheerful yellow paint. It was ten o'clock by the time she got back. She heard the phone ring as she came up the stairs but she didn't hurry. It would be Anderson & Lee wondering where she was. No it wouldn't, they hadn't got her phone number. They would have phoned Here Today, and that was who it would be. She hurried, practising.

I'm not well.

Well enough to get to the phone, Antonia.

She wasn't falling for that one.

And she wasn't going back to Here Today either, to be ordered about and told off. Never. They could get down on their knees. The phone stopped.

She changed into her painting clothes, cut-off brown cords and an old Capital Radio sweatshirt with holes under the arms. She'd got it by phoning up during a request programme and answering a simple question. All the girls in the office had dared her: 'Hello to Paul and everyone who knows me,' she'd said over the air. Paul, whom she'd only been going out with at the time, had missed it.

She tied her hair into bunches, turned on the radio and slapped stripper over the rest of the wallpaper, tearing and scraping and bundling it into a black bin liner. She heard a sound outside the front door. Post, Jehovah's Witnesses, burglars? A message from Mrs Hook, perhaps? A key turned. She switched off the radio and bounded out into the hallway: 'Paul, oh Paul.' She reached up to hug him and he looked back numbly, fending her off with a kiss on the cheek and a gesture at her dirty clothes, his own clean ones. A fine rain of dust was falling from her, like talc when she was getting ready to go out. He was in his office clothes. His hair was blond like hers but his was nearer golden, hers was nearer white. And he was the one with the curls.

'What's going on? What's all this mess?'

'It'll get worse before it gets better,' she said quickly. 'That's what you always used to say to me when we did decorating together, remember? Listen to me! Anyone would think we'd been separated for ten years –'

'Why? *Why?* Why have you pulled the wallpaper off the bathroom wall, Antonia?'

He was furious. She panicked and bowed her head but her hair was tied and wouldn't fall forward so she looked at him through her eyelashes instead. There was no getting round his anger which might even have an edge of fear to it as if he thought she'd gone mad, like hell she had. Who was he to say what she could do with the flat and what she couldn't? Had she asked him to leave it? 'It's something to do,' she said.

'Something to *do*? Haven't you got a job?'

'Only a stupid one.'

'It's finished, you mean?'

'I'm finished with it.'

'What a bloody mess.'

She tore off more wallpaper, flinging the wet bundle at his feet which he moved out of the way, mumbling, 'I didn't expect you to be here.'

'What did you come for, then?'

'I – er –' he wandered off towards the kitchen. 'I had a bit of a disaster last night. Put some milk on to heat and forgot about it.

Burned one of Mum's best pans. Lot on my mind.'

'Poor old Mum.'

'She said it didn't matter, but it's part of a set.'

'Oh.'

'Very similar to the ones Pat and Phil gave us for . . . I only need one. All right if I take one? Where are they?'

'Usual place.' How would he know? Couldn't even heat up milk. She heard him clanking about. He appeared in the bathroom doorway with one green pan in his hand. 'All right if I take this?'

'They're half yours.'

'Antonia –'

'They're all yours, actually. Pat and Philip are your friends, not mine. She rang up. Wanted us to go round and look at their slides of America.'

'What did you tell her?'

'That you couldn't come and she said forget it. Anyway, I'm just passing on the message. I see you kept your key.'

'It's my flat.'

'Put me out on the street then.'

Suddenly his face crumpled. For all his neat suit and his briefcase and his we-information-officers-know-where-to-look-things-up, he could collapse like a little boy. She'd seen it before but not often. The first time was when she became ill. He wasn't used to illness and her pain terrified him. The second time was when they found out what it was.

She'd often teased him about his lovely hair, said it was indecent on a grown man, looked like something a fond mama refused to have cut. Now she wanted to ruffle it and ruffle it and shove a chocolate in his mouth. The green saucepan dangled from his hand like a toy. He gulped. 'How are you, love?'

How are you? That was what strangers said, or friends who hadn't seen each other for ages.

'All right.' As he knew.

'Of course I'm not going to put you out on the street.' He had his composure back, he wasn't going to cry, he wasn't going to change his mind either. He was repeating his plan for a separation that would be as painless as possible in the circumstances. He didn't want to bring lawyers into it yet. They were grown people and they weren't enemies. (He could've fooled her.) He would keep up the payments on the flat for the time being while she saw about getting a proper, permanent job. Then they would see about the divorce and decide which of them was going to live where.

'You used to say my being a temp was a good compromise—' she began hopefully. It hurt to speak and she didn't know why she bothered, her last reminiscence hadn't got her anywhere, had it? *You ought to know, Antonia, before you marry me. I don't really approve of working mothers. Oh, neither do I. Not when the children are small.* Lovely fair-haired babies they'd have had. With brain damage.

'If I didn't find you so desirable,' he said softly, 'it might not matter. We could live as brother and sister—'

She wished he wouldn't say *desirable*. She wished he would say *sexy*.

The student had called her sexy. She refused to give him his name now, he was just the student. Student, what of? Literature, he'd said. Trust him to say *Literature* and not just *English*. And his thesis. Metalanguage and Byron. What that was when it was at home she still couldn't say and she'd typed it, finishing it with him at three one morning because he'd been messing around, he admitted, all the time he was supposed to be writing it and tomorrow was the deadline and all his work would be wasted if she didn't agree to help him get it in, *save my life* he'd said. *Will your husband mind? Shall I talk to him and convince him my intentions are honourable? They are, you know, and even if they weren't there isn't going to be time for any hanky panky* —

Hanky panky! Metalanguage! And then, *sexy. You look so sexy in the moonlight, Antonia. You can't go home at this hour, you can have my bed.* They'd opened the window to dilute the smells of coffee and work and cigarettes. It was a sharp winter's night and she'd shivered. He'd brought her a jacket and then not taken his hands away.

She'd loved him, of course. She wasn't the sort to have one-night stands with people she didn't love. Love, love, love, she was a person who could love others, she knew that, and Paul trusted her or he'd never have let her go, he'd never have guessed, it wouldn't have hurt him. Stephen couldn't have known what he had. That was his name, Stephen. She'd loved his cleverness and his determination to get his work done and the way he needed her and the way he admitted she'd have made a better research student than him because didn't being a temp take a similar kind of self-discipline to make a success of it and there was he, scrabbling around at the last minute, and there was she, temp of the year?

He'd been laughing at her.

A student forgodsake living off the income tax I pay week after week and Paul pays week after week so he can get some posh job and get other things and give them to some agency typist it doesn't matter to take a chance with –

She followed Paul to the front door as if she were saying goodbye to a guest. He carried his briefcase in one hand and his saucepan in the other. 'We'll give each other a breathing space,' he said.

Was she supposed to hope, then? She hunted round for something nice to say. 'Thanks for the taramasalata.'

'That's all right.'

'You're very thoughtful.'

'We're not enemies.' He kissed her cheek. He smelled of soap and the smell was all he left.

She bundled more wallpaper into the black plastic bag. It was perfectly good wallpaper too.

She had to have a job. Otherwise not only would she starve, she'd go crazy alone in the flat, pulling down wallpaper. Nothing would induce her to go back to Here Today now that she'd fouled up her chances at Anderson & Lee. She'd have to find another agency.

Catherine served three and a half weeks at Anderson & Lee. Three and a half weeks of Mr Parks' bizarre filing practices and fondness for calling her Cathy. Not that she minded first names, if used in full, but his seemed deadly secret. She had glimpsed his signature once and his initial was J. She thought about it. She had to think about something. James? John? Jeremy? *Next time he calls me Cathy, I'll say, And what's YOUR name, Mr Parks?* But she didn't. She lost her nerve. She had no nerve for anything. She considered putting an advertisement in a personal column somewhere: *SAMANTHA YARDLEY. Have You Been Raped? Contact* – She must be joking. She'd get all kinds of crank replies and probably end up raped herself. Anyway, what magazines did Samantha Yardley read? *Honey*? The *Tatler*? The *TLS*? On and on droned the interminable soap opera of Sheila's friends packing people in and being packed in by others. Such talk among her students used to enchant and intrigue her but now she had no right to feel distanced from it. She was part of it.

Suddenly the job ended. The flood of papers dried up with no indication as to why. 'We'll have to send you off to seek your fortune somewhere else, Cath,' said Mr Parks genially. 'Goodbye Mr Parks, and all the best,' she said. 'Call me Jason,' he replied.

She had a glorious day off, tidying the flat and listening to schools programmes on the radio. This made her sad after a while so she turned it off and read a new Virago Modern Classic. She couldn't concentrate. She looked up Forlex in the telephone directory. It was a NW1 address: Architectural & Engineering Consultants. (What had she expected, Rape & Sexual Harassment?) She didn't know whether to be pleased or sorry to find the place was real. It gave her a funny feeling to dial the number and hear it ringing in . . . in a perfectly ordinary office probably. When somebody answered she hung up, for what on earth would she say? Perhaps she'd pop round one day and have a look.

The women in her women's group fumed to hear that she'd been sacked without notice. 'Yes, they packed me in,' said Catherine, 'that's temping for you.' The friendliness of their indignation was welcome but if they thought she wanted the right to work out notice at Anderson & Lee they had another think coming. She told the group about Samantha and they wondered if she'd thought of phoning a rape crisis line for advice.

The call had its comic side. Lynn, the counsellor, took her cue from opening words that counsellors doubtless often heard – 'It's not about me, it's about a friend' – and proceeded with tremendous kindness to try and win Catherine's confidence. 'Our service is absolutely secret,' reassured Lynn, 'so you see I couldn't tell you whether your friend has been in touch with us or not.'

Antonia registered with five new agencies. They were full of promises but none of them came up with anything so she was able to finish the bathroom. It didn't look too bad at all, though she wasn't sure now about the yellow and it might have been better if she'd known how to put up lining paper instead of painting the bare plaster.

As she registered with more and more agencies she started getting odd days of work here and there, enough to keep going but only just. She went to the unemployment office and was shocked at how little money she was entitled to. If she wanted more she had to go to social security. But that would be as bad as asking Paul for money or going back to Here Today. She chose social security. Yes, they said, politely enough, they could top up her benefit, but they questioned her closely about Paul. She explained that he was keeping up the payments on the flat and she didn't want anything else from him. That's all very well, they said, but he's a liable relative. I don't know where he is, said Antonia. Don't worry, they said. We'll find him. Forget it, she said. She'd give up smoking. That would be worth a bit.

Bright Girls of Mayfair had, for the time being, nothing further for Catherine. She spent her time doing voluntary work, applying for teaching jobs and trying to maintain a cheerful attitude in the silence that followed. Occasional supply teaching came her way and when she left she would give her phone number to students who in her opinion would benefit from free private tutoring. They never took her up on it but she was glad to have offered.

She took on all her women's group's paperwork. She kept careful notes on her experience of unemployment with a view, perhaps, to submitting an article to *Spare Rib*. (Actually she could write a book but she would not presume to think that far.) And Mavis Ngonzi was still in prison. Mavis Ngonzi was the amnesty group's political prisoner. Catherine wrote every day to the South African government, urging her release and wondering how it felt to hold lives in the palm of your hand in Pretoria and be pestered about them from Hornsey. To Mavis herself she sent supportive notes and parcels containing soap, books, underclothes and tampons. She had a feeling that the tampons, besides being useful in themselves, would render the parcels less liable to confiscation. One night she had a gloomy fantasy about Mavis dying of toxic shock syndrome and becoming a *cause célèbre*.

She fought off depression with a strict nine-to-five working day. But she didn't make herself dress up. Mostly she wore a boiler suit from Laurence Corner. If anyone came to the door she would pretend to be embarrassed but really she thought she looked appealingly eccentric. Not that anyone was likely to come; she had never encouraged dropping in. People who said 'drop in any time' mystified her. Could they possibly mean it? If they didn't, weren't they taking the most terrible risk in saying it? If they did it must mean that they never did anything important or private in their homes: never had baths or read good books (or wrote them) or cooked souffles or made love or talked to themselves.

Catherine rarely made souffles, and as for making love . . . well, the chance would be a fine thing. Or would it? It did nothing for her self-esteem to know that it was not high principle – either Christian or feminist – that left her a thirty-year-old virgin, likely, in the fullness of time, to be a forty-year-old virgin and ultimately a dead virgin, but simple lack of opportunity . . . opportunity being that coincidence of time, place and mutual desire that had always eluded her but seemed such a commonplace in the lives of others. The women in her women's group, for example, debated the relative merits of men versus other women, as if it were a daily practical dilemma for them.

She thought a lot about food too, and ate rather less. Her knowledge of nutritional theory was more influential over her choice of meals than any appetite or preference. She had to watch herself. If you were at work, you tended to eat to be social. Alone she was capable of omitting food for whole days. Sometimes she wondered if she might be suffering from anorexia nervosa, she was certainly very thin, but she was conscious of no desire to be so. She wasn't repelled by food, it just didn't interest her. Even her stern resolution to eat a bowl of muesli each morning fell into disuse when a stone from the stone-ground oats broke one of her teeth, necessitating several trips to the dentist.

Not until Bright Girls of Mayfair rang up with a job for her did Catherine realize how cosy she had become. They wanted her to be a temp controller at their Moorgate office. One of their permanent staff had gone on maternity leave, and they always liked to fill in, where they could, with one of their own better-spoken temps.

41

CHAPTER FIVE

Voice of Calm

An itch, an ache, a tingle. Was this it coming back, or was it just frustration, loss?

Mustn't think about it. If ever there was a part of your body that responded, changed, with what you were thinking.

There was no way that she knew of controlling dreams.

Go on Antonia go on baby love darling let me let me –

She woke, groaning with disgust.

No style. No finesse. Naked need, arrogant demand, she could have been anyone. She turned on the radio.

All I wanted was to touch you, all I dreamed of you touching me, silly really, touching people only human, only me –

How desperate was she going to get and what on earth would she end up doing? She thought of stuff she'd read about doing it to yourself. Well of course I can, she thought in bewilderment, but what would that solve? You might as well suck a strong peppermint to take your mind off needing a three-course meal.

Thousands of people living in London's bedsitter jungle may be at risk from fire. In just a few hours the Prince and Princess of Wales will be setting off for their holiday retreat. And that's the news at two o'clock, good morning London.

Capital Radio, playing all you want to hear.

There must be lots of people who didn't have it, ever. Even married people. She'd read that. Married couples went to the doctor because the wife wasn't getting pregnant and the first thing the doctor had to do, before trying tests or anything, was to check that they were doing it right. He'd produce diagrams and plastic models and demonstrate and half the time it would turn out they'd been married for years and they hadn't done it properly once and apart from not having a baby they'd been perfectly happy.

Hello Mike this is Angie from Croydon –

And then there were nuns and people like that.

And ugly people who'd never in their lives been fancied but who probably had the same feelings as everybody else.

Hello Mike this is Angie from Croydon you don't know what it means to me to be able to talk to you Mike I haven't slept for seven months no really –

And people who were paralysed, there was an organization for them, Sexual Problems of the Disabled, SPOD.

And people who were married to people who didn't want to or couldn't but who loved them so much that they said, if it comes to a choice, having sex or having you, it's you, you, every time.

A chilly start to the day with rain this afternoon. Town-bound commuters can expect delays at the Polish war memorial. Here are this morning's cancellations from British Rail. London Transport running smoothly. So there's no excuse for being late for work.

If you're not going to work, settle back and listen to the Commodores.

Antonia went to the doctor's to ask for sleeping pills, but she caught her hands trembling in the waiting-room and walked out. If the doctor remembered what she'd come about before and guessed she was in a bad state he might think she planned to finish herself off. And it would be one of those conversations where if you denied it it proved it was true and if you didn't deny it it proved it was true. She looked in the medicine cupboard. Kaolin and morphine from last year's summer holidays. Morphine was a sleeping drug but didn't kaolin do something to your bowels? Fine thing if she was in deep sleep and they started playing up. Night Nurse was better, Night Nurse was best, knocked you doped into a heavy sandhill of sleep, really it wasn't right such stuff being available over the counter, someone ought to put a stop to it.

Hi, Antonia, you and Paul want to come to a party?

Paul wasn't telling people either, then. And everyone was

43

having parties. There ought to be some way of announcing it, like when they got engaged and Ruth, Antonia's new step-mother, put an announcement in the *Guardian*, not that anyone read it there. Antonia wouldn't mind going out, she longed to go out and cheer herself up a bit, if only she wouldn't have to tell people, if only she knew they knew, and they knew not to say anything.

One good thing about the fares going up again was that you could save yourself quite reasonable sums of money by walking a little distance. A couple of miles saved the price of a packet of cigarettes. She couldn't give up cigarettes. When she went to the unemployment office to sign on, she was tempted not to declare the days she'd worked, but she always did. This cut into her benefit but she didn't want to end up in prison as well as everything else. She gave up buying magazines but she still looked at them in shops and wished she was going to be able to afford the summer fashions, the summer holidays.

The day the phone bill arrived she had a job to go to which should last three weeks so she didn't worry about it too much. She put the bill aside and put on the clean dress she had prepared the night before. The job was from Max's Staff Bureau. The client was a West End dress shop with a backlog of invoices and letters needing to be typed. Another girl had been meant to go from Max's but she hadn't turned up. Max's were anxious that Antonia should restore the firm's good name. She checked her handbag (Kleenex, make-up, cigarettes, *A–Z*) and practised saying, 'Good morning. I'm from Max's Staff Bureau. So sorry about yesterday's misunderstanding.'

There was no separate office entrance, so she went in through the shop. It was hushed and dim, lit through chandeliers. It specialized in furs, jewelled evening dresses in protective plastic bags and good thick tweeds. None of the stock on display bore any price tickets. The saleslady wore a grey suit. 'Can I help you, madam?'

Antonia said where she was from. The lady said, 'But you're here.'

'Pardon?'

'The girl who was meant to come yesterday. She's arrived. At least, I *think* so. Just one moment, please, I could be mistaken.

44

And even if I'm not, we might be able to use two.' She went away, leaving Antonia alone in the shop. A customer came in, a tall, lean man with a deerstalker hat which he removed. Antonia said, 'Someone'll be along to help you in a minute.' He grunted and fingered a fur. The saleslady returned, noted his presence with her eyes, and said to Antonia, 'We can't use you, I'm afraid. So sorry you've been inconvenienced.'

'I'd be willing to – '

'Can I help you, sir?'

Paul always paid bills on time. The phone bill had special priority. 'It's the one thing,' he used to say, 'that they can cut off with no inconvenience to themselves and a lot of inconvenience to you.' She realized that she would have to phone him. His mother answered.

'Is that you, Antonia?'

'Yes.'

'I've been wanting so much to talk to you. But I didn't like to ring.'

'Yes?'

'I mean, I hope you and I can still be friends, dear. I'm so fond of you.'

'Yes. Is Paul there? I mean, thanks.'

'I'm not going to interfere. But if you could call some other time? He's in a funny mood. I think he might have been drinking.'

'I've got to talk to him now.'

'All right, dear. I'll go and get him.'

She heard footsteps, voices and the sound of the phone being picked up. He breathed in and out, waiting, but he didn't speak.

'Paul. I've got this phone bill.'

Now why did she do that? Straight into the phone bill without a hello or a how are you. Like cashing a cheque at the bank. Serve her right if he banged down the phone.

'What do you expect me to do about it?' He must know. She couldn't read his voice. His mother had said he'd been drinking. That was new. He drank less than Antonia did and used to kid her about visiting her in the alcoholics' home. Had he been drinking because he was sad? She'd never seen him sad until she made him sad.

'Thing is, I'll never get a job if people can't ring me up.'

'Get him to pay it then.'

'Who?' She was so shocked that the question *who?* was out before she could think. He meant the student of course. The student could pay because she'd slept with him. She was a prostitute, that was what Paul meant. The line crackled. *Who?*

He said, 'You mean there was more than one?'

Never, never, never had she meant to let him know that. She hadn't lied – it just hadn't come up. Sure there'd been more than one, but if she wouldn't say the number it wasn't just because she didn't want him to know. *She* didn't know. They were people, not numbers.

'More than one?' She tried sarcasm. 'There were hundreds, Paul. I thought you realized that.' Make him feel guilty. If he'd believe that – of course there hadn't been hundreds. It wouldn't even make double figures, she was sure; she'd count up when the conversation was over.

It wasn't over yet. 'Antonia, please tell me something.'

'What can I tell you? You're the information officer.'

Now why had she said *that?* Catty to the end. He might have been about to say something kind, to try to understand.

Whether he had been or he hadn't been, he wasn't now.

'What was he like?'

'Forget the phone bill, Paul.'

'Why? Send it to me. Send it to Lord Muck.'

'It's not – '

' – my responsibility? Of course it is. It's all my fault, I didn't fuck you properly so – '

She hung up. Paul never said that word. She'd got the wrong number, it wasn't Paul, it was an obscene caller. Laughter gurgled out of her like vomit, *she'd* phoned an obscene caller and given him more than he'd bargained for.

Properly?

Of course he'd done it properly. (He knew everything.)

She counted up. She'd been right, it didn't make double figures, even if she included the ones before she met Paul which even he admitted were none of his business.

I know you're experienced, Antonia, so am I. I don't hold it against you, may I hold this against you?

That old joke.

Didn't matter how old it was, she loved jokes in bed. Hearing them or making them. A good giggle after an orgasm. Or before

46

or during or even instead of.

Her first time after marrying Paul had been with an off-duty steward from an airline.

She remembered a conversation in the office, full of jokes and challenge, but she still didn't remember exactly why –

'We don't just serve drinks, you know.'

(What had she said to bring that on?)

'I know. You deliver babies too.'

'We're trained for every emergency.'

'All right. You're 30,000 feet up. There's a funny noise from the engine and the pilot drops dead. Can you save the passengers? *Can you land the plane?*'

'Sure.' She couldn't tell at first if he was kidding or not. 'At least, I can look it up in the manual of instructions.'

It turned out they did actually have a manual of instructions on the flight deck, reminding the pilot how to fly the thing.

She'd become hysterical. 'Like a washing machine. If engine emits knocking sound, rearrange load –'

'I've been thinking. I'd like to go to bed with you.'

'What? I'm married.'

'Have a fling.'

Concorde, she'd thought of calling him later. *Long and thin and faster than sound.* (She didn't, of course. She didn't because that wasn't the point, or at least the whole point. Two travellers getting close for an hour, that was the point. Making each other smile.)

Under her smile as she went home was, *why did I do that?*

She'd got away with it, though. And having got away with it, she'd never seen any reason to say no to other chances, if she wanted to say yes. Was that why? Because she could get away with it?

Paul's mother rang back. She wasn't going to admit to overhearing anything but she wanted Antonia to know that if there were any problems (she didn't say financial problems) that she could help with, Antonia was to be sure to ask. Antonia had often wondered whether something about her showed that she had never really had a mother. Her own had died in an accident before she could remember, and many women, from her childhood and even her more recent life, had been terribly kind to her, in ways that were both touching and embarrassing.

People had been amazed when her father married Ruth. Antonia had suspected that Ruth herself enjoyed her own family's shock. 'Coming down in the world' were the words she used, lacing them with laughter to show that that was only what *they* said. It had been quite romantic in its way. Antonia's father used to keep a newsagent's shop, he'd gone to the annual Christmas party of his confectionery wholesaler and started going out with the managing director's daughter, who was divorced.

Antonia didn't know what attracted them, but you often didn't in other couples. Her father was entitled to a bit of love and he seemed to be getting it. And Ruth had fixed up an office job for him, and it was probably nice for her to have a man around her Surrey house again, a father for ten-year-old Rex. They had a child of their own now as well, two-year-old Darcie.

Her father met her at the station. She wore a short-skirted blue cotton suit from last summer, with a wide red belt, matching handbag and sandals. She'd shaved her legs specially and oiled them smooth with baby oil. She didn't need tights. It was the first warm Sunday of the year.

They kissed, her sunglasses clashing with his spectacles. She clung to him, she hadn't touched anyone for ages, and he hugged her back but awkwardly. She broke the silence by winking at the flecks of mud on his freshly-pressed fawn trousers. 'Been gardening, Dad?'

He nodded. 'Up since six.'

'Got your alarm clock still.' It had been a childhood joke that he didn't need an alarm clock to get him up to open the shop, he had one right there inside his head. She used to imagine it shrilling away between his ears, cheerful-faced like the moon in picture books, dancing about with the vibrations of its own noise. He never asked her to get up with him and help but she loved to, making tea for them to share, and helping the delivery boys pack their shoulder bags.

He opened the door of the car, lifted a pile of unread Sunday papers with colour supplements off the passenger seat and put them in the back. She didn't want to go straight to the house with him. She wanted him to drive and drive. All she'd told him on the phone was that Paul had gone away for a while. She'd made clear that she didn't mean a holiday or a business trip but she hadn't told him anything else. Now she felt she could tell

48

him everything and he'd understand and take her side. Before he started to drive he handed her an envelope. It caught the sunlight and she could see that it contained a cheque. She opened her mouth to speak but he patted her hand. 'Not a word,' he said.

'You mean Ruth doesn't know you're giving it to me?'

'Of course she does, and this is from her as well as me. But we both thought you wouldn't want to talk about it in front of the children, and thanks are taken as said.' He didn't want to hear. Why would a happily-married couple want to hear such a nasty tale? He wasn't her father any more, he'd given her away at her wedding, and as for understanding . . . in the years between Antonia's mother's death and his meeting Ruth, she'd swear he'd never had another woman. He started the car, driving fast along the country lanes, slowing down once to let a riding school pass and turn left into a field.

Rex rushed out to open the white gates. He saluted as they went by. In his other hand he held a Rubik Cube. Darcie toddled out in shorts and a T-shirt, clutching a coreless peeled apple. The apple was beginning to turn brown and when Antonia picked her up to say hello, she wiped it all over her mouth.

'Ugh, Darcie! Oh, I see – you're giving me a bite. Thanks, mmm, delicious. How are you doing, Rex, all right? I've got some sweets in my bag –'

The boy squinted at her. 'We don't eat sweets.'

'What, never?'

'They're bad for our teeth.'

Antonia glanced at her father who was carrying the newspapers into the house. There was ivy round the big front doorway; it dwarfed him. 'Come on in.' She followed. The house was like a burrow, cool and dark. She breathed in deeply through her nose. 'Lovely smell.'

'Is somebody saying my house smells?' Ruth came smiling, ready either to kiss or not. Antonia let the moment pass, then wished she had kissed her. Ruth was a nice woman. She was tall and thickset with dark eyes and striking features. She wore beads and bangles and Dr Scholls under her long patchwork skirt. Antonia said, 'I only meant nice smells. Polish and wood –'

'Hm. Not drains? Or things fallen down behind the fridge?'

'I think it's a *lovely* house.'

'How about a nice cup of tea?' said her father.

'Or coffee?' said Ruth. 'Or is it time for a drink?'

Antonia hesitated: she asked for tea because she knew that was what her father always had. The three of them went into the kitchen which was huge, well equipped but oddly old fashioned with its rows of cast iron pans, sharp knives and wooden spoons hanging from hooks.

They carried trays out into the garden. It was carefully divided into a vegetable patch, a lawn and a play area with a home-made swing and three cricket stumps stuck in the grass. There were rose-bushes, fruit trees, raspberry canes and a potting shed. A fork stood upright in the earth, and when they had all had tea and Ruth began pouring drinks, Antonia's father took a sip from a glass of lager and went and got on with his digging.

Ruth smiled after him. 'Can't sit still for five minutes.'

'He's used to working hard.'

Ruth flicked through the newspapers and Antonia started to smoke.

Rex edged close and said, 'That's bad for you.'

Darcie climbed on to Antonia's lap and crawled all over her, trying to take away the cigarette.

For lunch they had cold breast of lamb rolled round sage-and-onion stuffing and tied with string. Rex wanted to chew the string when it was taken off, and Ruth said, 'Oh, how disgusting,' but let him. There were three salads, all different colours: a red one with beetroot, tomatoes and radishes, a white one with cubed potatoes and spring onions, and a green one. None of the salads was dressed. 'I never do,' Ruth explained. Instead she brought out a little tray with oil, vinegar, herbs and other ingredients, and pots and spoons for everyone to mix their own dressings. Antonia's father avoided her eyes and offered Ruth a spoonful of his own concoction to taste. She sipped thoughtfully: 'Bit heavy on the garlic, perhaps, darling. I've got to sleep with you.' Rex said, 'Shall I make you my special dressing, Antonia?' and ran off into the house to fetch something that had been forgotten.

'You've made a friend,' said Ruth approvingly. 'He doesn't usually reckon to wait on girls.'

'She's not exactly a girl, Ruth. She's a married woman and

his step-sister.'

They ate carefully, covering the silence with 'Mm,' and 'Delicious, Ruth,' and 'Is it all right?' Rex came back and mixed a dressing for Antonia. He seemed hurt that she had begun to eat without it. He wouldn't start his own meal until she had smothered several lettuce leaves with his oily mixture and pronounced it perfect. Ruth was impatient and amused. She brought out a summer pudding. When she sliced into its soft purple coating a tide of stewed berries and juice gushed out. They ate the pudding with cream, and Ruth went for coffee.

Rex said to Antonia, 'Will you play cricket now?'

'What, after all that?' She took out her cigarettes. Rex bent low over his empty plate. 'Oh don't,' he whispered, almost to himself. Antonia put the packet away. 'All right,' she said, 'I'll give it up.' She looked at where Rex's Rubik Cube lay on the grass. She picked it up. 'I'll have a go with this instead.' She fiddled with it, getting nowhere. 'I've got a book about it,' said Rex, and he ran into the house to fetch the book.

'It's sunbathing weather,' said Ruth, gathering up the lunch things. She didn't need help washing up, she said. It could all go into the machine. Darcie followed her into the house. Rex had given up trying to teach Antonia his Rubik Cube. He kept glancing meaningfully at the cricket stumps. 'You could bowl,' he said. Antonia's father said, 'Why don't you go and do some digging, Rex? I'll bowl at you later.' Rex went reluctantly. He kept staring back at Antonia and her father alone together.

'I think he's in love with you.'

'Not any more.'

'Sorry. I meant Rex.'

'I meant Paul.'

'Things'll work out.'

She sighed. 'They already have.'

'You mean he's coming back?'

She wanted so much to say yes. Not for herself – well, she did want it for herself, but that wasn't what she was feeling now. She wanted to say yes for her father so he could stop trying to say the right thing.

'No, he'll never come back.'

'It's early days yet.'

What used they to talk about, those mornings in the shop?

51

She supposed she must have had problems sometimes. Had she brought them to him? She couldn't remember.

Ruth returned in a bikini top. Her breasts were low and heavy and the flesh round her middle was striped with stretch marks. Darcie wore a nappy and plastic pants. Antonia searched her father's face quickly: she saw no passion there, just sun in his eyes and deep contentment.

'I don't suppose you thought to bring a sun-top, Antonia,' said Ruth. 'Sit in your bra, no one'll mind. Love – have a squint over the hedge and see if anyone's about. Antonia wants to peel off.' She added with a laugh, 'Not that anyone round here would be surprised if we took up *nude* sunbathing. They think we're beyond the pale anyway with our Labour posters in the window for the local elections.'

'Are you Labour now, Dad?'

'It's a secret ballot,' he replied.

Antonia didn't like being told by Ruth to undress. She stayed hot and uncomfortable. Her sleeves were too narrow to roll up. Rex snatched his Rubik Cube from her lap. 'Can you do it or not?' he demanded. 'Doesn't look like it.' she said. Ruth said, 'Rex, take Antonia up to my room and show her my scarf drawer. If you can choose something out of there, Antonia, and improvise a sun-top, feel free.'

She sighed and followed Rex. The house was very quiet. 'This way,' he said, his voice husky. The stairs were thickly carpeted, the colour of milky coffee. There were pictures everywhere, some old and valuable-looking, others more modern. Rex took her into the big bedroom. The double bed had brass knobs and a dip in the middle. Ruth's bedside table had a pile of books on it: *Testament of Friendship* and *The Bedside Guardian* and *The Computer Book*. Antonia's father appeared to be reading *The French Lieutenant's Woman*, a brand new paperback copy with a bookmark sticking out very near the beginning. Antonia had been to see the film with Paul; she'd enjoyed the Victorian bits. She'd heard the book was very different. She decided to read more books; she had a library ticket somewhere at home. There was a picture of her mother and another of Ruth's first husband on the mantelpiece; and a wedding shot of Antonia's father and Ruth outside the registry office; and a wedding shot of Antonia and Paul.

Rex opened the scarf drawer. Antonia gazed into the sea of

many-coloured silk and chiffon and cotton and wool. She found two wide strips of unhemmed crimson chiffon. She fingered them. The boy watched her.

'Thanks, Rex.'

'That's all right,' he said gravely.

'I'd like to be private now.'

'Aren't you coming down?'

'In a minute.' He shuffled over towards the door. 'Off you go.'

He went out. She waited, listening. Then she walked heavy-footed towards the door and heard him scamper away down the stairs. Soon she heard the sound of him bossing Darcie about in the garden. She took off her jacket and bra and stood in front of the dressing-table mirror, winding one of the scarves over and round her breasts, moving her arms up and down to test its security. She tied the other scarf in her hair, smoothing it down.

She returned to the garden, still wearing her skirt and carrying the jacket with her bra tucked out of sight in the sleeve. She realized she was expected to leave her things in the bedroom and waited for Ruth to say something, but she just said, 'Oh that *does* look nice, Antonia, I'd better give you those scarves to keep, I never wear them. I haven't asked you what the work situation's like in London these days.'

'It's all right.'

'I hear the temp is being squeezed rather.'

'What does that mean, Mummy?' Rex asked. 'Mummy, what does it mean?' He was sitting near them on the grass but not looking at Antonia.

'Just that there isn't much work for temps, Rex. Unless they're very good ones, like Antonia, and they've got a good agency. How is Mrs Hook?'

'What's a temp, Mummy?'

'Why don't you ask Antonia?'

Rex walked away.

'Have you ever thought of looking for something permanent, Antonia? Now that, er –'

'I'm not going to keep coming to you and Dad for money, if that's what you mean.'

Ruth smiled sadly. 'I'm sorry if it sounded as if that were what I meant.'

'No. You didn't. Sorry. People keep telling me I ought to. But I just can't seem to face up to things.'

'Of course. And it's early days yet. You know you're always welcome here, and if you need any help you've only got to ask either of us. I won't tell you to think of me as your mother, we should be more like sisters, but if you *do* want to talk about anything –'

Antonia looked at Ruth. She was leaning forward in her deck chair, her big breasts looming out of her bikini top, her dark eyes kind and eager. Antonia's smile flashed. 'Actually there was a job I was thinking of going for. Good salary and loads of responsibility.'

'Oh?'

'Only Margaret Thatcher's already got it.'

Ruth threw back her head and roared with laughter. Antonia could see all her fillings.

They went for a walk. No one talked much. Ruth held Antonia's father's hand and together they seemed to forget occasionally that anyone was with them. Then they would stop and wait for Antonia and the children to catch up, or trot forward to catch up with them. Darcie tugged at Antonia's fingers, or demanded to be carried. Rex hauled her down and ran off with her into a wood. Antonia walked alone. Rex was picking buttercups and cow parsley. He offloaded them on to his sister and whispered in her ear. She gave them to Antonia, who said, 'How lovely. Are they from both of you?' 'It was her idea,' said Rex.

They went home and had tea. Ruth said, 'We're not trying to get rid of you, Antonia, but we thought we'd go to church this evening. Shall your father drive you to the station, or would you like to come with us?' Antonia looked at her father in surprise. He fidgeted and said, 'Well, we do go sometimes.'

Antonia said, 'Last time I went to church was my wedding. And before that, yours.'

'That wasn't a wedding, it was a blessing,' said Rex. 'Why don't you go to church?'

'It's choral evensong,' said Ruth, 'but don't feel you have to come.'

She went with them. Everyone dressed smartly. The church was large and the service was quite well attended. The setting sun gleamed gold and red and blue through the stained glass windows. The choir wore purple and white. Darcie slept on her mother's lap. Antonia stood between her father, who mouthed the words but did not sing, and Rex, whose voice was high and true. The only tune she recognized from school was *Dear Lord and Father of Mankind*. Rex whispered, 'Sing, you've got to,' and she did, quite enjoying it until she heard what she was singing.

> *Breathe through the heat of our desires*
> *Thy coolness and thy balm*
> *Let sense be dumb, let flesh retire*
> *Speak through the earthquake, wind and fire*
> *O still small voice of calm, O still small voice of calm*

After the service they put her on the train with the remains of the breast of lamb wrapped in tin-foil, her father's cheque for a hundred pounds (more than enough for the phone bill), Ruth's chiffon scarves and Rex and Darcie's bunch of flowers drooping in her lap despite the wet cotton wool wrapped round their stems.

CHAPTER SIX

Madly Urgent

BOOKINGS NOW FOR TOP TEMPS MADLY URGENT!!!!

And madly urgent it looked too, chalked on a blackboard in the doorway of – what was this one? Bakerloo Temps – the chalker not even having found time to finish the list of rates or maybe they had been there so long they had got rubbed out or maybe they went up every day and had to be changed.

Or down.

Antonia went in and was breathlessly questioned.

'Shorthand and typing speeds?'

'100/50.'

'Don't need to give you a test do we. Audio?'

'Yes.'

'Accounts?'

'No.'

'Reception work?'

'Yes.'

'Word processing?'

'No.'

'Can you work a photocopier?'

'Do me a favour.'

The girl ticked 'yes'. 'Any other agencies?'

'No.'

'Right, then, Antonia. We'll be in touch.'

'It says immediate bookings outside.'

'That's word processors, dear. Will you be at this number?'

The party's over, Antonia. That was what Mrs Hook had said and she was right. It had been like a party, once. Every bit as good as

56

Antonia had hoped when she left school, the ads for temps loud in her ears from the radio or urging her on from the walls of escalators or the pages of evening papers. She remembered that final term, all the other girls applying for jobs and choosing what they'd do, she'd thought, *why one? Why have just one job when you can buzz around like a bee and have a try at everything?* Mrs Hook had chuckled in the way of older people seeing (or fancying they saw) in some youngster the way they used to be themselves. 'I don't usually use school leavers as permanent temps. They think it's a dead end and they're not reliable. The good name of my agency –'

'I'll be reliable.' *Dead end?* It was a hundred open roads. She did dream sometimes of the perfect job where she'd stay. Behind each attack of new job jitters – *will there be something here I can't do? Will there be someone I can't get on with? Am I following after some supertemp or perfect permanent?* – was the certainty. *This is the one! This is where they'll beg me to stay and I'll be promoted and promoted and have my own department and fly round the world –*

It hadn't happened but that was her own doing. She'd been asked often enough to go permanent. It had got so that if they didn't ask her she wondered what she'd done wrong. But she'd never wanted to stay. Three weeks, a month, were her limit. First week you were struggling to get the hang of things. Second week you were on top of it and everyone marvelled, you marvelled at yourself. Third week, the taste of staleness entered the air.

She liked temping. But she wasn't a temp any more, she was unemployed. And she'd promised to be out of the flat by August. She had to be something. What could she be with her skills and her O-level English? She'd always thought she'd be a wife and mother and proud of it. No point in going into all *that* again, what was done was done, it'd never happen. She could be a nurse if she didn't hate hospitals so much. She could be an air hostess only that didn't last for life and she needed something now that lasted for life. Everyone seemed to want girls to do engineering and carpentry and things like that these days, she was always reading articles about courses, but she wasn't sure she'd be any good and she was in no mood to try something so new. What she had to do was carry on temping and sooner or later she'd land up in something, hear of something, that she could stick at for the rest of her life or at least until August.

*

Bright Girls of Mayfair.

She was passing, she might as well give them a try.

She went in and there behind a desk was someone she recognized, someone she'd met on a job once, that ridiculous firm in Covent Garden, her last Here Today job. Catherine something. She looked different, very smart: a white frilly blouse of the kind Lady Di used to wear when she was still Lady Di, make-up that she'd made a bit of a mess of, and a new hairdo. There were curls everywhere. Antonia wouldn't have recognized her if she herself hadn't lit up in a friendly way and gushed: 'We can't go on meeting like this.'

'Pardon?'

'Joke cliché for when you meet someone unexpectedly. Like in all those adulterous thirties films.'

What was she on about? 'I don't remember the thirties,' Antonia said, not meaning to be quite as catty as she sounded.

'Neither do I. Did you fail your test?' Now what –? Vaguely she remembered telling Catherine something about Mrs Hook's ultimatum but she really didn't want to go into that.

'I decided I didn't want to do word processing.'

'Bravo,' said Catherine. 'Is it the health aspect you object to, or the unemployment aspect?'

'It's the being pushed around aspect.'

Catherine said, 'I'm sorry about that because I'm going to have to ask you to take a typing test.'

'Oh, that's all right.' Typing tests were the least of her worries. Catherine led her into a little cubicle where there was a desk with a typewriter, a nest of grey plastic trays containing paper of different sizes and thicknesses, and a dictaphone with a headset. Antonia picked up the headset and inspected the ear-pieces. She took out a Quickie from her bag and started wiping them. 'I'm sure the last girl was very nice,' she explained, 'only –'

'Risk of ear infection.' Catherine seemed pleased. 'Of course. Now, I'll leave you to it, I won't watch you, you'll be all thumbs.'

'I always listen to the tape straight through first.'

'That's sensible. I won't start timing till I hear you begin to type.' She left Antonia alone to load up the typewriter with paper and turn on the dictaphone. The ear-pieces were cold and damp in her ears. There was a buzz and a crackle and

Catherine's voice started, deafeningly loud. Antonia turned down the volume and listened.

'Capital D, capital S, Dear Sister, comma, new paragraph. Capital H. Have you ever considered that, comma, as a temp, comma, you are one of the most exploited members of the work-hyphen-force, question mark? New paragraph. Capital S, Shunted from job to job, comma, lacking security, comma, and not even well paid when you are working – '

Antonia took out the ear-pieces, went towards the doorway and stared across the office at Catherine who was talking with one of the other girls. Catherine saw her and shot her the subtlest of warning winks. Antonia shrugged and returned to her test. When she had finished typing, Catherine came back and they whispered together while Catherine pretended to check her work for errors.

'It's propaganda!'

'Of course,' said Catherine. 'I offered to make some new test tapes. I didn't say what I was putting on them. I never *guessed* at the abuses until I came to work here. D'you know this agency takes half as much again of what you earn? And they have favourites. Some women never work at all. Or get pushed into the domestic section. I didn't know they did cleaners too, but I've seen women come in here with perfectly good office skills and the next thing they know they're being offered glorified *charring*.'

'How do you get to be a favourite?'

'Pardon?'

'Well, it's all very interesting, but I've got to work, Catherine. I'm getting desperate, and I don't mean domestic work either.'

Catherine looked at her with an expression of deep hurt. As if she'd expected her to run out into the street with a banner the minute she heard the tape. She sighed. 'Don't worry, Antonia. I'll do my best for you.' She looked as if she would, too.

Antonia felt guilty. But then who was Catherine to go around saying things about other people's jobs? What did she expect? 'If it's against your principles, why do you work here?' she demanded.

'I'm subverting from within,' said Catherine. 'And I'm going to be organizing a meeting soon.'

Rather to Antonia's surprise, Bright Girls came up with a job. Someone called Judith phoned (it was Catherine's day off) at about half-past nine one morning when Antonia was still asleep. She lit a cigarette and propped herself up on her elbow, writing down the details Judith gave her. 'They've been clients of ours for years. The booking's for three weeks: one of their secretaries is going on holiday. Needless to say, they've left it till the last minute and they want you there five minutes ago.'

'No problem. Where?'

'Near Regent's Park. The name of the firm's Forlex.'

Antonia got out of bed. 'What kind of firm is it?'

'Architectural and Engineering Consultants.' Antonia was disappointed in Judith. Often temp controllers tried hard to make a job sound interesting but Judith might have been reading that from a phone book. What did Forlex build? What did they engineer? She had a feeling that this was going to be *it*, this was going to be the one, and she wanted to know what she was going to. And what to wear. She decided to play safe with her soft denim pinafore dress over her white cotton polo-neck sweater, and gold bangles.

The firm was part of a white-painted terrace round a semicircle of private garden which glowed with marigolds. On the walls of the dim, plant-filled lobby were paintings and blown-up colour photographs of what appeared to be hotels in exotic resorts. Just looking at them made her feel warm.

'Er, *just* one minute please.' The security man's tone was reproachful, even though she'd made no effort to go anywhere unauthorized. He wanted to know all about her, to take her picture and to issue her with a pass. For this he would require a deposit of five pounds, refundable when she left.

He looked a bit like the fat man in *Not the Nine O'Clock News*. He took her into a room with a white wall and flashed lights in her eyes, then asked again for the five pounds.

'Do me a favour,' said Antonia, trying to sound firm.

'That's right, Jim, do her a favour, it's bad enough for her that she's been sent to work here, no reason why she should pay for the privilege.' A scatty-looking girl in a wrap-around skirt was leaning on the handle of the door. She had a bundle of files under her arm. Papers fell from them and skimmed across the floor; she made no effort to pick them up.

'Never mind about that,' Jim grumbled. 'If a temp goes off with her ID, who gets it in the neck?' He fingered his neck where there was a faded scar with stitch-marks.

'I'll send you down five pounds from petty cash.' The girl looped her free arm into Antonia's and bore her away.

'Whew, thanks,' said Antonia. 'I thought I was going to get murdered.'

'Probably won't come to that,' said the girl, whose name was Audrey.

It was an open-plan office with men leaning over drawing-boards, bent in the middle like the Anglepoise lamps that lit up their work. They drew and ruled carefully on sheets of tracing paper which they then picked up and took to show each other.

'What are they doing?'

'I've always wondered,' said Audrey. 'Let's go and ask Barry, he's new so he can probably remember what they said at the interview.' Barry was a small, bird-like man with round spectacles and thinning sandy hair. He nodded and smiled at Antonia and Audrey. 'This the Bright Girl, then?'

'She'll have to be.'

'Oh I don't know so much, Aud. She's only got you to replace.'

'Don't worry, I'll be back in three weeks.'

'I suppose the time'll pass.'

'Her name's Antonia and she's got an enquiring mind. She wants to know what you and the other boffins do to earn your huge salaries.'

Barry beamed. 'I didn't know anyone cared. This project's a hotel and leisure complex for Larana.'

'Where's that?'

'You've heard of Majorca, Corsica, Crete – ?'

'It's not a bit like any of them,' said Audrey.

'Come and see my hotel.' Barry spread out a large drawing. 'All bedrooms overlook the sea. Kitchens here, pool there, miniature golf, disco, marina, what more could you want in a holiday paradise?'

'Sun?' suggested Audrey.

Barry gave her a friendly thump with a cardboard tube. 'You get that upstairs,' he said, 'in Electrical.'

Audrey's territory was about seven feet by ten, bordered by shelves full of papers and magazines, and filing cabinets. There were two desks, one with telephones and trays, one with a very new typewriter. 'You work for Len.' Len was a white shadow behind frosted glass. 'He makes all his own calls, so you don't have to worry about that. This is the international phone. He keeps it switched through so you can't phone your boyfriend in America. Not that you would. Now, if he wants you to type anything he puts it into the red tray, and things that want filing go in the blue tray, and if I've got time I'll show you the filing system, *system*! For want of a better word. Post goes here . . . whew, I'm exhausted.' Behind a wall of plants, a pot of very black coffee bubbled on a hot-plate. There was a packet of polystyrene cups all stuck inside each other like a snake, a bottle of milk, a packet of sugar and some Sweet 'n' Low. Audrey poured two cups and left Antonia to add what she wanted.

'Don't we make any for Len?'

'I never do. Better not or he'll start expecting it.' They walked back to Audrey's territory. 'Help yourself to magazines, try and put one in for every one you take out, all the girls do.' There was a vase on the magazine shelf with a single wilting rose. 'Oh, and every Friday you get a flower to keep on your desk. Fridays, right? So it has plenty of time to die over the weekend. Now don't do anything you're not paid for.'

'Such as?'

'Their personal stuff. See him over there – ' Audrey indicated a podgy man with nudes on his wall. 'That's Alan. Always firing off letters of complaint. I don't know what it is about him, one of life's losers. If ever he buys a coat, the buttons fall off within twenty-four hours. New shoes leak ditto. And his wife's always finding dead mice in tins of beans. He loves writing letters about it all, though, so that's some consolation, but it's no reason why you should type them. He has got a wife, by the way, whatever he may tell you.' Realizing he was being talked about, Alan looked over towards them, smiled invitingly and started to sharpen his pencil. 'See?' said Audrey.

'Not my type,' said Antonia.

Len, who looked a bit like Omar Sharif in a bad mood, emerged from his office. 'Is this the girl?'

'Yes, Len. This is Antonia.'

'Does she know where everything is?'

'I was in the middle of showing her.'

'Perhaps she could type this for me.' He gave Audrey a sheet of paper marked URGENT and went back behind his glass without looking at Antonia. Audrey put it into the red tray.

'We'll do it after lunch,' she said. 'In fact we'll go and get our lunch now, before the queues.'

The afternoon was spent typing and learning the filing system. At about half-past four Audrey said, 'Think you'll manage, then?'

'Why, are you off?'

'Got to do my packing.'

'Have a nice time.'

Antonia got on with typing a monthly report. It was three weeks late and it was a chapter of disasters. Len's prose lashed sloppy workmanship and missed completion dates in various foreign countries. Once she looked up and found him watching her.

'Will that be finished tonight?' he asked.

'It is a bit long.'

'You were late this morning.'

'I came as soon as the agency told me.'

'You'll need to stay tonight,' said Len, 'and finish it.'

Antonia raised her eyebrows, then shrugged. 'All right.'

Everyone except Antonia, Len and Alan disappeared on the dot of five. Antonia typed the last few pages. Len lurked behind the glass, pacing up and down. Alan sat among his nudes, writing desultorily and, from time to time, catching Antonia's eye. She pulled the last sheet of the report from the typewriter at ten to six. As she checked for errors, Alan sidled towards her. She walked past him into Len's office. Len snatched the report, put it into his briefcase, snapped it shut and left without a word. Alan leaned on her desk as she cleared away. He had curly grey hair, a pink face and pot belly. He held a sheet of paper in his hand. 'Off home then?' he said.

'That's right.'

'What do you think of it so far?'

'It's fine.'

'In a hurry, are you?'

'Yes.'

'Meeting the boyfriend? Or something?'

'Not exactly.'

'Because if you – er – '

'Must go.'

'Want to have a look at this?' His long, handwritten letter to the Prime Minister was headed 'Re Inland Revenue: Gross

Discourtesy of Inspector of Taxes'. 'I suppose it wouldn't be possible for – er –'

'Of course,' Antonia beamed.

'Oh good.'

She waved at the typewriter – 'Help yourself' – and left.

The front lobby was quiet and shadowy. No one was on duty. She looked for the signing-out book but it seemed to have been put away. So she wrote on a piece of paper 'A. Lyons, temp, six pm' and left it on the table. The door was bolted in three places. She felt sure she wasn't supposed to unlock it without authority but how else could she get out? The bolts were stiff but she managed. The evening was light and mild. The air smelled of cars and flowers. She pulled the door to behind her and started down the steps. As she reached the pavement somebody grabbed her from behind.

CHAPTER SEVEN

Original Sin

Catherine had been educated at church schools; her parents were not serious believers, but they had wanted her to have good manners.

Some of the teachings of Christianity had appeared increasingly improbable to her with the years – but original sin was a doctrine that had, in different forms, remained with her. Any fool could see (and the adolescent Catherine was no fool) that the life led by her and other whites in Rhodesia was a blasphemy against a God who purported to fill the hungry with good things and send the rich empty away; but besides feeling guilty and trying to be as nice as possible to the Africans, what on earth could she do about it? And if the very act of being born rendered all men sinful (Catherine saw no reason, in those days, for not including herself among all men), what chance was there for anyone once one was here? Original sin, then, was a leveller: it carried an element of consolation.

'We had the land. They brought the Bible. Now they have the land and we have the Bible.' She was unable to identify the precise moment of losing her faith, but the slogan of the black nationalists, devastating in its terse justice, had summed a few things up for her.

Her parents had urged her to go to England to do her teacher-training. With the guerilla war hotting up, her mother had said, 'You'll be safer overseas.' Her father's reasons were different: 'You'll want a qualification that'll be recognized world wide.' He still considered himself an English patriot though he never went near the place.

Neither of these considerations had influenced her final decision to leave Rhodesia. *We have outstayed our welcome here,* she thought, *if we ever were welcome; it's up to each of us to make our arrangements and go; they shouldn't have to fight a war to tell us this.* (None of which had stopped her wondering, once she was qualified, whether it might not be morally better to go back and teach in an African development project.)

Of course she'd discovered the women's movement with its critiques of, among other things, Christianity: some were scholarly, some wild, some could bash repeatedly on a kind of spiritual funnybone by being both. It turned out that powerful images of snakes, gardens, knowledge-bearing fruits and gods who died and returned in the springtime were as old as the human psyche. Often they had matriarchal meanings. There was no special reason to accept the Christian version.

No special reason to accept anything. Even her trained, enquiring mind, which she'd thought of as an asset, got her into trouble. At a recent meeting on women and unemployment she'd ventured to wonder aloud why the British ruling class had not reintroduced domestic service on a grand scale, a potential servant class being abundantly present. Her hearers were shocked; she was appalled by their shock; she had not been *advocating* it, for heaven's sake! Later, bruised and miserable, she admitted to herself that it had not been the most tactful of speculations. And anyway, not everyone had responded with hostility, just a few people who did not know her, did not listen, just sat alert for buzz words and buzzed: *she'll be abolishing social security next, and having some working-class woman cleaning her floors!* Others understood the academic spirit in which she had spoken, though they made it clear that playing devil's advocate was a piece of decadence which could not be afforded and might deservedly be misunderstood.

Everything was a dilemma. There was never an obviously right thing to do. For Christian guilt read liberal guilt. (*Amnesty International! What's needed is a spot of armed struggle, kill the bastards.*) Feminist guilt. (*Bastard means the child of an unmarried woman. How come I'm using it as a term of abuse?*) Braying middle-class do-gooder guilt. (*Who am I to organize temps?*) Complacency guilt. (*What do I do, then? Nothing?*)

Now that Catherine was working at Bright Girls of Mayfair, it was easy enough to find an address for Samantha Yardley. On a card in a box marked NTBOW (Not To Be Offered Work) she discovered that Samantha lived in a place called Honor Oak Park; was eighteen; and had scored low marks for both speaking voice and appearance. Nothing very revealing about that. A bad speaking voice might mean anything from a regional or foreign accent to total incoherence. A bandaged-up vagrant bearing carrier bags might get low marks for appearance, but then so might someone with the looks of a film star if her fashion sense happened not to coincide with that of the BGM interviewer.

Finding the address was one thing. What to do with it was something else. It was for the victim to decide what action to take over a rape. She might prefer to forget it.

Catherine looked up Honor Oak Park on a railway map but postponed her visit again and again. In the meantime, consciousness-raising among temps was the thing. Her test tapes were good conversation starters, and she hadn't so far been caught. As soon as there was enough interest, she would organize a meeting. At which she most certainly would *not* take the chair.

Honor Oak Park. The name of the place mingled with the gleaming heat of the Sunday afternoon in June when she went there, and became a dream of old England – honey still for tea. Thirteen minutes out of London Bridge the train stopped at a seemingly arbitrary point in the continuous stream of suburb. Its gutters revealed it as a neighbourhood keen on takeaway meals; its pavements showed that dogs were also popular.

The house was huge, Victorian, with servants' windows in the roof. It was too big for one family but it lacked the multiple doorbells that would suggest flats. Catherine's hand paused over the knocker as she realized it might be an institution of some kind. A refuge for battered women? Then she had no business even knowing its address, never mind coming round looking for somebody who quite possibly didn't want to be found.

The front door opened before she could knock or turn away. A boy and a girl came out, wrapped in each other's arms in a kind of desperation. They glanced at Catherine and left the door open as if they'd been expecting her. They kissed lasciviously and went on their way.

She walked towards a row of closed doors through hot stripes of air, each separate-scented: meat, soap, body odour, smoke. A washing machine vibrated far below. She could also hear some badly-recorded women's screams.

There were rotas and lists of rules on a notice board. Each sheet of paper was headed 'OVERNIGHT. Youngsters at Risk. Registered Charity.'

She opened a door. The room was dark and smoky. A dozen teenagers lounged on ill-matched chairs and bean bags. On the TV screen a woman was being pursued along a railway tunnel by a man with a meat hook.

'I'm looking for Samantha Yardley. I said I'm looking for Samantha Yardley, is she here?'

Not a head turned. But a voice bellowed, 'Smanfa! The law's come for yer!'

'I'm not the law. I'm . . .' What to say? 'Her sister.'

'Smanfa! Yer sister's here.'

The film froze on the victim's face, caught between meat hook and oncoming express. An argument started up with the boy operating the remote control. Some wanted the film to continue. Others wanted to watch something else.

A girl arrived with an air of firm nonchalance. She wasn't at anyone's beck and call. She was thin as a stick, gauntly pretty in a rust-coloured nightie. Her eyes were crusted with sleep and old mascara. She looked straight past Catherine and approached a packet of white bread that stood on a tray on the sideboard. She took out a slice and stuck it in a toaster. 'Where?' she said.

'Are you Samantha Yardley?'

A thread of blue smoke rose from the toaster. Samantha took out her slice, spread it with liquefied Blue Band and ate. She perched on the arm of someone's seat and stared forward at *Cut Out Her Heart*. 'Samantha Brown,' she said.

'Oh. Sorry,' said Catherine. Menacing music rasped out of the video. She tried to identify the person who had first summoned Samantha. 'I said Samantha Yardley and you called Samantha Brown.'

'*You* said you was her sister,' the reply came back, 'and you don't even know what she looks like.'

'Look. I'm not the police, the, er, law, and, all right, I'm not her sister. But I *am* looking for her and I was given this address.

It's entirely to her advantage. I mean I want to help her on a personal matter.'

Samantha Brown finished her toast. She asked the group, 'Is this what you woke me up for?' and stalked off. Catherine waited. *Cut Out Her Heart* was not much to the group's taste and they started to pay her some attention.

'Smanfa Yardley, which one was she?'

'Sort of ee ba goom, she was. From up north.'

'Yeah, Cambridge.'

'Cambridge ain't fucking north.'

'Fucking is.'

'Fucking ain't.'

'*Amanda*, that was. Not Samantha.'

'She used to go to the Clock Radio.'

'I slept wiv 'er a few times.'

'Samantha or Amanda?' asked Catherine.

'Bofe, I sleep wiv all the girls 'ere.'

'Oh yeah?'

'Oh yeah?'

'Not wiv me you don't.'

'Isn't anyone in charge here?' Catherine pleaded.

No one was. She wondered whether this was one of those run-by-the-residents we-don't-have-leaders set-ups, or whether someone had simply not bothered to turn up. Or get up. According to the rota in the hall, somebody was supposed to be on duty. Somebody called Dave. She went on to wonder if it was in keeping with the undoubted idealism of the charity's founders that the youngsters at risk should spend a sunny Sunday afternoon watching video nasties in a darkened room. Finally she wondered what business it was of hers.

She wrote a note to Dave asking him to phone her on an important matter which she would explain fully. She asked him to use the Bright Girls number, she didn't fancy leaving her home number here.

Halfway down the road she remembered something and went back. 'Excuse me.'

'Ssshh.'

'Yes, I will sshh and go away, but one of you said something about Samantha Yardley going to the Clock Radio.'

'Yeah?'

'What is it, please?'

'Disco.'

'Where, please?'

'Clapham.'

She took a deep breath for a final try. 'If you know she went there, you must know who she is.'

No one would admit it. They were too deeply absorbed in the carnage on the screen.

In lieu of several evenings' overtime at BGM, she had Monday off, which was welcome in theory but dragged a bit. It was good to have an excuse to phone in to BGM, to hear another human voice, to hear her own.

'Any messages for me?'

'Yes, actually, Catherine,' said Judith. 'Somebody called Dave.' Clearly Judith thought that Dave was Catherine's lover. To destroy this impression Catherine put a few more casual enquiries about her temps, as if they were of equal importance. This was how she learned that Antonia Lyons had been sent, this very morning, to work at Forlex. Catherine absorbed this information without thinking about it. She was keen to phone Dave. He sounded an affable enough chap, with a sleepy, laid-back voice. Yes, Samantha Yardley was on the books of Overnight, she'd stayed there from the beginning of the year till a date in April which Catherine recognized as a week after the rape. (*At Forlex.* Ye gods.) No, Dave didn't remember her, he was new. No, he didn't know where she'd gone.

Catherine raced round to Forlex, meaning to burst in but waiting instead to meet Antonia after work. There was a beautiful garden over the road but it was fenced off and locked. She stood sentry on the pavement from four-thirty onwards. She must have seen fifty or sixty people leave the building. She asked if there were another exit and was told there wasn't. At a quarter to six she tried the door but it was locked. At last she started to walk away. From a distance of about a hundred yards she looked back and saw Antonia walking down the Forlex steps. She looked tired but still fresh in soft blue and white. Breathlessly Catherine caught up with her as she started walking in the other direction. She grabbed her from behind: 'Antonia, Antonia, are you all right?' For a reply Antonia spun round, lashed out in shock, lost her balance and fell over.

'Oh Antonia, I'm terribly sorry. Are you all right – really?'

70

Antonia's eyes were hard with pain and unamusement as she got to her feet. 'No I'm not if people keep giving me a fright and knocking me over.'

'I'm sorry, but – '

'I suppose you know what tights cost.' She indicated where hers had been torn by the fall.

'I'll pay for them. And let me buy you a drink. I need to talk to you.' Antonia glared as if she wanted to refuse. But she hesitated, and Catherine was reminded of that evening at Anderson & Lee when Antonia had seemed to seek with bleak desperation for a reason not to go home. She still didn't want to go home, though she didn't think much of Catherine as the alternative either, that was clear. Her indecision was transparent and pathetic. Finally she hunched her shoulders, let them droop in a shrug of fake indifference, and followed Catherine as if she were doing her a huge favour.

'I expect you'd prefer a wine bar,' said Catherine, not quite sure why she'd said it except that Antonia seemed to be the wine bar type.

'Who's paying?'

'Me,' said Catherine.

'Well, sorry, but I haven't got a lot of cash on me.'

You mean you haven't got a lot of cash full stop. I know what you earn and it's not enough. I know you're married. I wonder what your husband does and why you don't want to go home to him. I'm not going to ask. You're all strung up tight and I'm not going to say the wrong thing.

Catherine tried to make her story as lively as possible. 'Ever hear of a place called Honor Oak Park?' She laughed. 'Talk about the sticks.'

'South of the river.' Antonia nodded. 'That's where I live.'

'Oh really?' They walked along in silence. 'Well, anyway, the address turned out to be a hostel for homeless – '

'Might be useful for me.'

' – teenagers. Pardon?'

'Nothing.'

They found a wine bar off the Euston Road. Catherine bought a half carafe of house white. She saw Antonia eyeing a blackboard that offered lasagne, giant sausages and various quiches.

71

'Hungry?' Catherine asked.

'Well, if they've got any crisps,' said Antonia, obviously still worrying about the cost. They had none so Catherine ordered a platter of biscuits and cheese 'for us to share', she said, though she ate little, while Antonia wolfed it down, drank, chain-smoked and relaxed a little. Catherine reminded herself to look for a convenient moment delicately to offer a pound for the ruined tights, and proceeded with her story. She hoped she wasn't talking too much, but Antonia must think her behaviour rather extraordinary and she wanted to make her understand so that she could enlist her co-operation.

Antonia wouldn't hear a word against Forlex or its men. And from what she said of her day's work it sounded like a fairly pleasant place, despite the compulsory overtime. 'How do you account for it, then?' Catherine demanded.

'Account for what?'

'Samantha saying – '

'She might have been lying.'

She might. But why? Catherine didn't want to fall out with Antonia but if she were now going to say something about rape victims asking for it or making it up, she would have to make a few serious points.

'There is a reason,' Antonia said, 'why a temp might make up an excuse – you know, something pretty awful like that – for leaving a firm *and* leaving an agency.' She drank more wine and lit another cigarette. 'I've been asked lots of times.'

'What, to say you've been – '

'*No*. To go permanent. Sometimes it's all above board, you know, the firm pays the agency a commission and that's that. Sometimes you come to an arrangement. The temp *leaves* the agency, *pretends* to leave the firm but goes back there. As a permanent. And they split the commission between them.'

'I *see*. If you're right, Samantha's still there.'

Antonia shrugged. 'Suppose so.'

'Could you, you know, look for her?'

'I'm not going to go around accusing people.'

'Of course not, but . . . well, watch out for yourself too.'

'So I don't get raped.' Antonia laughed bitterly. The carafe was empty. She said, 'Shall I get some more?'

Catherine said, 'No, I will,' but Antonia had already gone over to the bar. Catherine marvelled at her strong head. She

72

herself had drunk little but was feeling distinctly woozy.

They changed the subject. They loosened up. They chatted. At least, Catherine tried to. But she realized she had hardly any small talk that was not immediately political or did not lead there, and she did not want to ram politics down Antonia's throat. They swapped stories about teaching and temping. Antonia said she loved to temp and never wanted to be anything else. She let slip that she was separated from her husband. She said she had a father and a stepmother, of whom she was reminded by Catherine. Catherine wondered if this was good or bad. It turned into quite a pleasant evening, Catherine thought, considering its bad start.

She pondered Antonia's suggested explanation for Samantha's behaviour. If the rape story did turn out to be a lie, that ought to be good news; no, not *ought to be*, *would* be, a real rape was never good even if the alternative was a woman lying about it in order to swindle an employment agency.

She decided to phone Forlex and ask for Samantha in a tone of voice that took for granted that she would be there. The call would come from a call box so there would be no suspicion that it was the agency checking up.

Catherine did this; the switchboard assured her that no one of that name worked at Forlex. Catherine then said that Samantha Yardley might be a temp. The switchboard said they used a lot of temps, didn't even try to keep track of their names. Catherine said she might be a former temp who'd joined the permanent staff; the switchboard said that in that case they'd know; she'd be in the internal telephone directory; but they didn't and she wasn't.

CHAPTER EIGHT

Appetite for Stars

Saturday night and I'm going to a disco.

Hang on a minute, Saturday night and I'm going to a disco with Catherine. What am I going to a disco with CATHERINE for?

Been saying for ages I need new friends.

More to the point, why did she ask me to go with her? Hasn't she got a man to go with?

I suppose she'd rather be with another girl in case she does find Samantha.

Can't remember when I last went to a disco with a girl.

Sorry, I'm with my husband.

Sorry, I'm with my friend.

'You've got rain on your face,' said Catherine.

'It's my make-up,' said Antonia.

They stood in the queue and rain fell on them. Tonight was a Capital d-j night so it was a long queue. Under Catherine's plastic rainhood her hair looked freshly washed and flyaway. Antonia wondered what she was wearing under her mackintosh and what they would find to talk about for a whole evening.

Flyposted stickers rippled across corrugated-iron hoardings round a building site over the road.

GRAPE PICKING WORK IN THE SUN.

THERE AIN'T NO BLACK IN THE UNION JACK SO SEND THEM BACK.

'Bloody cheek,' said Antonia, for something to say.

'What is?'

'It's our flag, isn't it? Our country.'

'Oh, but – '

'Not just those stupid National Front loonies who hate coloured people.'

Catherine smiled.

Catherine paid for the tickets. 'I still owe you for the tights,' she said, which was true. They headed for the ladies' where Antonia whisked off her coat and changed her shoes. Catherine made no comment on her black and silver catsuit but Antonia could see the other girls taking note as they did their hair. Catherine was wearing a neat tartan skirt, a silky blouse and black shoes with little heels. 'Will I do?' she enquired.

'Eh?'

'If you don't want to be seen with me, you only have to say.'

Antonia looked away. 'I'm starving,' she said.

There were a few tables in a dimly-lit alcove near the dancing area. Fast music thudded through. *Who cares, baby, if you love me, Who cares if there's fighting in the streets* – A waitress in jeans and a T-shirt brought a plastic menu. 'Maybe that's Samantha Yardley,' Antonia hissed. 'Why don't you ask her?'

'It could be anybody. I ought to have a photo.'

'I'll have a Hawaiiburger,' said Antonia. 'With chips.'

'I don't think I want anything,' said Catherine, but the waitress said she had to have something if she was going to occupy a table. 'Just have a plain hamburger,' Antonia suggested. 'I'll eat it if you don't.'

The Hawaiiburger had a slice of tinned pineapple inside it which made the bun difficult to hold. Antonia ate it, shrugged and started on Catherine's.

'The amount you eat,' said Catherine, 'it's a wonder you aren't fat.'

'The amount you eat, it's a wonder you aren't dead.'

Antonia finished eating, yawned and looked round the place. It was set up to look like the inside of a clock radio. Wires as thick as arms twirled around the ceiling, in and out of copper-coloured fittings. Enormous batteries made of foil and cardboard swayed above the dance floor reflecting waves and particles of light on to the small group dancing below. There were some good dancers. Luminous green digits glowed from a wall in the form of a clock face. On another wall there was a list of records, the letters all made up of dots. You could communicate to the disc-jockey what you wanted played next by tapping out a number on a keyboard. The celebrity d-j wasn't on yet. His sidekick, dressed in a check shirt and a red waistcoat, was changing old records without comment.

'I can think of people who'd envy us,' said Antonia, making an effort.

'Why?'

'You because you can sit in front of a hamburger and not want to eat it and me because I can eat it and not get fat.'

'Slimmers, you mean?' Catherine was making an effort too. 'I once knew someone who, if she wanted a doughnut, used to buy three so that the shop assistant wouldn't know it was for her.' Antonia said she knew people like that too. Catherine said, 'There's some interesting psychology there but it beats me.'

Inter-esting psy-chology. Do me a favour. Antonia had to get away from her and see if there was anyone here that she knew. 'D'you want a drink?'

'Not really, but I suppose I have to.'

'What would you like?'

'Choose me something.'

A couple of triple gins might liven you up a bit. Antonia settled for two Bacardi and Cokes. She took her time getting them and had a look round. There was nobody she recognized. She was disappointed and relieved. She paid for the drinks, they cost a lot but never mind, it was Saturday night, eyes were on her, she glittered and gleamed, each speck of silver reflected an eye watching, wondering, watching. *Shine for me,* the singer pleaded, *shining girl shine star you are*

She offered Catherine a cigarette.

Catherine said, 'Do you know, I think I might.'

The famous disc-jockey perched himself on his stool, sitting with care in his tight shiny green trousers.

'Doesn't look like his voice, does he?'

'What's this we're drinking? I could do with another.'

'*Midnight Train to Clapham Junction,*' the d-j announced. '*Sorr-ee. Midnight Train to Georgia.*'

'Are we going to dance or what?' demanded Catherine, who obviously didn't want to.

'What?' said Antonia, mesmerised by the wistful sweet music of a lover coming home.

'I'm a lousy dancer but I could learn – '

'It's too slow,' Antonia snapped. She could smash that d-j's face in. What was he doing playing slow sexy music this early? What about people who hadn't got partners, how did he think they'd feel?

Catherine went for more drinks. The music slithered round Antonia's heart like a snake till she thought she would cry or be sick or have to go home. Then it changed and she was all right, it was *Going round in straight lines*, it was fast, she knew it, she went quickly to the dance floor with Catherine still at the bar. She looked through the crowd to see if there was anyone trying to catch her eye. No one. She closed her eyes. *Straight lines, cutting edges, circle makes a square...* – hands waving, feet and beat and brain. 'Might've waited for me,' said Catherine, and there she was, imitating Antonia with a self conscious silly expression on her face. Antonia put herself into a trance and moved away, limbs flying. The digital clock glowed through her eyelids. She watched it flash: 22.37.00, 22.37.01, 22.37.02. . . . there was a bloke on his own, good dancer, smart dresser, velvet . . . 22.37.29, 22.37.30, 22.37.31 . . . no, he was with a girl in a suit like hers . . . 22.37.59, 22.38.00, 22.38.01 . . . . and a whole minute gone.

'I told you you don't have to be seen with me,' said Catherine, halfway through another Bacardi and Coke, when she got back.

'Sorry,' said Antonia. Catherine did look rather miserable and it must feel bad to be so out of place. Globules of light, red, purple and blue, slithered across the ceiling and strobes turned the dancers into jerky puppets. 'I've heard those things can give you epileptic fits,' said Catherine.

'You're not going to have one are you?'

'No, but I think I'd like to go outside for a bit. You don't have to come with me.' But Antonia felt guilty, so she did.

The man on the door stamped purple marks on their arms so that they could get in again. The rain had stopped but it was cold. Catherine looked up at the stars. 'So many. So many more than we can see. Aren't they *wonderful*?'

Embarrassment made Antonia catty. 'I think you're drunk, head girl.'

'*What* did you call me?'

'That's what you remind me of.'

77

'I was, too. In another life do you know what I would have been? A nun.'

Antonia could see she was going to end up taking Catherine home if she couldn't sober her down a bit. 'Shall we go and look for Samantha Yardley now?'

'But is it the *right thing* to look for Samantha Yardley? Nuns never have to ask themselves whether they're doing the right thing. I have few appetites, Antonia, but one I have is for doing the right thing.'

'Why?'

'That's an excellent and disturbing question. I suppose I think it brings me closer to the god in whom I don't believe. God – excellence – the stars. It's all the same. I have an appetite for stars. Attainable – for nuns – through poverty, chastity and obedience. Obedience is the rock on which I would have stumbled – apparently having unintelligent superiors is one of the main reasons why intellectual women leave convents. Poverty and chastity would not have been a problem.'

Antonia was pacing up and down to keep warm. 'If you step on a crack,' she said, 'a bear round the corner will eat you. Did you play that? I don't suppose you played anything. You were studying to be head girl.'

'You don't *study* to be head girl,' said Catherine. 'It is thrust upon you.'

'Oh – have some Glitterglow,' said Antonia, getting out her little bottle.

'What? Stop it.'

'Go on, go on.' Antonia tipped and dabbed at Catherine's face and Catherine let her, simpering. 'Go mad. It looks nice. What do you want to be a nun for? Or a head girl? I don't think you're any better than me, you know.'

'I never said – '

'No, you didn't. I'll give you that. But I can think of lots of people who'd say what's she making friends with *you* for, with all her education? She's after something, and she'll look down on you.'

'I'm not –' Catherine was suddenly sober and very distressed, lines appearing in her twinkling face. 'I hope I never – '

'*No.* That's what I'm saying. I don't think you're any better than me, head girl or not. At least I know how to enjoy myself.'

'And d'you think I'd enjoy myself more if I wore make-up and dressed . . .' she hesitated '. . . in the fashion?'

'Tell you something. I filled in a questionnaire once. It was called "What is Your Best Beauty Feature?" You could tell what the right answers were but I was honest. I thought I was doing pretty well. Getting top marks for everything. Then I turned the page. Know what it said?'

'No.'

'"Think quite a lot of yourself, don't you. Beware. Vanity can ruin everything."' Antonia laughed. Catherine looked as if she didn't know what to say. Well, she didn't have to say anything. It was just a story. Pretty nasty. Antonia had thought it at the time but she didn't mind any more. She couldn't, could she, or she wouldn't be telling the story against herself.

They went back inside. Catherine went to the bar, to make some enquiries, she said.

Comfort me with apples babe; drink my wine, feed among the lilies lilywhite and fine, someone out there wants you to be mine —

Antonia danced alone. She could hear her ear-rings tinkle as her soft hair brushed her face. Probably her hair was her best beauty feature. She could do anything with it. She'd tried other styles but she always came back to one where she could feel it touch the place where her chin met her cheek and her neck.

The d-j writhed, howled, devoured cigarettes, urged the dancers on. Urged her on in a sea of tigerskin and denim and fur and silk and gold, leather and lace and flowers, ear-rings and nose-rings and finger-rings, dreadlocks and skinheads and curls, spotlit by random beams. And flesh. Arms and legs and faces. And here and there a navel, a nipple, the pupil of an eye.

The pupil of an eye hard on her. Check shirt, designer jeans, waistcoat. She knew his face. Where from? Was he looking at her or was he looking at everybody? She did know him. He'd gone. There he was. Lots of movement on the floor but he was never far away.

He cocked an eyebrow. 'Hi.'

'Hi.'

He moved away again. *Be like that then.*

The disc-jockey cried, 'How's - about - the - Boat - Dance?' And everyone sat on the floor in a long line, each between the legs of the one behind. Antonia didn't need to look to know who was behind her. She knew who he was now: the guy who'd been putting the records on before the main d-j arrived.

As they swayed back and forth he said, 'I was watching you.' She didn't look at him. 'Oh yeah?'

'We have to – ' He spoke in short bursts when the rowing motion brought their heads close. '– us d-js. You have to find one face in the crowd – so you're talking to one person – otherwise you'd go mad – anonymous, impersonal–'

She smiled, wondering if it was true. 'Come here often?'

'I get around. By yourself – are you?'

'Kind of.'

'Want to have – a drink with me – ?'

She smiled over her shoulder at him. 'If I'm thirsty.'

The music changed.

All I wanted was to touch you, all I dreamed of

Everyone stood up and it was twos again, couples everywhere, the world glued together in twos. He held out his arms.

you touching me, silly really, touching people

She went to him. The alternative would have been to walk away alone through the couples.

Only human, only me.

He was surprisingly skinny. But he had nice hair, brown, but soft like hers, and he held her as if it might be at least half true, what he'd said about picking her out.

'Want to go on somewhere with me after?'

She said, 'I'm with my friend.'

He said, 'Oh.'

She said, 'I'll ask her.'

He said, 'Don't be long, then.'

Catherine was talking to people at the bar. They were trying not to laugh at her serious, glittery face. Antonia heard her say blearily, 'No, I don't know what she looks like. I wish I did.'

Antonia said, 'I'm off.'

Catherine shrugged. 'Okay, might as well, I'm not making very startling progress here.'

'Well – '

'What?'

'*You* don't have to leave just because I am.'

Catherine folded her arms. 'I see.'

'Don't mind, do you? Look, I've thought of something about

Samantha. What you need's a photograph of her.'

'Why didn't I think of that?'

'I can get one.'

'How?'

'The security man at Forlex has photographs of everybody.'

'*Brilliant*. Only why does that mean you have to leave now?'

Antonia hadn't meant to imply there was any connection. She'd just thought of it on the spur of the moment as a good way of mollifying Catherine.

I've thought up the first helpful idea in this whole Samantha Yardley business and all she does is sulk, thought Antonia as she got her coat.

CHAPTER NINE

All I Dreamed Of You Touching Me

'Cold, innit?' he said. 'You live far?'

Under the street lights he looked very young. She said, 'I thought we were going to your place.'

'It's not up to much.'

'I thought all you d-j's lived in penthouses in the Barbican.'

'I'm just starting out.'

He hailed a taxi. Sitting in the back, he nuzzled the corner of her cheek and planted a dry kiss there. The taxi dropped them in a street of semis with small neat gardens. He paid reluctantly, from a zip-up purse.

'You wait round the corner,' he said.

'Why?'

'Gotta check they're all asleep.'

'Who?'

'My – my landlady.'

He sent her up an alley. She'd never thought of disc-jockeys as people who might have difficult landladies but she supposed he had to live somewhere. A fried chicken box spilled bones and batter on to the ground. She lit a cigarette. Somewhere nearby a train rumbled and she began to think *what am I doing?* She took a few steps. He caught up with her.

'It's all right,' he said. 'They've gone to bed.' He grinned uneasily. 'Not walking out on me are you?'

'I thought you had on me.'

'Not likely. Not when – '

'When what?'

'I never thought you would – you know.'

82

He opened the glass-panelled front door with a latchkey. The house smelled of polish. He didn't put any lights on. He pointed at a table with a pot plant on it, warning her not to walk into it. At the top of the thickly-carpeted stairs were three doors, shut and very close together. He opened one.

His room was neat and clean. The duvet cover on the narrow bed matched the curtains. There was a desk with a lamp, a pile of files and a jam jar containing biros, rulers and pencils with very sharp points. She looked at the titles in the home-built bookcase. *The Day of the Jackal. The Catcher in the Rye. The Joy of Sex. A-Level Mathematics.* 'You're not a disc-jockey,' she said. 'You're a schoolboy.'

There was a long silence. She started to say it again, more loudly. He said, 'Sssh.' He whispered, 'I'm the school d-j. My brother-in-law owns the Clock Radio, he lets me do warm-ups. I run a fanzine, want to see it?'

'No. And this isn't really your place, is it? *Landlady. Barbican apartment.* This is your parents' house and that's them sleeping next door. And that's your homework there. And on Monday you're going back to school as usual. I knew you were lying.' She hadn't known, though. She'd believed every word. Because she'd known what she wanted and had to have something to believe to make it all right. He'd played on that. How could she accuse him of playing on it when he was just a kid and they'd only just met? Never mind how. She hated him. There was nothing she wouldn't do to get back at him and he'd deserve everything he got. She spoke loudly, enjoying his cringing. 'And what are Mummy and Daddy going to say when they find me here in the morning? Eh?'

He said sulkily, 'You'd be gone by then.'

'How old are you?'

'Eighteen.'

'Do me a favour.'

'Sixteen and a half.'

'Thought it was about time you had a girl, eh? Couldn't believe your luck when I said yes.'

'Ssshh,' he pleaded. 'What's wrong with that?' he challenged.

'Nothing,' she said softly. 'Nothing at all.'

She asked for the bathroom. He said she wasn't to pull the chain in case it woke anybody. She locked the door. Locked, trapped. She looked at herself in the mirror. The Glitterglow on her face looked absurd, like something spilt.

A disc-jockey's sure to have been around, I thought. He'll have heard of it, I won't have to go into details. Might even have it himself, lots of top people have.

Oh, I'd've told him. It's only fair. But he wouldn't have gone all neurotic like Paul.

He'd've said, if you never take a risk you'll never cross the road. He'd've said, all I dreamed of, you touching me.

The moon shone through the window into the clean blue bathroom. Under the basin there was Gumption for the floor, Frish for the toilet, Clean-Pine for General Hygiene. On the shelf there was Colgate for teeth, Listerine for breath, soaps and lotions and gargles. So many ways of keeping clean, so many places and parts to need it. She felt her spine crawl.

She hadn't thought through anything of the kind. Only now that she realized he wasn't a disc-jockey was she pretending it would have been all right if he had been.

She had not planned to tell him anything.

She wouldn't know where to start.

How lovely and soft his mother kept her towels. She reached out and felt their fluffiness, three blue bathtowels on a rail.

Silently she opened the bathroom door. In five strides she was past his room. She took the stairs like a cat. She managed the locks on the front door as if she had lived in the house all her life. Outside, the cold struck her skin like a slap of spite.

She was in time for the last train.

The carriage was empty except for a middle-aged man with watchful grey eyes. He sat at the far end. He had mud on his clothes.

Antonia sat where she could see him but as far away as possible. Their eyes met. She looked away. When she looked back he was still watching her.

The train moved away from the lights of the station into a tunnel that Antonia did not recognize. The man started walking towards her.

'Excuse me,' said Antonia. 'Excuse me.'

He accommodated the sway of the carriage with perfect balance. She wondered about that and the mud on his clothes.

Maybe he was some kind of horseman. The leather belt on his hips slanted with his stride. Before he could reach her the train stopped at another station. He sat down, out of sight. Antonia listened for the sound of someone else getting on. No one did. She looked out of the window. Too late to change carriages: the train was moving again.

He was the tallest man she had ever seen. His long-legged strides ate up the distance between them along the corridor. There were hairs on the backs of his knuckles which were white as he gripped the backs of seats to steady himself against the sway of the train.

'Excuse me, would you stop walking towards me like that please?'

'Why?'

She knew without looking at her watch that they were two minutes out of the station. She knew there were four minutes between stations. He was in the compartment with her now, looking down at her.

She said faintly, 'I'll pull the cord.'

'Why? I only want a light.'

'This is a no-smoking carriage,' she said.

'But you,' he said, 'are smoking.'

She looked at her hand. A cigarette burned there, with a long lip of ash.

'This is a no-smoking carriage,' he said. 'I could have you arrested.' He sat opposite her, his legs spread wide. He could snap them together and crush her. 'I could have you fined.'

'Please no.' Her voice was a whimper. 'I can't afford to pay a fine.'

'Then I will have to punish you myself. Taking risks with your own health is one thing; you have no right to inflict them on others.'

'But I didn't –' Where was the station? She must be on the wrong train, on and on it went.

He seemed confident that it wouldn't stop, he took off his belt very slowly. 'I'm going to beat you and fuck you, then beat you again.'

Before he could do it the carriage door opened and she was staring from her bed into the empty depths of Paul's wardrobe. She was lying on top of the covers, dressed in her disco clothes, alone.

She undressed, shivering, and got into bed, not bothering to wash. Her face itched and she rubbed it with her hands. She looked at her fingers, tipped with Glitterglow in the darkness, eight of them and two thumbs, stretching and straining to separate from each other and fly away like birds – sparrows, seagulls, vultures.

Sunday morning. The sky hung grey and still over the lines of rooftops and the sad squares of garden. She thought of her father up digging while his family slept. She wished she had a garden to dig, except that she'd never stick to it. Commitment, that was what a garden needed.

She turned on the radio. She didn't want the pop music stations this morning. BBC World Service announcers read the news in their proud clear tones. On Radio Four there was a programme for immigrants. 'Poor old immigrants,' she said, turning it off. 'Expect you to get up early, don't they?'

She lay feeling scratchy, promising herself a deep hot bath and a big breakfast with lots of coffee.

She went out and bought an *Express*. Nothing much in it. There was nothing to clean in the flat, she'd done that yesterday, except for the windows. She polished them until looking through them was like looking through nothing.

She turned on the television. A woman said with a smile, 'We must concentrate on the things we can do, rather than mourning for what we cannot.' The camera moved back to show that she was sitting in a wheelchair. Her legs were still as sticks in finely tailored trousers. Antonia switched channels to a room full of women working word processors. A man strode out in front of them. 'Basically stupid and mechanical,' he said, 'That's what computers are. They can do clever things but only if you tell them how. They understand only the simplest instructions: if yes, do this. If no, do that.' Antonia decided to manicure her nails and went to fetch her set. 'Let's see how it works in practice,' said the man. Concorde took off and flew over a traffic jam. 'From directing traffic,' he said, 'to affairs of the heart.' Two good-looking young people met in a pub. 'You must be Katy,' said the boy. 'You must be Richard,' said the girl. Wedding bells rang and a knife cut into a cake. 'No need to ask,' said the man, 'whether computer dating has worked for Richard and Katy.'

'I said I was looking for a girl with brown eyes who was interested in football,' said Richard.

'Right, let's stop there. We coded all Richard and Katy's answers and the computer read them. If you like, it asked, has this girl got brown eyes? If no, forget it. If yes, move on to the next question. Is she interested in football?'

'I am quite,' said Katy against a chorus of roars, and she went off on honeymoon with Richard. Later she was pregnant and knitting. 'Basically,' she said, 'you can do two things with the wool. Pass it *under* the needle or *over*. But look at all the different patterns that can produce.' The camera panned over a display of knitted goods.

The presenter sat with Richard playing Twenty Questions. 'Have I got one?' 'No.' 'Can you eat it?' 'Yes.' 'Is it a sandwich?' 'Yes.' 'Is the filling sweet?' 'No.' 'Savoury, then. Is it a marmite sandwich?' 'Yes! It's a *marmite sandwich*!' The man calmed down. 'By receiving the answer "yes" or "no" to twenty questions,' he explained, 'a skilled player has access to virtually all the concepts in the world. That's how it is with a computer. Its whole thought process hinges on whether the current is turned on or off. One or zero. Yes or no.'

Antonia phoned Catherine who was very cool. 'Just wanted to make sure you got home all right,' said Antonia.

'Yes. I did.'

'Can I ask you something?'

'You seem to be doing so.'

Antonia made a face but this was something she had to know. 'Are computers and word processors the same?'

'I imagine word processors are a kind of computer but does it matter at this time in the morning?'

No. It didn't. Or at any other time either. The moment had passed, the moment when she'd thought she'd understood the programme and thought that if she could get herself on to a word-processing course it might not be a dead end after all, it might be a way into a career with computers, even though she hadn't got any qualifications, after all, computers were the thing of the future.

'Did I wake you up?'

'Yes.'

'Did you manage to find anything out?'

'Do you care?'

87

'Wouldn't be asking if I didn't, would I?'

Catherine yawned. 'As a matter of fact,' she said, 'I didn't.'

'I meant what I said,' said Antonia, 'about getting a photograph from Jim.'

'Antonia, what exactly is the purpose of this call?'

How dare Catherine take that tone? What did she think Antonia was – a schoolkid? A social work case? Some spinster who pestered people on Sunday mornings just to hear the sound of another voice? She hung up. Catherine hadn't asked whether *she* had got home all right, Antonia noticed. But that was Catherine's type all over, go to endless trouble for a stranger, wouldn't spare the time of day for somebody they knew.

CHAPTER TEN

So Nice To Me
This Morning

Then came the news that Audrey would not be returning to Forlex after her holiday. She had resigned apparently, giving no notice. And nobody knew why.

Antonia heard about the resignation one morning when she was a little late for work. Jim on the door was very nice about her lateness, averting his eyes as she signed in for the proper time. She was irritated with herself for getting into a position where Jim was doing her favours. She would prefer to find a way to make *him* indebted to *her*, so that it would be easier, when the right moment came, to get him to show her Samantha Yardley's pass. Jim wasn't the kind of person who did a lot of favours for people. He would reckon one was enough.

'Glad you could make it,' said the draughtsmen, already at their boards. 'Good of you to drop in.'

'Looks as if she has just dropped in and all,' said Alan, running his eyes over Antonia's pink jumpsuit. 'By parachute.'

She put out her tongue and went to her desk.

Alan stayed with his joke. 'Maybe she'd've got in on time,' he said, 'if it hadn't opened.'

'Sticks and stones,' said Antonia, getting on with her work.

An inter-office memo had arrived, saying that a representative from Chestnut Computers UK would be calling to demonstrate some of his firm's products and all secretarial staff who could be spared were to attend. The memo didn't say whether this included temps but along the bottom was written in red ink: 'Since you appear to have very little to do, I suggest you go to this. E. Forbes.'

Mrs Forbes was the senior secretary of the floor, not a great achievement since the only other one was Audrey. When she wasn't supervising the photocopier she liked to swan about making tsk-tsk noises if Antonia was having a chat with anyone between jobs.

'She thinks I'm lazy,' Antonia fumed to Barry. 'What does she know? The only person who's entitled to tell me I'm lazy is Len, and he never complains.' He never praised or thanked her either, it was true, and Antonia resented this a little because she kept up well with the work; but he was probably only shy, some bosses were with all their responsibilities, and she'd thaw him out eventually, it was a challenge.

'You might get offered a permanent job here,' said Barry, 'if you don't watch out.'

'What d'you mean?'

That was when he told her about Audrey. He told her as if it was the most normal thing in the world for Forlex staff to go off on holiday and not come back. Apparently Len was in a lousy mood about it. Barry did an imitation of him saying how would Audrey like it if he sent *her* a postcard (that was all she'd sent, a postcard) saying her services were no longer required. Barry seemed undisturbed – amused if anything, cock-a-hoop. But Antonia felt as if a cold wind had blown on a warm day; she didn't know why. She hadn't known Audrey long enough to miss her. People were entitled to go on holiday. And they were entitled not to come back, if they didn't want to.

What if she asked Barry if he knew of anyone else who'd disappeared from Forlex in mysterious circumstances? But it would sound ridiculous, suspicious, rude. She'd already made up her mind to check out the business of the passes with Jim, to please Catherine. She couldn't make two such enquiries in one day.

What if she *was* asked to stay on at Forlex? She liked it. She liked the clean, light office, the flowers on her desk, the international telexes and most of the people. But she wasn't going to get her hopes up.

Barry seemed convinced that they would ask her to replace Audrey. He took the summons to the Chestnut presentation as clear proof and not an example of Mrs Forbes being spiteful.

Antonia turned up her nose. 'What is it, word processors? I hate them.'

'Ever used one?'

'No.'

'Then don't be so feeble.'

She stalked off to make a cup of coffee for Jim on the door. He reddened. 'Audrey never done that,' he said.

'Audrey's a bit lazy if you ask me. And you were so nice to me this morning.'

'I was? What'd I do?'

'I was late and you let me – '

'You was *what*? I let you what? Don't sound like me at all.'

'Anyway, I thought you might fancy some coffee. I mean, I get it for the others and you're always left out.'

'Story of my life,' said Jim.

'I bet. Except when things go wrong.'

'Too right. Then I – '

'Get the blame?'

'No one understands that.'

'Trust a temp to understand it. I've known firms who get a temp in for two weeks every year *on principle*, whether they've got any work for her or not.'

'Why's that?'

'So they've got someone to blame for everything that goes wrong for the next fifty years. Weeks, I mean. More coffee?'

'No thanks.' He looked at his watch.

'Jim.'

'What?'

'I expect you have to guard those old passes like the crown jewels, don't you?'

'Thing is, you see,' said Jim, 'you can't have people walking about in possession of a Forlex security pass when they don't work here no more and they've got no legitimate right to be in the building.'

'*Of course* not. Because then you could have any Tom, Dick or Harry walking in, couldn't you? Or any Mary, Jane or Samantha.' He didn't react. 'So I suppose the best thing is for you to destroy the passes when they're not needed any more.'

'Yes,' he said slowly. 'Yes, that's the best thing.'

'Put them through a shredder, do you?'

'What is all this?'

'Nothing.'

'You better get back to work then, or we'll both be handing in our passes sooner than we thought.'

'I'm looking for a picture of a friend of mine.'

'Who's that?'

'Samantha Yardley. Temp from Bright Girls. She was here in March.'

'What's she look like?'

'Oh . . . sort of . . . nothing special. You know?'

'Pretty?'

'Depends what you like.'

'Sounds as if she was a really good friend of yours. What colour hair did she have?'

'What d'you mean, *did* she have? Anyone would think she was dead.'

'You can dye your hair,' said Jim.

Antonia turned away.

Jim said, 'You're worried about her, aren't you?' Antonia had hoped it didn't show. Anyway, she wasn't. She was more worried about herself. 'Come in here,' said Jim. She followed him into the room where he had first taken her picture. She hesitated in the doorway as he rummaged in a cupboard for a large biscuit tin sealed up with masking tape. 'What's the matter, nervous?' he said. 'Don't you trust me?'

'Why shouldn't I?' she said. 'You're not doing anything wrong, keeping all these . . .' she swallowed hard as she opened the tin '. . . photographs.'

Photographs. That was all they were. Not passes. Just the photographs cut out from the passes, plastic backed like square counters for tiddleywinks. Dozens of girls, head and shoulders. Like the victims of the Yorkshire Ripper, only none of them had names. She ran her fingers along the hard plastic edges. The pictures clicked softly together as she looked through them in the silent little room. She shivered.

'What do you do with the passes, Jim?' she asked calmly as she could.

'Once someone's left it's my responsibility to destroy them.'

'But you keep the pictures?'

'Are those real?' he said. He seemed to be looking straight at her breasts. 'Them zips?' There were six gold zips on her jumpsuit. Two covered pockets, the rest were for decoration. 'Suits you,' he said. 'You go to a lot of trouble, don't you? Make the best of yourself. I like that. But you can't turn round and complain if we notice, can you?'

'Why do you keep the pictures, Jim?'

'There's a shop near me where you can get them blown up. Life size. Or bigger.' She shuddered. 'Costs, though,' he said. 'I only do that with the *really* pretty ones. I'll probably get you blown up when you leave.'

She made towards the door. 'You will not. You won't know when I leave.'

'If you don't hand in your pass you won't get your five pounds back.'

'I didn't pay five pounds,' said Antonia.

Mrs Forbes raised the platen cover of the photocopier and took out the confidential report of which Antonia was making five copies. 'This should not be done here,' she said. 'It should be done in the print room.'

'Len said I was to do it.'

'Because it's late going out, I suppose?'

'I only got it today.'

'As a temp, you do not photocopy confidential materials. You take this to the print room. And get them to sign for it.'

'Want me to keep my eyes shut on the way?'

Mrs Forbes said that taking that tone would get Antonia nowhere. She would photocopy the document herself. She did so at great speed. She was sealing the copies into envelopes with swift dabs of her pink tongue as Antonia strutted away.

'Only her spit's good enough I suppose,' grumbled Antonia to Barry who had observed the incident from afar with an amused expression. 'It says perfectly clearly in the manual for staff that only orders of twelve sheets or more are to go to the print room. I'm going to be really popular, aren't I, running down there every time Len decides he's got another secret.'

'So *that's* what you do all day! Learn the staff manual off by heart.'

'No, but Barry – '

He laid a gentle hand on her brow. 'Are you paid to think?' He took it away but she still felt it there. 'Are you? Just go with the tide, Antonia. It's easier in the long run.'

'No, but what is all this confidential business? What's confidential about hotels?'

'Who's to say they're really hotels? You think they are. I

think they are. But that's what we're supposed to think. They might be top-secret bomber bases for all I know.' He yawned. 'Or care. Is it time to go home yet?'

'No, but it's getting on for lunchtime. Why can't anyone give a straight answer to a straight question in this place, that's what I don't understand.'

'Any firm's got its competitors, Antonia. Even us. It's not impossible that once in a while Len delivers himself of some prose that might be of interest to them.'

'What kind of place is Larana?'

'Oh, a paradise,' he said. 'One of the wonders of the world. A something jewel set in a silver sea. How should I know?'

'Never heard of it till I came here.'

'That's because our security's so good,' said Barry, and Mrs Forbes came by. Barry and Antonia chorused in whispers to her back, 'There's a lot of time being wasted today,' and broke up with giggles. Alan came over with a sheet of paper and the hesitant smile of someone arriving late at a party but determined to have a good time.

'If you want to look busy, Antonia, I've got a few letters,' he said.

'I was doing some photocopying but I've been made redundant. Who are your letters to, the queen?'

'I should be nice to Alan, Antonia,' said Barry. 'He might take you to Larana on a staff visit.'

Alan said, 'She'd have to join us permanently for that. Temps can't go on staff visits.'

'Go on with you,' said Barry, 'I'm always hearing you telling temps, do as I say and I'll take you to Larana.'

It was impossible to tell who was joking now and who wasn't. It was nearly impossible for Antonia to find her voice.

'Did Samantha go with you?' she croaked.

'Who?'

'Samantha Yardley.'

'Who? What's he been saying about me? I'm a respectable married man.'

Barry laughed. 'It's true, Antonia. Alan hasn't had a day out of the office in all the time I've known him. Hasn't looked at another girl, either.' There was a lot of winking and laughter. Alan went away. 'But then I haven't known him all that long,' said Barry.

94

CHAPTER ELEVEN

User Friendly

When Catherine went along to the Clerical Workers' Union she was hoping they would have a women's officer; but as soon as she had explained her business she was taken through to meet someone called Frank Spivey, a gnome-like little figure with a neat pot belly and a beard that made his age impossible to guess.

He was courteous and friendly, treated her as if she were the one person he'd been hoping would call. She tried to talk but his phone rang a lot. And he was one of these people who didn't just talk on the phone, he performed.

'Will I speak to Tim Bird of the S & G? Of course I'll speak to Tim Bird of the S & G. Can't think of anything I'd rather do than –' Frank put his hand over the mouthpiece and whispered, 'Sorry about this. I'll get rid of him. Tim, my old mate. How are you doing?' Frank's face showed muted pain as Tim talked. 'One phrase I will never sanction my members signing, Tim,' he said, 'is "so far as reasonably practicable". Why? *Why?* (a) Because it's unnecessary. It goes without saying, Tim, that my members would never ask for anything that isn't reasonably practicable; I can't speak for yours. And (b) because employers have lawyers, Tim. And once they've driven their coach and four through a phrase like that, it ends up meaning "as long as the employers feel like it". No, Tim. It's not on.' The call ended without resolution. Frank sang softly as he put the phone down. '"The people's flag is palest pink, it's not as red as you might think." Coffee?'

'Yes please.'

The phone rang again. Leaving it, he went to the door and called, 'Tina? Could you be an angel and bring two coffees? Milk and sugar, Catherine?'

'Neither, thanks. In fact, no coffee. I've changed my mind.'

This call seemed to be about someone with a bad back. Huge with sympathy, Frank enumerated a few points concerning the law on compensation and put the call through to someone else. 'Health & Safety should deal with that. Trouble with recruitment is, once you've recruited someone you're the face of the union to them. They all think of you as Mr Fix-It. What sort of response have you been getting to these tapes of yours?'

Catherine was startled and impressed. She hadn't thought he'd been listening. She started to tell him the response had been good and she needed advice as to what to do next, but the phone cut in.

Leave it, can't you?

'Leave it, shall I?'

'Up to you,' said Catherine.

'It's annoying you, though, isn't it, and you think I'm not paying attention. I could get Tina to stop all the calls and deal with them, only you wouldn't like that either, would you, eh?' He picked up the phone before she could reply, mouthed at her that it was the General Secretary and made great play of sitting up straight. But he said, 'Sorry, Phil, I've got someone with me right now. I'll come up this afternoon.'

The calls died away. 'Lunchtime,' he said. 'It's the only time I ever get anything done.'

'Perhaps you'd like me to leave?'

'Nonsense, we've only just started. Now, you did want coffee, didn't you? If I make it? Milk and sugar? Have you had lunch?' He brought a mug for himself, a cup with a saucer for her and two unmatched chipped side-plates. He took two home-made ham sandwiches out of a paper bag in his brief-case and offered her one on a plate. Touched, she ate.

'Could you get a meeting together?' he said. 'I could come along and put the position. Get people to join there and then, group pressure works best.'

'You'd send a speaker, would you?'

'I'll try and fit it in myself.' He pulled out a diary. She chewed hard on the stale bread.

'It might be better,' she said, 'if you were to send a woman.'

He paused in mid-bite and pointed a rhetorical finger at her. 'You give us a hard time, you know that? If we set up a separate women's division, that's tokenism. If we say – as *we* in the CWU say – that all officials ought to be equally involved in the problems of all workers, that's not right either.'

She felt sympathy for him. He too knew what it was to be damned if you did and damned if you didn't. But she must be firm. 'I want to get one of the temps themselves to actually run the meeting.'

'Fine. You tell me when to speak, I'll speak. And at an agreed signal I'll shut my mouth.' He started to chuckle. He looked more like a gnome than ever.

'What now?' said Catherine.

His laughter blew out of him like a breeze. 'Subverting the test tapes. I like it. I love it.'

She finished her sandwich and coffee and felt it was time to go. They agreed a date for the meeting.

'Will I see you before that?' he said.

'I don't know.' She blushed, realizing it was an invitation and she had treated it like an enquiry. They stared at each other. 'I'll try again,' he said. 'Do you drink?'

'Not much. Er, sometimes.'

'Eat?'

'Oh yes.'

'Right,' he said. 'There's this place I know that does great curries.'

The word processor was smaller than Antonia had expected. It was cream coloured with a still green screen. It didn't look as if it would do anyone any harm.

The salesman, who had DESMOND written on his badge, addressed the secretaries. 'Now I expect some of you girls have seen these on television.'

Somebody said, 'Yeah, I saw a programme about how we're all going to be on the dole.'

'The new technology,' said Desmond, 'is going to *create* jobs.'

Liar, thought Antonia, perched on a stool at the back of the room. She didn't like Desmond. He reminded her of Mrs Hook. All right, if Forlex was going over to word processors and she was going to stay at Forlex, she'd have to learn how to use them whether she liked it or not. She wasn't saying she didn't like. But she hadn't decided whether to stay either. It was a big decision and she'd take her time. Just no one push her, that was all. She looked round at the Forlex secretaries. She'd seen some of them before: on her way to the print room, or when they came to swap magazines in Audrey's pile. She supposed if she stayed she'd get to know them, make some new friends. Their expressions seemed to divide into two: those who hated word processors and those who would probably end up buying one.

'They're bad for your eyes,' said someone. 'You can go blind.'

'They said that about sex a hundred years ago,' said Desmond impishly. No one laughed. 'Seriously though, that's a very responsible question. Flicker and glare from the VDUs on other models have been blamed for eyestrain. You should be grateful to your employers for choosing Chestnut. But don't take my word for it.' *We weren't going to.* 'Everybody look at the screen for ten seconds without blinking.' They did. He timed them on his watch. 'Now shut your eyes. Can you still see any glare? There you are, then. May I have a volunteer, please – someone who hasn't *already* got a headache from the noise of an ordinary typewriter?' A girl with long black hair went forward and sat before the keyboard. Desmond picked up what looked like a record still in its sleeve and stuck it into a slot in one of the wired-up boxes. 'Floppy disk,' he said.

The machine whirred and letters appeared on the screen. WELCOME TO NUTSHELL. 'Nutshell's the name of our introductory word-processing teaching package,' Desmond explained.

WHAT'S YOUR NAME? asked the machine. The girl with the long black hair gave a little squeal and bent closer.

'Gather round, everyone,' ordered Desmond. Antonia moved a little bit closer so that she could see but she stayed on the edge of the group.

'Type in your name. Go on, don't be scared, it's a perfectly ordinary keyboard.'

The girl typed LIZ but her hand slipped with nerves and it came out as LIZX. She blushed. Desmond said, 'Don't worry, I'll show you how to delete in a minute.'

GOOD DAY LIZX AND WELCOME TO YOUR FIRST LESSON. DO YOU WISH TO OPEN A FILE?

Liz grinned up at Desmond. 'I don't know. Do I?'

He explained that if she called her file LIZX then forever afterwards everything she typed would be stored in the computer's memory and could be recalled in seconds if she asked for it by name. But she would have to say LIZX. The computer wouldn't recognize LIZ.

'One day computers'll know more than we know,' said someone.

'They can't know anything we don't tell them,' Antonia announced. 'They're basically stupid and mechanical.'

'Er, yes,' said Desmond. 'I'll demonstrate the Global Search Function. Suppose it's ten to five.' Antonia muttered, 'Wish it was,' but nobody heard. All eyes were on Desmond who had hustled Liz from her seat and taken it himself. He was busily fiddling with disks and keys while the screen filled up with rapidly shifting text.

'Suppose it's ten to five and you've just typed a thirteen-page report about a firm called Johnson Limited, and your boss looks at it and says it's not Johnson, it's *Johnstone*, and I can't let you use Tippex and it's got to go out tonight.' All the secretaries nodded, remembering occasions when just this sort of thing had happened.

Antonia said, 'I wouldn't stand for it, not if he told me wrong in the first place.'

'You press,' said Desmond, 'the Global Search key and ask it to locate all the Johnsons and turn them into Johnstones. Like this. It'll do all the corrections in the time it takes you to collect up your bits and pieces and say goodnight to your friends.'

'If they haven't all been fired.'

Desmond smiled at Antonia. 'You haven't tried it yet, have you?'

'I don't want – '

'You can be next. Fear of innovation, you know, often arises from ignorance and inexperience.' Someone laughed. Antonia went forward and Desmond whispered, '*Touché?*'

It was a QWERTY keyboard with a few extras: arrows pointing in different directions, words like DELETE, CONTROL, PAGE, ACCEPT and new things like CHAR and CURSOR. Desmond asked her name. She didn't answer. He asked again.

'Just a *minute*. I'm having a look. It's Antonia.'

'We've already got a file called Antonia. From the last lesson.' Anyone would think it was her fault. 'We'll have to get rid of it.'

She stared intently at him while he told her how to do this. She kept her eyes hard and her mouth a tight line. She wanted him to know that she didn't mind listening to him if he had something worth saying but she didn't like him. Soon she pressed her first key on her first word processor. It was DELETE. The screen shook itself into alertness. Luminous green worms uncoiled into letters.

DELETE WHICH FILE?

'Delete Antonia,' said Desmond.

DELETE ANTONIA.

ARE YOU SURE?

Antonia laughed 'Talks back, does it?'

'Yes. Like you. It's the anti-error feature. Tell it again.'

DELETE ANTONIA.

ARE YOU REALLY SURE?

'Bit cheeky, isn't it?'

'User Friendly, we call it. You have to tell it three times before it deletes a file. Could be serious. There was a lady writer working on a machine without this feature once and she deleted a book by mistake. Six hundred pages. Now you can delete all the others for practice, they're only training files.'

DELETE ANTONIA DELETE JANE DELETE SANDY DELETE LIZX ARE YOU SURE ARE YOU REALLY SURE DELETE SAMANTHA.

'Fine,' said Desmond.

'Delete Samantha.'

'Girl at another firm.'

'What can I do now?'

'It's someone else's turn now.'

'But I haven't done anything except delete people.'

'We'll never get her away from it now,' said Desmond to the rest of the girls. 'All right, you can do some standard letters.' By typing the letter only once you could produce hundreds of different versions, personalized for different people. Some of the other secretaries wanted their turn but Antonia didn't move. Desmond gave her a plastic-backed training card. The instructions were easy to follow if you concentrated. First you typed the letter. The keys yielded to the slightest touch, the beautiful green characters arranging themselves neatly on the screen. Then you typed the variables in a list: Mr Smith, carbon paper, £10 a ream; Mrs Jones, push-chair, £15.50; Miss Harris, make-up box, £3.

'Now we activate the printer – ' The wired-up box jolted and hummed. A tiny wheel of letters spun faster than the eye could follow. 'Two hundred characters a second,' whispered Desmond. Out came the sheets of paper, perfect originals. Dear Mr Smith, we confirm that our special carbon paper is available at £10 a ream. Dear Mrs Jones, we confirm that our special push-chair is available at £15.50. Dear Miss Harris–

'Wow,' Antonia breathed.

'Good, eh?' said Desmond.

'Mm.'

You learned fast. That's a difficult function. You're a natural.'

'What else can it do?'

He showed how it could rearrange lines and pages of text to accommodate a correction. He showed how it could do underlining and italics. He changed the disk in the disk drive. Now it could do accounts, stock control, drawings. He said, 'That's enough for today, I think.' He said he looked forward to meeting those girls selected by Forlex for the full training course. 'One last thing,' he said, proffering a bottle of aspirins. 'Headaches, eyestrain, anybody?' The girl who had mentioned eyestrain blushed and was nudged by her friend. Desmond gave everybody a coloured booklet to take away, called *Word Processing, a New Chestnut*.

Antonia went back to the drawing office. *He said I was a natural*.

'How did it go?' said Barry. 'Seen Audrey's postcard?' He pointed to a new addition to the cards on the noticeboard: The Needles, Isle of Wight. He took it down for her.

'He said I was a natural.'

'What did I tell you?' Barry mimicked her: '"I hate word processors. I can't do it because I've never tried it."'

'It's almost human. It talks to you. Of course it's program-med, it can't do anything it hasn't been programmed to do. It all comes down to yes and no–'

'Don't most things in life? See what's happened to Aud?'

'You have to stick a disk in it to tell it what it is.'

'I beg your pardon?'

'No, Barry, *sshh*. It all comes down to yes and no. If yes do this. If no, do that. If you want to underline something you have

101

to press the underline key. You have to decide before you do it what's important. Only it doesn't matter if you make a mistake because you can correct it and it doesn't leave a mark, the whole thing rearranges itself as if you'd never –' Barry was grinning at her. She reached out a hand for the card. 'What's this?' she asked dully, 'Audrey's resignation letter?'

'No, this is another one, just arrived. The Real Truth, for popular consumption.'

Antonia read the card. '"I'm IN LOVE!!! The boy next door, would you believe. He was always CREEPISSIMO when we were growing up but suddenly he's transformed! So I'm staying on with Mum and Dad for a while – " She's staying with her *parents*?'

'On the Isle of Wight, yes. Apparently that's where she always goes. Not a great traveller, our Aud.'

In love on the Isle of Wight. Oh well. Good luck to her. Good luck to everyone who was in love, wherever they were.

'So the Chestnut salesman's had his way with you, has he?' said Barry.

'Do me a favour.'

'Be glad to, how would dinner suit you?' He turned pink under his sandy hair.

'When?'

'Tomorrow?'

'I'm tied up this week.'

'Well – '

'And next.'

'All right, Antonia, some time, eh?'

'Aren't you married, Barry?'

'I'm divorced.'

'Oh. Okay, then. Some time.' She smiled to show that she did like him.

Frank collected Catherine on a motorbike, bringing a spare helmet for her to wear. He rode the machine with great dash and aplomb, but stopping was a problem: he had to tilt it dangerously (it felt dangerous to Catherine) to get a foot to the ground, his legs were so short. 'Suppose I put my feet down,' she said. 'Then you can get off.'

'Brilliant.'

He ordered enormous quantities of curried things and side

102

dishes for himself; she just asked for a vegetable biryani but she still felt hungry when she'd finished it so she helped him finish his. He continued to perform and, rather than talk to her, address her on matters of union business; but she didn't mind, she recognized the signs of someone so conscientious and committed that they never switched off, and she was fascinated. And every so often he would glance at his watch: 'Look, we've been listening to my voice for ten minutes solid. Tell me something about *you*.' Then he would ask delicious probing questions. When she offered to pay her half he wouldn't have it – 'I chose the restaurant. But I promise I'll still respect you if you pay next time.' *Feminist man*, she thought; *half-trained*. 'Trouble is,' he said, 'if you do try to be supportive, as a man, and encourage women with their painting or whatever, all they do is leave you and go to live in America.' In spite of the impersonal 'you' and the plurals, she guessed that this was how he had started to be trained, and had his training cut short. She had visions of a stream of artistic young women with suitcases and folded-up easels making their way out of his front door and down his steps. The suitcases all had Pan Am labels attached.

It was Friday afternoon. Antonia took her time sheet in for Len to sign as usual. Looking at a point somewhere beyond her left shoulder, he said, 'Are you up to date with the filing?'

'Yes, Len.'

'And has the progress report gone out?'

'Yes.'

'Good.'

He scribbled on her time sheet and gave it back to her. She returned to her territory and looked at it. She went back to Len. He was on the phone. She waited for him to finish. She said, 'Excuse me, Len. Did you mean to put "no" here? It means you don't want me back next week.'

'I have a new permanent girl starting next week. Audrey has resigned.'

'I know, but . . .'

He was spreading a drawing out on his desk. He was having trouble getting the corners to lie flat. He glanced up once: Antonia was still there. He thrust out his damp hand for her to shake. 'Good luck in the future,' he said.

She stormed over to Barry. 'Good luck in the future,' she said.

103

'Eh?'

'That's what he said to me. I thought you said he was going to ask me to stay. He's got someone else starting next week.'

Barry scratched his ear with a pencil and looked dumbfounded, disbelieving, furious. 'The ass. The stupid *ass*.'

'What is it, Barry? What have I done wrong? I'm entitled to know. Is it because I was late, once?'

Alan overheard and ambled towards them with the look of a schoolboy who had just heard a dirty story. Barry was still fuming. 'What a prat Len is. I thought he was joking – '

'Len never jokes about sacred matters,' Alan put in. 'Let's tell Antonia, she'll probably be flattered.'

'I'd be ashamed to tell her anything so petty,' said Barry.

Antonia turned her back on him and faced Alan. 'Well?'

'He says you're too pretty,' said Alan. 'He says you keep distracting us from our work. He says first of all Mrs Forbes complained so he let her stop you walking through the office to go to the photocopier, and then he noticed it himself. He says next time he's going to get another old bag like her, with her hair in a bun, and productivity in the department will treble. Don't look at me like that, Antonia, I'm only telling you what he said. I mean, it's better than being sacked for rank incompetence, isn't it?'

It was like watching a film in which the sound suddenly broke down and the camera went crazy, darting round and focussing on little things that seemed unconnected but suddenly made a pattern: cups of coffee and bottles of ink next to intricate drawings; lamps perched on the edges of tables; slender-stemmed rubber plants; Mrs Forbes' flower vase made of the finest china; the glass walls round Len's office . . .

The sound came back. 'I could smash this place up,' she was saying, wonderingly.

'I'm sorry I spoke,' said Alan, pretending to shield his head.

'I wouldn't stay in this place if it was the last job left in the world.'

'That's the spirit,' said Barry.

She turned on him. 'Don't you that's-the-spirit me. I must've been mad to come here in the first place. I'm lucky to get away with my life, I reckon.' Alan walked off sheepishly and sat among his nudes. 'What about them?' Antonia shouted across the office. 'Aren't *they* a distraction?'

'They don't chat to us,' said Alan.

Barry stood protectively between his drawings and Antonia. 'Don't do anything rash, Antonia. Not that I'd blame you.'

'You're not worth it,' she retorted.

She went back to her territory. She looked at her watch. It was 3.20. She had put 5.00 on her time sheet and Len had signed it. In her tray were some handwritten letters marked MOST URGENT. She tore them up. She went through her stationery supplies and took Sellotape, notebooks, envelopes, Biros and headed notepaper in case she ever needed a reference. Then she started a leisurely sort through the secretaries' magazines to see if there were any she hadn't read yet. At the bottom she found an issue of *Girl in London*, several months old. 'S. Yardley' was written in pencil on the cover.

She sealed the magazine up in an envelope with a With Compliments slip, addressed it to Catherine and put it in the postal tray marked First Class. Len darted like a guilty lizard out of his office and put three more sheets of typing in her typing tray. She tipped the tray into the waste paper basket before his eyes. On her way out Barry approached her and hesitantly repeated his invitation to dinner. She gave him her phone number. In the lobby she handed Jim her pass and he gave her five pounds.

CHAPTER TWELVE

Against the Cuts

The boutique was having a closing-down sale. There was a blue and white cotton gingham dress in the window, fresh and summery, at £5.99. It had half sleeves, a tight bodice and flared skirt.

Antonia had two five-pound notes in her purse. She went into the shop. Kate Bush was playing. She hummed as she tried on the dress, which fitted perfectly. She fluffed out her hair over her shoulders.

'Shall I wrap the dress up?' offered the assistant.

'No, I'll wear it now,' said Antonia. She gave the assistant the clothes she'd come in to wrap.

'Hi, Antonia,' said the doctor. He looked like Billy Connolly and had an accent like Catherine's. He wore desert boots, jeans and a white coat. His badge said DR DAVE DAY. Another badge said DOCTORS AGAINST THE CUTS.

'Congratulations,' she said.

'Pardon?'

'Got my name right.'

'I looked in the file. What can we do for you?'

The little room was very cold. She looked down at her lap and the blues and whites of her new dress. She followed the threads with her eyes. There was one thread that had been woven wrong or dyed wrong. It was white in the blue squares and blue in the white. She hadn't noticed this in the shop.

She explained that she wanted a check-up and got ready.

'Didn't need to take the dress off,' said Dr Dave Day.

'It's new.'

A nurse draped a sheet across her knees.

'I don't know what this is in aid of,' said Dr Dave Day. 'We can see everything, why shouldn't the patient?'

Antonia said, 'Please leave it there.'

'This'll feel a bit cold, sorry. You're very tense.'

'I know.'

'Wiggle your toes.'

She wiggled them.

'Just the one attack and no problems since?'

'No problems since.'

'Looks like you're one of the lucky ones, then. Everything okay with the IUD?'

She laughed. 'Must be. I'd forgotten it was there.' She remembered thinking she'd have it taken out, forget the whole thing. She could ask him to do it now. Just pull the string and out it would come. On the other hand it wasn't doing any harm.

Wasn't doing any good either.

She ought to start leaving off her wedding ring too.

'No problems,' said Dr Dave Day, after a long silence interrupted only by the soft *cling* of instruments in dishes. 'Would you like to get dressed?'

Once she was dressed he seemed to expect her to go but she sat on the chair by his desk and looked down at her skirt, scratching at the odd thread with her fingernail. A loop came loose. 'How,' she asked, 'can you be sure?'

'I'm as sure as I can be. You look very healthy. You want a second opinion?'

'How can *anyone* be sure when it's incurable?'

'Antonia, the common *cold*'s incurable.'

'Do me a – don't give me that.'

'I'm not sure what you're asking me.'

Not much you're not. Won't look at me, will you? Your notes with my life written on them. She held the loose thread and tried to straighten the skirt so that the blue bit would go into a blue square and the white bit into a white square. 'Is it true that once you've got it even if you think you're not having an attack you can still be infectious?' The words were surprisingly easy to find once it came to it. They came out in a rush.

'Don't spoil your nice dress,' he said softly. Too late. The thread broke, a hole appeared in the skirt, getting bigger and

107

bigger. The fabric was collapsing, she could see her tights. '*Oh,*' he said, as if it were a great tragedy. 'I'll answer your question,' he said. 'The overwhelming consensus is no, you can't. There's a small minority of researchers who think yes, you can.'

'Thanks a lot.'

'I'll give you the references if you like,' he said, 'and you can weigh the evidence for yourself.'

'What do you think? If I was your girlfriend, what would you think?'

'I can't answer that.'

'I know why you can't. You don't think there's any point in telling me I can't ever have sex again because you think I don't know how to say no.' She started to pace in her torn dress. 'You think I'm a nymphomaniac, well I haven't touched a man since all this and don't think I haven't had the chance.'

He closed the screens round the bed for her to change her clothes. He went on talking to her through the screens. 'Some of the nicest people I've ever met,' he said, 'I've met here.'

'Is it all right if I have a cigarette?'

'Of course.' He passed an ashtray in to her.

'"Why doesn't your doctor smoke?"' she said softly. '"Because he's seen too many patients who do."'

'Pardon?'

'Advert I saw once.' Her deep sucks hauled the flame along the cigarette like a forest fire. It hurt her throat but she went on talking. 'Scared the life out of me so I changed to low tars.'

'Me too,' said Dr Dave Day.

'*Really?* Want one?'

'Better not.'

'What would you do if you got lung cancer?'

'Die probably. What do you mean, what would I do?'

She came out from behind the screen dressed in her old clothes, carrying the new dress. 'All right if I put this in your bin?'

'It's a shame – '

'It's no good.'

'If you mean wouldn't it feel terrible to know my own silly habits and weakness had caused my death, then yes, of course. But I hope I'd live long enough to come to terms – to say oh well, I enjoyed the cigarettes and weakness is part of the person I am. Was.'

'Got any ideas about how to tell people?'

'You do change the subject a lot, don't you?'

'No. First time you go out with them? They might say, "Fancy yourself, don't you? I wasn't planning on sleeping with you in any case."'

'It's difficult,' he conceded. 'Just try and bring it naturally into the conversation. Don't make a big drama of it.'

'Oh, right. Thanks.'

'You're really giving yourself a hard time, aren't you? The thing about nymphomaniacs, as you put it, is that they don't *care* about their partners. You wouldn't find a real card-carrying nymphomaniac letting a thing like this turn her into a nun.'

She dashed her eyes with the back of her hand. 'I can't be one then, can I?'

She'd arranged to meet Barry in a pub. She arrived early and walked round the block. Three minutes late she went in and saw him at a table, reading a *Standard* and drinking a pint. She waited for him to turn a page and glance up and see her. She waited for his face to light up. That lighting up would tell her that everything was all right. She would go over to him and perhaps he would kiss her on the cheek and perhaps she would tell him she had bought a new dress and torn it. What else would she tell him? The trouble was, she couldn't even imagine the answer she wanted to hear. *That's all right, I've got it too?* She knew she'd be disgusted, crazy but she would. *That's all right, if we get that far, you be careful and I'll risk it.* Why should anyone say that? Only if they were madly in love with you, then they might. But it wasn't fair to let them fall madly in love with you without knowing. He read on. She backed out of the pub and went away.

'D'you think it was a mistake,' Catherine frowned, 'to have men here?'

Antonia had arrived late at the meeting. At least, she'd thought she'd be late. Well, she'd thought she wouldn't come at all. 'Sorry, I've got a date,' she'd told Catherine, 'but good luck and let me know what happens.' The answer was nothing, nothing was happening.

Not that there weren't plenty of people there, perched two to a chair some of them. It was mainly girls and women though

109

there were a few men who looked like students or actors. 'Some of the Bright Girls are boys,' Catherine explained. 'I just hope they don't take over.'

Antonia wished someone would. A girl came over, frantic and pink-cheeked with a pile of papers in her hand and rather nasty patent leather shoes, and had an anguished conversation with Catherine who was trying to reassure her. 'When you're ready,' said Catherine. 'I'll say shhh.'

'I'll give these out first,' said the girl. She seemed relieved.

'Who's that?' Antonia demanded.

'Her name's Lisa. I persuaded her to be chairperson. She's actually very militant only now she's terrified.'

'Why her?'

Catherine gave her a crooked look. 'Why? Would you have done it if I'd asked you?'

'No fear. I mean, why not you?'

'I'm not going to be head girl any more.'

Antonia looked at the sheet of paper Lisa had given her. She felt annoyed; if the meeting wasn't going to be properly organized why bother? The paper was headed 'A New Charter for Temps: Draft Demands for Discussion'. *We'd never get these in a million years.* '(1) a 50% increase in hourly rates, (2) one week's notice or pay in lieu, (3) union recognition, (4) no sexual harassment and (5) no use of temps to replace workers made redundant.'

'Can we have some order please?' Lisa croaked, and Catherine went 'Shhh!', nudging Antonia until she went 'Shhh!' too. At last there was silence except for the sound of Lisa's papers quivering in her hand. 'Now, does, er, anyone want to say anything about any of these demands?'

'Some of them are obviously more crucial than others,' said one of the male students at once. Catherine grimaced but Lisa looked at him with gratitude: 'Would you like to, er –'

'Numbers one to three, for example,' he said, standing up. 'Five isn't really anything to do with the agencies. It's up to permanent staff in the workplace to ensure that that doesn't happen. We have to be clear who we're making demands *of.*'

'*I – don't – believe – it!*' Catherine looked as if she could spit bullets although she was only whispering.

'What?'

'See how he's done it? We've been going five minutes and

110

he's rendered the one demand that's specific to women – sexual harassment – *invisible*!'

'Say something then.'

'I'm not going to impose . . . *you* say something.'

'Me!'

'Tell them about why you got fired from Forlex.'

And have everyone think, 'Too pretty? Who's she think she is?'

'Would you mind if I told them?' Catherine pressed.

'You mention it and I'm going home.'

'But it *proves* – '

'Why don't *you* tell them about Samantha Yardley? Hey, have you thought, she might be here.'

'I've found out something pretty important about that,' said Catherine. 'Thanks for sending the magazine.'

Another man had arrived, hairy and scruffy and short, pushing his way to the front of the meeting with a brief-case under his arm. Catherine suddenly looked tense and very, very pleased. She whispered, 'I'll tell you later,' and leant forward to hear the man speak.

'If I, er, could just intervene here?' He shoved his hands into his pockets and waited for silence. 'Frank Spivey, Clerical Workers' Union. I'm very pleased to have been asked here this evening.'

'I did ask them to send a woman,' Catherine whispered, 'but . . .'

'The CWU hasn't had a lot of luck with temps,' he continued. 'Working in different parts of town, isolated from each other and the branch – '

'Frank,' said Lisa, scarlet in the face but firm, 'if you want to say anything, could you please do it through the, er, chair?'

'Oh. Sorry, Lisa.'

'That's right, Frank. Do as you're told and keep quiet,' whispered Catherine, but only for Antonia to hear. So Catherine knew Frank already. And so did Lisa. They were all friends together.

Someone said, 'But I want to know about the union; we were just wasting time before.'

'No we weren't, we were getting to know each other.'

'Getting to know the men, you mean,' said someone else. 'Why isn't this meeting women only?'

'The speech on the union comes later,' said Lisa. It was

111

impossible to imagine her going any redder but her voice was firm and Frank Spivey sat down. He was soon called upon to speak again, though. There was a lot of discussion about whether the agencies could afford the first two demands. Some said they'd price themselves out of the market, others said they could take it out of their commissions. But it all came down to how they should set about asking. Frank Spivey sat silent and expectant as the discussion came back again and again to the union.

'We'll have to stick together,' said someone, 'all for one and one for all.'

'Are we a majority of BGM temps?' someone else wanted to know.

'No,' Catherine admitted, 'but once we've got a branch and recognition it'll be easier to recruit the others.'

Frank Spivey said, 'Trouble's been in the past that temps who join unions suddenly find the agency isn't giving them any work. For some reason which I can't for the life of me explain.' Everyone booed cheerfully. 'So it's important to get a majority as soon as possible, even think about a closed shop.' Some didn't approve of that. 'I'm not saying the union's the answer to all your problems, comrades, but if that's what you decide to do, I'm at your service.' An all-out recruitment drive at Bright Girls of Mayfair, followed by a demand for recognition, was decided upon. Frank produced a sheaf of forms from his brief-case.

'Lisa! You were fantastic!' Lisa had been circulating the forms with Frank and had now come over to be praised by Catherine. She'd stopped blushing all over, though her cheeks were still bright pink like a sporty schoolgirl's.

'Was I all right?' she breathed.

Catherine's just said, you were fantastic.

'I was so nervous!'

'Yes, I thought you were,' said Antonia, then she wondered why she was being so catty. Some people might think it was because she was jealous that Catherine seemed to have taken Lisa up now but Antonia knew she didn't get like that about girlfriends.

'You can fill this in now,' said Lisa nicely, handing Antonia a form. 'And I'll take your pound.'

112

'I'll think about it,' said Antonia, wishing she hadn't come. She hadn't thought she'd be put on the spot.

'What's there to think about?'

'Look, I agree with all this, but I need to work.'

'Who doesn't? Can't make an omelette without breaking eggs. Think of the –' Lisa's face went blank.

'Tolpuddle Martyrs?' Catherine supplied. 'You see Antonia, the sooner there's one hundred per cent membership, the sooner we'll have power. And management won't even know you've joined until there's enough people to –'

'What if they find out?'

'What is this?' said Lisa. 'Everyone else has joined.'

'Yes, well, I bet most of them are living at home or they've got husbands supporting them. Didn't think to ask that, did you?'

'God's gift to management, you are.'

'I think we ought to take Rosa Luxemburg here for a drink, don't you, Cath?' said Frank, joining them. He meant Lisa.

'We'll *all* go for a drink,' said Catherine quickly, including Antonia.

'I didn't think much about it at first,' said Catherine. 'A women's magazine is a women's magazine. It only proves she *did* work there, and we knew that already.'

'I thought it might be helpful,' said Antonia.

'Oh, it was. Because I was reading this article about food allergies and there was a page missing.'

'Elementary,' said Frank, quaffing his pint.

'So I went along to the magazine's office, got a back number and guess what had been cut out?'

'Tell us,' said Lisa, who was obviously in on this too.

'An advertisement for an outfit called HooRay Holidays. And what was interesting was that they had a special offer for temps. Something like "Not working next week? You could be lying in the sun, on one of our last-minute bargains."'

'Oh, why haven't I ever thought of that?' said Antonia lighting a cigarette. No one else smoked. 'I mean, all those times I've been unemployed, I could have gone on holiday if only I'd thought of it.'

'*Exactly*. Now, doesn't it strike you as a bit funny that Samantha Yardley, two weeks after being raped – out of work and living in a doss house – should take herself off to Larana even if it was a cut-price bargain?'

'How do you know she did that?'

'I went to HooRay holidays of course,' said Catherine, 'and checked.'

'Larana?' said Antonia.

'Heard of it?'

'We build hotels there.'

'You do?'

'I mean Forlex does.'

There was an awed silence.

'Did she go alone?' said Frank.

'I asked that, but they went all prim. "We can't give you that information." They probably thought I was a jealous wife.'

'Did you get the name of the hotel?'

'HooRay only have one hotel there. The Excelsior. Is that one of Forlex's?'

'I don't recognize it,' said Antonia.

'Well,' said Frank after another pause, 'seems to me it's your civic duty, Catherine, to go there and suss it out. Blimey, I wish I could think of an excuse like that for having a holiday.'

They talked about other things. Lisa kept dropping dark hints about people who wouldn't join unions. She didn't seem to realize that this made it less, not more, likely that Antonia would ever join. Antonia said she had to go, and the others said they had to as well. Antonia walked off in the opposite direction from Lisa. From the end of the street she looked back and saw Catherine and Frank shooting off on a motorbike. Catherine looked absurd with a helmet on, like a long-stalked mushroom.

CHAPTER THIRTEEN

The Recovery Section

HyperMail Limited. Everything for the Modern Home Delivered To Your Doorstep on Easy Terms. The warehouse was in Northampton; the London office was near Liverpool Street, up three flights of sooty stairs which coiled round a defunct lift shaft.

Antonia was to be in the Recovery Section with six other temps, all from different agencies, and three permanent typists, one of whom was Rosa the supervisor. Rosa was middle aged with thick legs, a tired smile and a foreign accent.

The Recovery Section sent off personal letters to people who owed the firm money. There were ten desks in the small room which led off a much larger open-plan office where men went through files, worked things out on calculators and spoke into dictaphones. The men then brought the files and the dictaphone tapes into the typing room.

Rosa warned that at the end of the day she had to write in a ledger the number of letters each girl had done. They should aim at fifty. 'It is not difficult,' she reassured. 'Most letters are the same. And if you make a little mistake, leave it, and they will send it back for re-type if they notice. Then it counts for two.'

Workmen were drilling the road outside. Rosa closed the window and said, 'Now you must start.' She pressed a master-switch and ten electric typewriters hummed. Three of them began to rattle like guns as the permanent girls set to work. Everybody was smoking. Sandwiched between two permanent girls, Antonia untangled the wires of her headphones. The ear-pieces were grubby and sticky to the touch. Antonia spat on a Kleenex and wiped them.

The letters were short and sinister. Like Mrs Hook. *Here Tomorrow is flourishing, thank you, dear. How nice of you to ask. Bright Girls of Mayfair? Yes, I'd heard they were having some trouble with their temps. What a sensible decision.* (Catherine had been fired from BGM. Lisa soldiered on, undetected.) *My temps have never felt the need for trades unions . . . Maggie? Would you come in, dear? Antonia has something to say to us. We can be gracious, can't we? When's the next word-processing course we're sending temps on? Not till October? Well, then, Antonia. You have till October . . .*

The letters threatened further action. The man on Antonia's tape sounded drunk. The tape was very old. In the background there were echoes of previous letters that had not been properly wiped.

Take a tip, Antonia, stick at this one, okay? She's had it up to here with you . . .

She had to look in the files for the full addresses of the debtors because the voice usually said just, 'To Mrs Forrest, Dagenham.' Sometimes there were letters in the file, in quavering handwriting: 'My husband is under the doctor with "ANKYLOSING SPONDYLITIS" and has been off work for six weeks, I will pay by instalments, I can pay 50p per week, I will start next week.' Sometimes there were reports from debt collectors. 'The house has good carpets and furniture. In my opinion the Named Person is well able to pay.'

'Work, you must work,' Rosa insisted, mouthing above the roar of the typewriters when she saw Antonia reading the files. The voice on the tape faded out of hearing. Antonia fiddled with the volume control. The voice boomed back into her eardrum.

She picked her way over coils of flex and went to Rosa. 'I can't hear my tapes properly.'

'Try, you must try,' said Rosa. She said something else which Antonia could not hear, so Rosa wrote it down. 'If the machine is sent for repairing you will not be able to work.'

Antonia sighed and returned to her desk, lighting another cigarette. The ear-pieces roared and itched in her ears. The room shook. Every now and then the door opened and a man strode in with another pile of files and tapes. Antonia finished her third letter and looked at her watch. She had been working for an hour. The permanent girls' letters were piling up. Even the other temps were making better progress than she was.

She stopped reading the files and tried to concentrate on the letters. The typewriter seized up and the tape went dead. She was in the middle of a word and her finger slipped, grazing itself between two immobilized keys. Thick silence descended on the room. Cigarette smoke lay in still layers. Even the road drill seemed far away.

Antonia said, 'Power cut? Thank God for that.' She pulled her ear-pieces out of her ears.

'Not a power cut, coffee break,' beamed Rosa, standing over the master-switch.

They had fifteen minutes for coffee. Antonia said she would just take five and catch up, but Rosa kept the master-switch turned off. 'If you work in the coffee break, he will say we can all work in the coffee break.' There was a kettle in the corner, with mugs with brown-stained insides and a carton of milk. Antonia made coffee for everyone who wanted it; the others had cans of Coke and One-Cal and Cariba. Rosa told the story of her fight for the coffee break. 'I said to him, what do you think we are, machines? He said, *my* people have no coffee break. I said you must be joking. You people outside have a break whenever you want. You don't have a plug in your ear. You have a chat, how's the wife, had a good weekend? Et cetera. In here we are like machines, plugged in, type, type, type, and in any case the type-writers are getting overheated. He said, oh, in *that* case –' One of the permanent girls started reading out everybody's horoscope. Antonia went to the washroom to clean her ear-pieces.

Once they were clean, the second half of the morning's work seemed easier. She did twelve letters before lunch. At one o'clock Rosa turned the power off again. The girls took out salads and the smell of cheese hung on the air. Antonia asked if anyone wanted to go to the pub but no one did so she went alone. She had a lager and lime and a ploughman's, and saw one of the men who kept bringing in files. She smiled at him but he looked right through her.

She got back at ten to two. The room was empty except for Rosa who was reading the *Complete Works of Shakespeare*. A smoky haze hung over the desks. Through it Rosa nodded approvingly: 'You are early, Antonia.' She pronounced it Anton-*ee*-yah. 'You are a good worker. Slow but getting faster. I will tell him and maybe he will offer you a permanent job.'

'Thanks, but I'm not looking for a permanent job. If I do all right here. I'm going on a word-processing course.' Antonia looked round the room. 'One machine could do all this.'

'Word processor! They only got electric typewriters for us a year ago.'

Antonia managed seventeen letters before tea. Rosa was full of praise. She came over to her desk with a letter in her hand. 'You are an educated girl,' she began.

'Well. Not very.'

'Look at this, please, and tell me if it is good English. I typed it straight from the tape and the tape is spoken by an *Englishman*.' The letter said, 'I beg to acknowledge receipt of £5, please confirm in what respect the sum relates to.'

'Doesn't sound right, does it?' Antonia agreed. Did it matter? Rosa went triumphantly back to her desk and thumped her Shakespeare with her fist: 'The preposition is in the wrong place!'

'I suppose so.'

'You suppose so? It is your language, not mine. You should be proud of it and angry when it is maltreated.' The break ended. Rosa was still muttering 'in what respect the sum relates to' as she turned on the master-switch.

Delete Antonia.

Yes I'm Sure.

It wasn't a word processor and it hadn't said that. It was the television and she'd fallen asleep in front of it. She had it in her bedroom now. Why mess up two rooms? Furiously she turned the dial. She'd missed the end of the film she was watching and now it was snowflakes, snowflakes, snowflakes. In America the television stayed on all night. Maybe she could go and live in America.

God's gift to management, said Dr Dave Day, chasing her; she couldn't run but he couldn't catch her. He was a virus with green tentacles, he would trap her in a suitcase and send her to Larana in the hold of a plane. *I'll be with you always,* he said. *I'll be with you in your spine.* He threw himself on her and inserted himself into her spine.

She got out of bed. Keeping the flat in darkness she ran herself a bath. She tried to smoke but the cigarette kept getting wet. She

118

scrubbed and sponged at her body but it wouldn't get any cleaner. She remembered she'd already bathed this evening . . . yesterday evening; it was three am.

Might as well walk to work. She'd been neglecting exercise and the articles said maintain a good level of general health. Well, they would, wouldn't they? Who ever wrote an article saying neglect your health? She dressed in office clothes and her winter coat.

The trees on Clapham Common rustled and whistled at her but she saw no one.

She walked by the river, through the waking West End and the City. Sometimes she dawdled or found herself resting on benches, which was ridiculous really because she wasn't in the least bit tired. She could have been working all night, all this time. Why on earth hadn't she thought of it before? It was just before seven when she reached HyperMail and even Liverpool Street Station sparkled with freshness. She reckoned she could get at least fifteen letters under her belt before Rosa arrived.

But HyperMail was locked. She should have thought of that. Never mind, she'd have breakfast. She went into a sandwich bar and had coffee and a Danish pastry. The place was full of workmen and railwaymen who smiled at her and said she was up early. She smiled back. Really they were the nicest kinds of men, the nicest of the lot, much better than disc-jockeys and stewards and information officers, how come she'd never gone out with one? There was a time when she could have gone out with anyone she wanted.

She stayed in the sandwich bar till eight, then returned to the office and found a side door open. She climbed the stairs in the quiet building. There was a man in the Ladies, fitting a new roller towel. Antonia said good morning, hesitated, what the hell, and ducked straight into the loo. He was gone when she came out. She filled a basin with cold water, washed her face and put on her make-up.

The sun shone in wide beams across the quiet typing room. The road menders hadn't started yet. Antonia turned on the master-switch. She half expected it to fuse and shoot blue sparks. It didn't. Funny how you didn't quite trust electricity.

Rosa was impressed and disturbed to find her. 'You must go home early,' she said, 'or he will say, that girl starts at eight o'clock, you all can start at eight o'clock.'

'But I want my time sheet to look good for Mrs Hook.'

Rosa grumbled and the other girls came in.

'I want her to know I know what hard work is.' Antonia insisted. She was typing so fast her keys jammed and her fingernails were breaking one by one. She was finishing ten letters an hour. That would be seventy in the day, eighty if she could persuade Rosa not to make her have lunch. The letters were to council housing departments: 'I understand that a Mr Patrick Schaffly is now a tenant of yours, and would be grateful if you would assist me to ascertain his whereabouts as it is of an urgent nature that I contact him.' 'I understand that Mrs M. L. Rice is now . . .'

God's gift to a word processor.

'Coffee,' said Rosa.

'I don't want any – '

Rosa turned the electricity off. Antonia screamed, 'Leave it, let me finish.' Looking as if she had been punched, Rosa turned it back on. She brought Antonia coffee at her desk with an air of high dudgeon. 'I understand that a Miss A. J. Pine is . . .' *It's a rotten shame,* thought Antonia, *going after people when they haven't got any money.* Then it was like two voices in her head, three if she counted the voice on the tape piercing the area between her ears. *They shouldn't order stuff if they can't pay for it. They didn't know, what if somebody died? If they paid their debts you wouldn't have this job. If they got word processors you wouldn't have this job. I would, it's the others that wouldn't, I'd be the one working the word processor.* She glared triumphantly at the coffee drinkers. Grinning at her and mouthing, now what was so funny? 'Having an interesting conversation with yourself?' they asked as she pulled out her ear-pieces. 'It's the first sign of madness,' said Rosa, 'when you talk to yourself.'

'Rosa.'

'Yes?'

'When I do my time sheet, can I put the number of letters on it as well as my hours?'

'Get us all fired, you will,' said a girl. Antonia typed on grimly. Five minutes before lunch she looked at the page she was typing and saw nothing but dirty marks. The ribbon had run out and she'd done a whole paragraph without noticing. Furiously she grasped at the carriage return lever and it broke. There was no one in the building who knew how to mend typewriters. There were no spare typewriters. She could go home and come back tomorrow.

She looked horrible, reflected against the wall and the pipes outside the tube. She was blotchy and flushed, there was ink in her hair. Her hands looked as if she had just murdered somebody whose blood was black.

She could hardly raise her feet as she walked out of the station towards the flat. And Paul was in the flat, with a woman.

Not that they were doing anything. Nor had they been, she'd swear to that. She marched straight past them in the hall and checked the bed, first thing to do; it was as she'd left it.

'Burnt some more pans, Paul?' she said cheerily, without any hellos either way. She wouldn't look at the woman. Why should she look at her? She wasn't a woman anyway, more like a schoolgirl, which figured. Paul wouldn't want a sophisticated woman, or an attractive one.

'Hello, Antonia. This is Patricia.'

'Hello, Patricia.'

'This is Antonia.'

'Hello, Antonia.'

Antonia swallowed and closed her eyes and opened them again dizzily. Paul put his arm out. She dodged his arm and ran for the bathroom. She slammed the door and locked it. The ghastly yellow walls made her retch but nothing came out. She lay down in the bath with her clothes on and put the plug in and ran cold water. She heard Paul talking to Patricia in a low voice. She heard the front door close as Patricia went out. Paul beat manfully on the bathroom door, shouting above the rush of water. 'Antonia let me in. What are you doing?'

'Washing,' she said, lying there in the bath with her clothes on.

Eventually she let him in. She stood before him, dripping on to the lino. 'Get those things off,' he ordered. 'I'll bring you something dry.'

'Who is she?'

'I can't live with you.'

'You could if you tried. You could live with me and keep her in a shed for sex.'

He turned his back, went into the bedroom and brought her

121

dressing-gown. He closed the bathroom door on her while she changed.

'Come here often?' she snarled through the door. 'With *Patricia*?' Either he didn't answer or she didn't hear. She took her time drying herself and buttoning up her dressing-gown. 'You're quite safe,' she said at last, opening the door.

'She hasn't been here before,' he said gruffly. It seemed to matter to him that she believed him. She did, actually, but she wouldn't let it show. 'I believe you,' she sneered.

'She only wanted to see it. We were passing . . .'

'Her new home.'

'Perhaps. Antonia, I never wanted this to be so unpleasant. Haven't I given you time? Haven't I given you the choice? Haven't I been fair?'

'I promised you,' she said, 'that I'd leave by August.' She felt desperately tired.

'August is next week,' he said.

'August is next week?'

'August is next week.'

'Give me till September then.'

He took a deep breath. 'On September the first,' he said, 'either you've moved out or I stop paying the mortgage. Then neither of us will have the flat.' She nodded and went into the bedroom and lay down. He stood over her for a while, all the muscles of his face moving under his skin. She wished she could shut him out. She realized she could, simply by going to sleep. Nothing in life was too bad as long as you could go to sleep.

She woke in a panic. The flat was empty and it was dusk. She phoned Catherine. 'Can he throw me out or not?' Catherine would know.

Catherine didn't reply. Antonia remembered that she was angry with her because she wouldn't join the union. She thought of hanging up. Everybody hated her now, why bother, why bother about anything, she would go and live in a hostel for homeless teenagers, she didn't look her age. Catherine asked her to explain what she was talking about and listened while she did. Then she said, 'I think probably not, not while you're still married. Possession's nine tenths of the law in this sort of case. But look, nothing can happen in two weeks, can it? I'll find out all I can for you when I get back.'

'Back?'

'I'm going away.'

'Where to?'

'Larana.'

Antonia felt hurt, she didn't know why. 'Have a nice time,' she said. 'You wouldn't catch me going there, personally. Especially on my own.'

'I'm going with Frank.'

'Oh.'

'And when I get back I'll help you find a solicitor.'

'D'you think I could stop Paul coming here?' *With Patricia*, she meant, but she wouldn't say that.

'You might get a court order if there's been violence . . .'

Antonia laughed. Then she panicked again. Catherine was going away, her only friend at the moment. If she stayed in the flat she'd never dare go out. She'd never know what she'd find when she came back.

'Paul doesn't want to bring solicitors into it.'

'Why?'

'He says it'll be too unpleasant.'

'More unpleasant than what's just happened? How much does he know about the law?'

'He knows everything.'

'Then he probably knows he'll get the flat eventually but he'll have to divorce you first. But he also knows it'll be a damn sight easier *and cheaper* for him if you just move out and disappear.'

'That's what I want to do.'

'Come here then.'

'What?'

'You can look after my flat while I'm away.'

'I can live in your flat?'

'Tell me I'm wrong and to mind my own business if you want. But it sounds to me as if you're both pretending this isn't really happening. He's harassing you to get out of the flat when you both know perfectly well that you won't until he makes you. Maybe he hasn't made up his mind yet, and he knows that the moment he talks to a solicitor he'll have to.'

'But if he hasn't made up his mind to divorce me yet I don't want him to!'

'Exactly! So move out! Show a bit of initiative! Let him wonder where you've gone!'

Would he wonder?

He might not even notice.

He would if she sent him a note.

Catherine urged, 'Get a taxi and come straight round.'

'No, I can't, Catherine. I've got to think about it.'

'Don't think about it.'

'I haven't got any money.'

'I'll pay for the taxi when you get here.'

It took her a long time to make up her mind. She supposed she had made up her mind, she was packing so she must have. She wasn't thinking clearly about what to take. She found herself putting winter clothes and boots into the suitcase and took them out again. It was only for two weeks. She chose work clothes, weekend clothes and plenty of clean underwear. She put the manila folder in which she kept her tax papers and passport and other important documents in her shoulder bag. She gathered together some saucepans and plates but they wouldn't go in the case . . . what was she doing, Catherine had a proper kitchen surely, even if she didn't eat much. Antonia stared at the telephone and dithered. She wrote a letter instead. *Dear Paul.* 'Dear Paul,' she wrote, 'Dear Paul. You can have the flat. I'm going away.' She phoned three minicab companies but none could manage a car for her in less than forty minutes. She'd almost made up her mind not to go when one finally arrived. She got him to stop on the way while she posted the letter. It was late when she reached Catherine's flat and the flat was empty. She beat and beat on the door and looked in at the windows. There was no reply. She asked the driver to take her home but he'd guessed by now that she couldn't pay and he was furious. He left her with her suitcase on Catherine's doorstep.

CHAPTER FOURTEEN

A Good Time For Giving Up

She waited in a pub, making a half of lager last till closing time. She asked the barman to watch her suitcase while she nipped out to see if Catherine was back yet.

'Sorry,' he said. 'No unattended packages.'

'Is there a phone here?'

'Not a public one, no.'

She fumed and worried alternately. The pub closed. With very little hope she hauled her suitcase back towards Catherine's flat. A light was on and Catherine was there. As soon as she saw Antonia she flung her hand dramatically to her forehead. 'Oh God! You! I forgot.' She seemed wildly cheerful about something.

'Thanks very much.'

'Frank's had an accident.' It wasn't cheerfulness, it was hysteria. 'He's all right, though. Honestly! He is all right!' Antonia took charge, forcing Catherine to sit down and explain. Frank had been on his way round to stay the night before setting off with Catherine in the morning. His luggage had unbalanced the bike and he'd come off on a roundabout, broken both legs, three inches had saved him from being crushed by a bus. 'The hospital phoned just after you did. All I could think of was getting there.'

'Don't worry, as long as he's all right.'

'The doctor said he would be, only he'd have a bit of a limp.' Catherine gave a watery smile. 'And Frank opened his eyes and said. "A bit of a limp what?" Then he sort of drifted off. He keeps doing that: saying something, then drifting off. He's concussed.'

'Will you be able to get a refund on the holiday?'

'Oh sure. Less ninety per cent cancellation charge. Like a fool I let him book it and he thought he'd save a few quid by not taking out insurance.'

'That's a bit rough on you.'

'He said I should go anyway.'

'By yourself?'

'He said I've got to. He said if I turn up at visiting time tomorrow when I'm supposed to be in Larana, there'll be trouble. Not that he'd be able to make much in the way of trouble, he's all plaster and pulleys. But he said it was his fault about the insurance, which it is, and he knows I want to go, which I do, and he doesn't want us to spend the rest of our lives together with me wondering about Samantha and thinking I let her down.'

'Are you engaged, then?'

'I don't really believe in marriage. What time is it?' It was nearly one. 'God, it's hardly worth going to sleep.'

'I've got to.'

'Of course you have. I'll show you where everything is. You'd better have the bed.'

'No, you're travelling in the morning, you have it.'

Catherine made her a bed on the floor with pillows and blankets and eiderdowns. She finished her packing and set the alarm for five o'clock. 'I'll try not to wake you.'

Antonia was yawning continuously. 'I could sleep for a week. Can you set it again for eight when you go?'

She seemed only just to have nodded off in the makeshift bed when she heard Catherine get up and pad to the phone in her striped pyjamas. Antonia hadn't heard the phone ring. She heard Catherine enquire after Frank. She heard her say, 'Yes, thanks, sorry to trouble you. When he wakes up will you tell him Catherine sends her love.' She heard her go back to bed and, a few minutes later, she heard her start to sob.

Antonia waited a while, then went to her and sat on the bed. 'What did they say?'

'That he's asleep and fine.'

'Still, I don't blame you, being worried.'

Catherine blew her nose and scoffed at herself. 'People break their legs every day, they don't die of it.'

'No, but when you love someone you always think they're

going to die.'

'Do you? Does everyone? I thought it was only me.'

'What time is it?' Antonia asked.

'Half-past three . . .'

'This time yesterday I was just getting up.'

'Sorry. I'll be quiet now.' She lay on her back like a corpse. Antonia went back to bed. She was just drifting off again when Catherine said, 'Antonia. Come with me.'

'What?'

'To Larana.'

'How can I?'

'Of course you can't.'

There was further silence. Catherine started talking to herself. 'How am I going to *stop* myself *worrying?* Especially if I'm on my own.'

'Look, I've got a job to go to.'

'Good one?'

'I hate it. But Mrs Hook – '

'It was a stupid idea, forget it,' said Catherine. 'I don't suppose you've even got your passport, and if you tried to travel on Frank's – '

'They might spot the difference,' said Antonia, giggling to cover up the fact that she knew she had her own.

What with the sleepless night and Catherine being so pathetic and persuasive and the imminence of another day in the Recovery Section, Antonia did find herself packing a suitcase in the morning with things that might be suitable for a holiday in the sun. But she couldn't believe she'd really have the nerve to go. For one thing she'd never pass herself off as Frank when they got to the check-in desk.

'I'll just see you off,' she said, as they boarded the Gatwick train at Victoria.

Catherine was vague and gloomy. The morning was warm but a fine rain had started to fall. An unread copy of the *Guardian* lay on her lap. 'Yes,' she said, 'then back to work. What is your job?'

'It *stinks*. It's enough to put you right off smoking, that place. In fact – ' Antonia opened her bag and took out her packet of cigarettes. There were seven left. She broke them in half, spilling shreds of tobacco. She shoved them back into the packet, crushed it and put it under the seat. 'There,' she said. 'I've given up. Going on holiday's a good time for giving up, I've heard that.'

'But I thought you weren't coming,' said Catherine.

Antonia began to smile. Catherine looked vague and didn't smile back. As if something had been bothering her for some time and she'd only just resolved to do something about it she said, 'Excuse me,' pushed Antonia out of the way, picked up the crushed cigarette packet and put it in her bag.

Antonia said, 'Thinking of taking it up, are you?' and abandoned her smile. She said, 'I'm not coming, of course I'm not, I don't know why I've brought all that stuff up there.' She nodded at her suitcase on the rack. 'I haven't got any money for a start.'

'It's all paid for,' sighed Catherine. 'Full board at the Hotel Excelsior. Where Samantha went.'

'No, but I mean for spending. If we wanted to go out.'

'That's the least of our worries.'

'Look, I *know* you're wishing you hadn't asked me and it's all right, I'm not coming. I'll phone the office from the airport and tell them I'll be late. I mean, I know you've been to college and everything and you'd find me dead boring for two whole weeks.'

'I'm sorry if you think that,' said Catherine, but she didn't deny it.

'Is there a buffet on this train?'

'Go and see.'

'Give me that rubbish, then.' Catherine handed over the cigarette packet. Antonia found a bin but no buffet. When she came back Catherine was reading her paper. She looked up from it with a very bright smile. 'I *do* want you to come, Antonia. If I seem ratty it's because I'm still worried.'

'If I *do* come,' said Antonia slowly, 'I'm going to pay you back. You and Frank. Because I've got this feeling we're going to have a wonderful time and my luck's turned and I'm going to sort myself out and when I get back the most plum job's going to land in my lap, fantastic salary, and when Frank's better I'm going to send you and him away on the most romantic holiday you ever had.'

The mention of Frank turned Catherine's mouth down at the corners again. 'I've never been on a romantic holiday.'

'Oh Catherine, I know he's going to be all right!'

The train reached Gatwick and they got out. The station platform was sheltered but rain poured on to the tracks on either side. Catherine seemed overcome with weakness. Her feet dragged and she trailed her luggage like a reluctant dog. Antonia took it from her. Her own was heavier and she hadn't even planned to come away. She heard Paul's voice and banished it but not before it had said, *One suitcase only, please, Antonia. I know who'll end up carrying it.*

In the airport building everything was bright. The floors shone, outgoing travellers were cheerful in new clothes, returners were tired and tanned, their trolleys loaded high with suitcases and plastic bags from duty free shops. The tannoy drowned the sounds of the rain with talk of Nairobi, Majorca, Nice. Catherine became businesslike again. 'First thing we've got to do,' she said, 'is suss out the HooRay Holidays desk and see what the procedures are and how we can get round them.'

There were huge queues everywhere except at the HooRay desk where a surly hostess sat in her green-and-white uniform, reading a magazine and sending away anyone who approached her trying to check in. 'Probably a temp,' said Antonia.

'They've gone bankrupt more likely,' said Catherine, 'and absconded with our money to South America.' They watched people checking in at the other desks.

Antonia said, 'It's no good. They're checking the names on the tickets against people's passports.'

'Yes, but then they're handing over boarding cards. They don't put names on boarding cards, do they?'

'What are you thinking?'

'We'll wait till there's a crowd. Keep you out of sight. I'll say Frank's with me but he's gone to the loo. I'll check him in, then give you his boarding card.' Catherine seemed pleased with her plan, then her face fell. 'How long do you get for fraud, do you know?'

Antonia nudged her. 'Honestly. You're the one who fiddled those tapes at Bright Girls. President Nixon had nothing on you.'

'Yes, and look what happened to him. Oh well. Will you wait with the luggage and listen to see if we're called? I'm going to go and phone the hospital.' When she came back she just said,

129

'He's still asleep,' and wouldn't say more.

An announcement came over the tannoy that said the HooRay flight to Larana had been delayed three hours due to operational reasons. 'What's *that* supposed to mean?' Catherine stormed. 'It's been delayed because it's been delayed.'

They went and had coffee. There was a clean ashtray on the table. Antonia firmly removed it and had a doughnut. Catherine didn't want one. She read her paper, glanced at various books from her bag and stared into space. Antonia looked at the clock. It was too late to go to work now. Catherine went once again to the telephone and came back without comment.

It was midday when the call came for travellers to Larana to check in at the HooRay Holidays desk. Catherine put down her newspaper. Her face was chalk-white. She took out the tickets, Frank's passport and her own. She picked up all the luggage.

'Shall I help you?' said Antonia.

'No, keep out the way,' Catherine replied crossly. 'Remember, you don't exist. I wonder if we're going to get away with this.'

Antonia waited and waited. She bought some magazines and some peppermints for the flight. She had hardly any cash. She saw a bank and made for it, taking out her cheque-book. According to her counterfoils she had £17.00 in her account, but with her cheque-card she was able to draw out £50. She went back to the table where she had agreed to meet Catherine. There was no sign of her. She went to a balcony overlooking the HooRay desk. It was besieged by queues. There seemed to be a lot of arguing going on but she couldn't see Catherine. She had another coffee and waited.

'He's in a coma.'

Catherine dropped two green-and-white boarding cards on to the table.

'What?'

'"Asleep" was what they said. What they always say. But I know he's in a coma. Who sleeps at twelve o'clock in the morning?'

'Someone who's . . . been hurt might.'

'Someone who's dying might!' Tears streamed from Catherine's eyes. 'I only wanted to talk to him!' The tannoy urged passengers for Larana to proceed to the departure lounge. Catherine blew her nose, composed herself. 'Come on, then,' she said. 'We're off.'

'Did you manage to check us in all right?'

'No problem at all. Everyone else in the queue was shouting at the poor girl, I was polite, she practically kissed me. Now look, have a ticket. Put it away, you won't need it again till we come back. You show your passport at passport control and your boarding card when we get on the plane.'

'All right, all right, I know,' said Antonia crossly.

They joined the queue at passport control.

'I can't go,' said Catherine.

Antonia stared at her. The queue edged forward. 'But –' Catherine's eyes reddened over and her mouth trembled. 'No,' said Antonia quietly, 'of course we can't go.'

'I really can't.'

'I understand. It was a bit of a daft idea –'

'Not without hearing his voice again. Just to know he's all right.'

'Trouble is, I expect the luggage'll be on the plane by now,' said Antonia.

'That's all right, you can pick it up at Larana.'

Antonia stared. 'I'm not going by myself!' Already Catherine was edging out of the queue. 'Catherine! I've never been on holiday by myself!'

Catherine placed reassuring hands on her shoulders. Firmly they held her in her place in the queue. 'You won't be by yourself! You'll make lots of friends. All these people – ' She waved at the queue. She said excitedly, 'And anyway, you're going to find Samantha.'

'But I don't know what Samantha –'

Catherine drooped again. 'If you really won't go by yourself, then I'll come with you. I owe you a holiday, I promised. You've given up your flat and you'll have lost your job by now.'

'I don't want you to come if you don't want to,' said Antonia sullenly.

'No, that's understandable. It's settled, then? Have a wonderful time.' She was gone, heading back towards the trains.

'If I do find Samantha,' Antonia shouted, 'what then?' There was no reply. People stared. The queue moved forward and the passport control man took Antonia's passport out of her hand; he looked at it and gave it back to her; and then she was passing through a wired-up metal doorway that would bleep if she were carrying firearms.

There were more delays. Other airlines announced free refreshments for their stranded passengers but there was nothing from HooRay Holidays. Antonia wandered round the duty free shop and gazed at the long boxes of cheap cigarettes. There was nowhere to sit in the packed lounge. Several times she went to the ladies and drank water from the tap. She checked her money, fingered her ticket – MS CATHERINE LAMBERT: STRICTLY NOT TRANSFERABLE.

At last, with darkness starting to fall, the flight was called. A gaunt, impatient-looking stewardess looked at her boarding card. 'Are you by yourself, madam?' 'Yes, I mean no, I mean yes.' 'Smoking or non-smoking?' 'Smoking, I mean non-smoking' 'There's only smoking left,' said the stewardess.

Flames clicked into life throughout the stuffy cabin immediately after take-off. The couple next to Antonia shared a strong-smelling cigar, giggling and kissing each other. 'Spirits, tobacco, perfume, gifts?' offered the stewardess from behind her trolley. 'Two hundred Silk Cut please,' said Antonia. She paid for them and stowed them away unopened in her bag. 'They're not for me, they're for handing round at parties,' she said.

PART TWO

CHAPTER FIFTEEN

HooRay Holidays

A ribbon of tissue paper held down the lid of the toilet. It would be impossible to use the toilet without breaking the ribbon. YOUR ASSURANCE OF HYGIENE, it said, in five languages.

The twin-bedded room with bath was clean, bare, whitewashed and stuffy. Antonia pulled back the curtains and opened the glass door on to the balcony. She was five floors up. The air was dark, warm and windless, full of sounds of drunkenness, music and the sea.

She put the luggage, her own and Catherine's, on to one of the beds. She threw herself on the other bed and groaned. The groan ended in a chuckle.

At the airport (no more than a row of prefabs in a field, with queues of arrivals and departures winding out into the night), a male courier, prancing with agitation, sunglasses perched in his white-blond hair, had demanded her name. 'HooRay Holidays. I'm Ray – Hoo are you?' was how he put it, over and over again with little snorts of laughter.

'Catherine Lambert,' she had replied alertly. 'I'm with Frank Spivey, where's he got to?' Ray had checked off the two names on his clipboard and dispatched her to a coach.

And when the coach reached the hotel, one of a tall white row with their names in neon blazing through the darkness, she had been alert again. There were more name checks and this time they wanted passports. Antonia had spotted Catherine's name upside down on a list, read the room number and grabbed the key from the desk. 'Passport?' said the receptionist. 'It's there,' she had replied, pointing to the pile he had already gathered. She had ducked into a lift; and now she had her room.

A photocopied note on the dressing-table told her that Hoo-Ray Holidays hoped she would meet Ray in the bar for a champagne welcome at 10 am, five and a half hours from now.

'I'm Ray. Hoo are you?'

She hadn't meant to get up for the champagne welcome. But a heavy-footed maid had come barging in with a trolley and mops. At the sight of Antonia still in bed she had glared and slammed out again, but there was no sleeping after that. Antonia had showered, made up lightly, and now, on her way out to explore, she had been caught by Ray. He was dressed as he had been at the airport, in tight white jeans and a green jacket, but now his sunglasses were over his eyes. She couldn't see their expression as he asked her name. She said, 'Antonia. I mean Catherine.'

'Ah yes, Antonia, lovely name, my mother's name. I remember, we met last night. Don't run away, darling, you'll miss the party.' He steered her towards the bar where people she recognized from last night sat sullenly yawning and twiddling champagne glasses. A maid with a single bottle scuttled from one to the other, pouring tiny portions of fizz.

'I'm Ray. Hoo are you?'

'Pip,' growled a red-haired man, 'and Judy.'

'Punch and Judy, did you say? Ha ha! I remember, we met last night, don't run away –'

The people in the bar were restive as they waited for the party to start.

'It's a bit much if you ask me.'

'Absolutely ridiculous.'

'A whole day lost. That's the way I look at it. Do we get an extra day at the end?'

'That's no good to me, I'm needed at the office.'

'This is it.'

'Ladies and gentlemen,' said Ray, 'on behalf of HooRay Holidays, welcome to Larana.'

'Gatwick Airport Holidays is more like it,' Pip exploded.

A few people muttered rebellious agreement into their champagne – which wasn't – but the mutters died away as Ray raised his sunglasses, narrowed his eyes and pointed a long sinuous arm at Pip. 'Everyone's waiting,' he said silkily, 'for you.'

Pip squared up. 'No one talks to me like that.' Ray sat in a chair and put his feet on a table. Pip looked round the silent bar for support.

Ray beamed. 'Mustn't let a few late nights spoil our sense of humour, must we? All got a drink? *Good.* It's a funny place, Larana. Some ways they want the best of both worlds, some ways they've got it. If the twentieth century gives them tourists throwing their money around, fine with them. But there's a lot in their culture that's medieval. *Medieval.*' He shrugged. 'There's tours to the traditional villages if any of you lot are interested.'

The maid seemed to have acquired a second bottle and everyone was trying to catch her eye. 'Fill it up, love, not worth dirtying the glass for that.'

'Property's one thing,' said Ray. 'They don't believe in property, see? So to them stealing's not the crime it'd be to us. I'm not going to say a word against them and you'd better not in my hearing either. But I'd strongly advise you to hire safe-deposit boxes for your valuables. What's five quid for peace of mind? Either currency will do.' He went round the room taking money off people and giving them tiny keys off a ring.

Antonia said, 'No thanks, I haven't got any valuables.'

'Your funeral, darling,' he replied.

'What about drinking water?' someone wanted to know.

'What about it?'

'Is it all right – ?'

'What d'you mean, is it all right?'

'To drink the water?'

Ray rolled his eyes. 'Blimey. I don't know why some people come abroad in the first place. What d'you think the locals drink?'

'I just thought – '

'I'll tell you this. The rivers around here are cleaner than what you lot are used to from your *taps.*' His nostrils flared. 'One more thing. The police are a bit – well, it's not Dixon of Dock Green, let's put it that way. I'm not going to say a word against them. They've never bothered me, but then I've never bothered them.' He sniffed cryptically.

Someone said, 'Could you be a bit more – '

'We'll put it this way if you prefer,' said Ray patiently. 'They like the tourists but they don't want riff-raff. Now it's not for me

137

to say who's riff-raff and who isn't. Fact remains, HooRay is at the economy end of the price spectrum and that means we sometimes get . . .' He eyed Pip and Judy. ' 'nuff said, 'nuff said. No brawling, no walking out of anywhere without paying, no screwing the local crumpet, no sleeping on the beach, no stealing from the hotels. *Particularly* no stealing from the hotels. Or even borrowing. You might think, what's a towel here or there? It's a close-knit community. And if the chief of police sees you on the beach spilling your Ambre Sol on one of his brother-in-law's towels, you'll know all about it.' There was a ripple of laughter. 'Blimey,' said Ray, 'I'm *serious*. I don't have to spend my time telling you this. You break the rules, you'll be surprised what can happen. They're trying to raise the tone of this place. If you're lucky they'll deport you. If you're not – ' He mimed a bunch of fives, a knee in the groin. 'Not that I'll say anything against them, mind. Bit of discipline in the streets is what England needs, if you ask me.' He finished by handing out lists of excursions they could go on at extra cost; and shops where they should mention his name.

While she was still in the shade of the tall white hotels the heat bathed her like a warm shower. When she rounded a corner on to the sea-front it was like a blow to the head. The sun seemed to part her hair and scorch through to her scalp.

Groups and couples ambled along the dazzling pavement. Through her screwed-up eyes the beach looked miles away, multicoloured, immobile till she focussed on a particular place and saw it shifting, changing, as people turned over, rubbed oil on each other, went for a swim. Here and there she spotted an unoccupied patch of white sand but it vanished as she went towards it and others got there first, covering it with their towels and bags and beach beds.

The pavement was blocked with tables and chairs. She must get some sunglasses, her eyes kept going funny, seeing things the wrong size: huge teeth biting into sandwiches, splitting the crusts, throats throbbing as glistening lager went down. Once she'd had a fad for always eating and drinking things that matched her clothes if she was out with someone. Salad if she was wearing green, pasta with pale colours. Her first date with Paul had been at a Greek restaurant. 'Hey, that taramasalata matches your dress,' he'd said, and she'd said, 'Does it?'

138

In front of her walked a mother and daughter in shorts. The mother's legs were nicely shaped but webbed with blue veins.

If ever I get veins like that I won't wear shorts.

Behind her two men spoke in German.

No one's alone, except me.

Do you go mad if you go two weeks without talking to anyone? What's it like to go mad? People go mad in solitary confinement. But they're probably a bit mad to start with or they wouldn't be in solitary confinement. But they have the guards to talk to. But the guards may be under orders not to talk to them.

Everyone was wearing huge sunglasses. She was reflected in a hundred dark screens, walking, walking towards herself.

She was going to be careful about money but she had to have some sunglasses. She went into a bank and changed her fifty pounds.

Shops spilled out their wares on tables: fringed dresses and woven rugs, beads and lace, wooden bottle openers, napkin rings, cruets, leather purses. She saw a bikini, the colour of her eyes. An assistant offered it to her encouragingly. She tried it on in a cool, curtained cubicle. It skimmed her ribs and hips, it was only a bra and pants, she had plenty of those. She felt for bulges in her flesh where the fabric sat but there weren't any. She was tight and trim. 'I'll take it,' she said, picking up a bottle of sun tan lotion, some sunglasses and nail varnish to go with them. The total cost was nearly ten pounds.

She must have walked a mile from the hotel and still there was no space on the beach.

The restaurants had pictures painted on the glass of their windows – hot dogs, foaming tankards, sundae dishes with strawberries embedded in clouds of cream. If she were with someone she'd wear pink and white and ask for one of those sundaes.

Bells jingled and a mule trotted by, pulling a carriage with a couple in the back with their arms round each other.

Further from the centre of town the shops gave way to street stalls, hippies selling junk or handicrafts or offering to paint your portrait, buskers. She started to feel nervous in case she got lost. She knew she'd walked in a straight line from the hotel and could get back easily, but what if something did happen? Who was there to know?

139

Most of the women and girls were topless but she put on both halves of her bikini to swim. She'd meant to tire herself out with swimming but she soon got bored; what was there to do but swim up and down? She looked at all the naked breasts. Sooner or later she'd dare that too but it was her first day and she was alone. It wasn't just beautiful young girls who were topless either, there were drooping, mottled old women, not worrying what anyone thought. Antonia jerked her head away just too late to avoid seeing the woman with only one breast. There was a long neat scar on the flat surface of her chest and the surviving breast was firm. Antonia wouldn't look at her face, wouldn't see how young she was. The one-breasted woman came into the sea and Antonia got out. She would need to buy a towel too, the sand stuck to her as she tried to sunbathe. A man in a T-shirt offered her a plastic beach-bed. He wrote the price in the sand with his finger. She sent him away. One thing, it was more than twenty-four hours since she'd smoked a cigarette and she hadn't even wanted one. The thought made her hungry and she started back towards the hotel, stopping on the way to buy a towel.

It was help yourself. As she shuffled by the silvery trays of food on the white cloths nobody could tell that she was alone. She loaded up her plate with garlic sausage, egg mayonnaise, yogurt and cucumber, olives, stuffed courgettes, slices of red and green tomato, kidney beans, little potatoes showered with chopped mint, wafers of carrot and smoked fish. Then there was the hot table but Antonia had enough. Her plateful was fragrant and wholesome.

'This plate is too small,' the woman ahead of her complained to the waiter who was carving roast pork.

'Then take another plate, madam.'

'It's all right. I'll just have a little piece.' She permitted a sliver of meat to be added. 'I'll come back for more,' she warned.

'*Bon appetit*, madam,' said the waiter.

Antonia found an empty table in a corner and put on her sunglasses to eat even though the room was quite dim. Salad was all she'd eat while she was here, she resolved; nothing looked worse than a greedy girl on her own. Two maids laboured round the room with a trolley, scraping abandoned plates into pig buckets. A man summoned them to his table and handed over his half-eaten meal. Their expressions enquired if anything was wrong. He ignored them and joined the queue again, getting himself something else. He stopped by Antonia's table. 'Got your sunglasses on,' he said.

The nights were the worst. There was plenty to do, she knew, and she did not lack invitations. Men were always approaching her as she lay alone on the beach, men who spoke no English and didn't seem to care that she spoke nothing else. They would mention the names of discos she had seen advertised, and move the hands or digits of their watches to indicate the time she must be there. It was always late – eleven o'clock or midnight. She would nod and smile, meaning to go. After dinner she would retreat to her room to wait. She would lie on her bed, listening to the night life starting up in the street below. She would fall asleep, waking at half-past one or two to stare at the wall till morning came.

She must have slept for the wall seemed to lighten quite suddenly. It was rough stone, whitewashed. *What if I was in prison, how would it be different? What if I couldn't get up and walk out of here any time I liked? What if I couldn't go swimming or for walks? What if it was four o'clock in the afternoon and I'd just had my last meal till breakfast, meat pie, potatoes and rice pudding? What if there were three other women locked in here with me, murderers and thieves? What if we had to use chamber pots? How I'd wish for what I've got now.*

It's a miracle I'm not smoking.

Breakfast was from eight till ten. Breakfast ought to be the best of the three meals; at least the dining-room wasn't full and no one took any notice of her and there were other people alone, people who got up at different times from their partners. But she hated the way some couples sat, ignoring everyone, making little remarks, filling themselves with warm rolls and butter, coffee, cigarette smoke and each other. She ate extra rolls and planned to skip lunch. But she knew she'd be there as usual, queueing up. Without mealtimes the whole thing would be impossible and she couldn't afford to eat out.

CHAPTER SIXTEEN

Jellyfish

The mayonnaise in the egg mayonnaise was fluffy and delicious with a pungent tang of garlic. She feasted on it twice a day with bread and lettuce. One morning very early it made her sick.

She ran from the bed to the bathroom, squatting helplessly on the toilet, unable to reach the basin or anything that would protect the floor from the eggy stream that spouted from her mouth. She sat gasping and sweating till the spasms passed.

She cleared up the mess with a hotel towel. She put the towel to soak in the basin and had a shower. Under the water she felt dizzy again. She turned off the taps and made for the bed. Her wet feet slipped and the floor came up to meet her chin. It was a loud blow but it didn't hurt. It wasn't till she had crawled on to the bed that she realized she had blood all down her front. She gathered up bunches of sheet and pressed them to her face.

Slivers of light came through the curtains, growing brighter and brighter as she trekked between bathroom and bed. Once she was sure her insides were still and the bleeding had stopped she abandoned the bloodstained bed and lay on the other.

The room stank. She opened the windows wide.

The maid knocked peremptorily and pushed open the door with her linen trolley. She looked and sniffed and went away.

'I'm sorry,' said Antonia. She wished they had room service in this hotel. She wished she could get someone to bring her a cup of strong black coffee.

She pulled on jeans and a T-shirt. Barefoot, her hair uncombed and still wet, the red wound weeping on her chin, she went down to the dining-room. On the way she met the maid who was carrying a large bottle of disinfectant.

A little girl with wiry hair and towelling dungarees left her parents' table and came to inspect Antonia. She looked at the wound, fingered her own chin and started to cry.

The child's father came to get her. He was large and florid with a beard, olive-green shirt and matching shorts. 'Sorry about that,' he said, scooping up his daughter. Back at their table he spoke concernedly with his wife; neither of them looked at Antonia, so she knew they were discussing her.

She wondered if they had any cigarettes. She needed one after the shock but she didn't want to open the duty free box in her room; she knew that would be the end of everything.

The husband was coming towards her again. Just one cigarette.

'My wife,' he said, 'is a nurse. Would you like her to have a look at your face?'

Their names were Chris and Anne and the child's name was Eva. They took Antonia up to their room which was exactly the same as hers except for an extra bed. Anne cleaned the wound and put on an Elastoplast while Chris got Eva ready for the beach. Chris was a lecturer in computer science, at least he used to be till he lost his job; when he got back to London he was going into industry. They were enjoying their holiday but they weren't seeing much night-life because of Eva.

Antonia examined her chin in the mirror. 'I look like a patchwork quilt.'

'It doesn't notice,' said Anne.

'If you want to go to a disco or something,' said Antonia, 'I wouldn't mind babysitting.'

'Discos aren't quite our scene,' said Chris.

'But thanks for the offer,' said Anne. 'Are you feeling better yet?'

'I'm all right.'

'Because if you'd like to come on the beach with us . . .'

'Sure I wouldn't be a nuisance?'

'What are you planning to do?' said Anne. 'Flick water all over us?' And she laughed as if she didn't often make jokes.

Chris said, 'I don't think Antonia would do a thing like that, Anne.'

A girl approached Chris and Anne while Antonia was playing with Eva in the sea. Eva had just started to enjoy the waves and

143

she grizzled when Antonia insisted that they go back. 'You've had enough, Eva,' she said firmly.

The girl was thin as a stick with stringy red hair and small bee-sting breasts. The bottom half of her bikini was no more than a ribbon. She was making a great fuss about having lost something.

'My towel and my beach bag,' she sobbed. 'And oh-oh-oh all my money.'

If you're as young as you look, and such a cry-baby, you shouldn't be out on your own, Antonia thought furiously as the girl squatted down, adopting them.

Anne obviously thought the same but she was kinder. 'Where are you staying?'

Suzi – that was her name, she spelled it out, S-U-Z-I – named a resort five miles down the coast. 'It's really *boring*. My mum and dad won't let me do this, won't let me do that. It's like a blooming concentration camp. So I bunked off. And now I'm stuck.' She was obviously after money and wasn't going to budge till she got it. Antonia would gladly have given her her bus fare, to get rid of her. People like Suzi got people like Antonia a bad name; Antonia wasn't looking for any favours from Chris and Anne. A little way away a man was cooking sausages over charcoal and selling them wrapped in bread. Suzi sniffed and licked her lips quite blatantly. Chris said, 'Want one?' and Suzi said she could eat two.

'Antonia?'

'No thanks.' Actually she'd have loved one. Her stomach felt better but was aching now with emptiness. 'You don't know what's in those sausages, could be anything.'

'What did you do to your face?' Suzi enquired, and Antonia muttered that she'd had a fall.

Suzi ate her sausages, then sauntered on her way dressed in Chris's shirt, clutching money for her bus fare, much more than she needed Antonia would bet.

After half an hour another girl approached them. Anne said, 'We must have gullible faces,' but this girl wasn't after anything, she was handing out free tickets for a display of gypsy dancing. 'Why don't you go, you two, I could babysit,' said Antonia. They thanked her and said they might, in the meantime they were thinking of going to a restaurant for lunch as a change from hotel food. Would she like to join them? She remembered the remark about gullible faces and said she felt slightly sick again, she'd just go back to the hotel.

After her hotel lunch, she went again to the beach.

A man came hobbling from the sea with red blotches on his legs. The word went round as Antonia sat alone.

'Jellyfish, jellyfish!'

The man seemed to be in a lot of pain and soon his wife was leading him away, supporting him. After five or six casualties a chill of anxiety settled over the beach and the sea emptied of swimmers. Further out the wind surfers carried on arrogantly with their sport; but even they moved away in time.

Thwarted swimmers gathered at the water's edge to watch the pink malicious lumps beach themselves on the sand. Plimsolled feet kicked them into heaps. Children reached out to touch and were grabbed away. There were dozens of jellyfish suddenly, hundreds. All committing suicide, *a bit like those animals that jump into the water*, thought Antonia, *lemmings, only they do it the other way round*. She felt rather sorry for them. They were beautiful if you didn't know what they were.

Theories abounded among the speakers of English.

'It's the sewage attracts them.'

'Ships emptying out their tanks.'

'Medusa, that's what they call them in some languages, you know? One look turns you to stone.'

Not all of the jellyfish floated aimlessly to their death. Some seemed to be trying to swim, somersaulting, pulsating in the middle of their long ribbons of sting.

Nets were brought from somewhere and then it became a hunt, some people venturing in up to their knees, pursuing and scooping. Several piles built up on the sand, pink jelly with purple threads, like some grotesque dessert, throbbing in the sun. People threw stones and handfuls of sand. A fleck of grit bounced into Antonia's eye; she shouted 'Don't!'

'Don't what, love? Oh look, did you get stung on your chin?'

'Don't bury them. It's silly, someone might tread on them.'

'Makes sense I suppose.'

'How do you kill them then?' someone wanted to know. Someone else knew. 'Leave them to fry.'

Antonia was starting to wonder whether the sun, solitude

and sickness had turned her a little mad. First there had been her hostility to Suzi, for whom she ought to have felt sorry. Now, instead, she was feeling sorry for jellyfish.

She turned to go back to the hotel to get ready for dinner. Oohs and aahs drew her back to the water.

A long-haired man in a neat pair of tight trunks had walked in fearlessly, up to his waist. His back was packed with muscle and he was very, very brown. He carried no net. He examined the water carefully. He paused, prepared, aimed and scooped. He returned to the beach, his hands full of dripping jellyfish.

His face was a surprise: older and more crinkly than the rest of him, with shaggy, almost white eyebrows over blank blue eyes. Like a sea-captain. He dropped his jellyfish in a pile and went for more.

There were excited squeals. 'How's he do it, how's he do it?'

He didn't answer, probably didn't speak English. With a secretive smile he displayed his hands, smooth and unstung. Some men made to follow him into the water to learn his trick, but he indicated that he did not advise it. He was probably fed up with tourists.

She sat on the balcony of Chris and Anne's room, two floors up from her own, painting her toenails and watching the sun go down. She had hoped that babysitting would mean another chance to play with Eva, but the child was asleep. Anne's copy of *The Thorn Birds* lay at Antonia's side; she had always meant to read it, everybody said it was very good.

She could see clearly into the strip cartoon of the hotel opposite: eight floors, eight rooms to each with balconies and little bits of life going on inside them. She numbered them one to eight, A to H. In A1 a plump brown girl was squeezing herself into an evening pantsuit while the man she was with did up the zip. A2 had four beds crammed into a space meant for two. A mother was crawling over the beds kissing children goodnight. In B3 clothes hung from a washing line, a lacy bra, men's and women's knickers, and a pair of bleached jeans with square pockets. On B5's balcony two young men lounged with magazines and beer cans. One wore a T-shirt that said NO MUFF TOO TUFF. He caught sight of Antonia reading it and waved excitedly, pointing to himself: 'Want a fuck, love?' She started to read *The Thorn Birds*.

Chris and Anne came back early and disgusted from their free gypsy dancing. Chris said, 'It wasn't free and it wasn't gypsy dancing.' 'Apart from that it was fine,' said Anne. 'They kept having these horrible acts and saying the gypsy dancing was next and in the meantime you had to drink their drinks at five pounds a go.'

'It wasn't quite five pounds,' said Chris, and Anne snapped, 'Don't split hairs,' very crossly.

Antonia peeled the cellophane from the box of cigarettes she'd bought on the plane. She opened the box. There was more cellophane round the individual packets. She stopped herself. She went for a walk.

It was after midnight but the air was warm and the streets were light from the bars and open air cafés. She walked near the beach and heard scuffles and groans. She pretended not to hear. There was nothing she could do. Two policemen walked by, fast. They were walking away from the scuffles. She nearly called to them, then she remembered what the courier had said. It might have been them beating somebody up for stealing a towel.

What am I doing, where am I going? I'm going for a walk so I won't smoke. Where are all these people going, what are they trying to get away from?

The streets were still crowded. No one seemed to care what time it was. Some looked the same as they had on the beach, wearing shorts and sun-tops. Others were dressed for a grand night out, the men in jackets, the women in long dresses.

There are no rules, we're all on our holidays. What a stroke of luck, thought I wouldn't get a holiday this year.

And I'm having a great time, aren't I, not doing anything very much, just taking it easy. Lots of people have asked me out. I've met Chris and Anne and Eva. I've got a sun tan.

Masks of make-up hung in the darkness after each woman passed, masks and breasts, loose and free or great thrusting trussed-up breasts behind satin or cotton or cheesecloth, pushing through the night and never a hint whether they were

147

real or fake, cut away to nothing like that woman she'd seen on the beach with the flat scar.

And I've got a good book to read and I've broken the back of this smoking business. I'll take the box of duty frees back and give them to somebody. Shame I've torn the cellophane.

A sign up a side-street glowed: BAR SAMANTHA.

The first week's gone and I'm supposed to be doing something more than having a holiday. I'm supposed to be looking for somebody.

BAR SAMANTHA flashed on and off.

Haven't really been thinking about it, but I suppose I ought to have something to tell Catherine. Some effort I've made.

She walked past the place twice before going in. Inside it was plushy and dark. Deep crimson predominated in the fittings and lights. Most of the customers were lone men. She'd have left immediately, but a familiar voice said, 'Hi. I thought it wouldn't be long before you turned up.'

CHAPTER SEVENTEEN

It's My Job

'Thought it wouldn't be long,' Ray repeated, 'before some of the HooRay mob followed me here.' He was wearing a white linen suit with a blue kipper tie and a matching handkerchief in his breast pocket. 'Night off? Don't make me laugh.'

'I'm not a mob.' She walked over to the fruit machine. All the men were watching her. It was a kind she'd never seen before, no whirling wheels, just computerized dots arranging themselves into cherries, pears, bananas. She pressed in a coin.

Ray said in her ear, 'I've just lost a fortune in that. Can't figure it out.'

'You probably think too much,' she said, collecting up her winnings.

'The least you can do is buy me a drink.'

'Sorry, can't afford it. Too busy paying your salary.'

'Suppose I'll have to get you one then.'

'Don't do me any favours.'

'From the looks of things you've had enough already.' He eyed the plaster on her chin. 'All right for some, that's what I say. All right for people who've got nothing better to do than drink till they can't stand up straight. Want to know what I've been doing today? Three hours' sleep. Toddled off to the airport to meet a flight – not one of ours. I owed one of the other reps a favour. Wouldn't have minded except for the gear they make you put on. Met the flight, got their miserable lot stowed away in their hotel, then I had to go to the police station and persuade them not to actually kill a bunch of Swindon drunks who'd been smashing windows. And that was my day off. When I get back tonight I've got paperwork to do.'

She squinted at him. 'You happy in your work or what? I should have your problems.'

'Looking for a job, are you?'

'No, why?'

'You wouldn't be the first to think, oh, anyone could do what old Ray does. It's all fun in the sun and it beats Pay As You Earn and the Jubilee Line.'

'I'm not looking for a job, I'm looking for a drink.'

He laughed, sat her at a table and called a waitress, who was quite old, wearing high-heeled boots, net tights and a feathery swimsuit. Some of the feathers had fallen off, leaving bald patches. The swimsuit stopped short of her breasts. At first they looked full and youthful. But they weren't, they were little and wrinkled, pushed up on a pair of platforms. She reminded Antonia of a man she'd once seen at an office party. Wearing a paper crown, he'd been called away to the phone. She'd happened to go by his door while he was still talking. On and on he'd gone about quality criteria and production quotas, looking not so much funny as sad because he'd forgotten the party hat on his head and was trying to be serious. This waitress was the same, bored out of her mind in her sexy swimsuit, chewing on a bit of gum.

'Get you anything, Ray?'

He ordered two somethings. Antonia didn't catch the name.

'She's English?'

'Linda started life on the Mile End Road. But she's almost a native now.'

'Why's it called Samantha's?'

'Because it's easier for foreigners to say than the Ploughman's Arms.'

Linda brought two thick-bottomed glasses of bitter syrup. Antonia said, 'You could clean your car with this.'

'It's the local spirit, love. Have to drink it if you want to go native.'

'Got a cigarette?'

He sighed and gave her one. She smoked it halfway down then put it out, having got more pleasure from it than a whole packet used to give her before.

'Would you remember a girl called Samantha Yardley, who came out in April,' she enquired casually, 'on a last-minute special bargain from a magazine?'

'It's none of my business how they come,' he said, 'as long as they've paid. And I never remember names, I can't even remember yours.'

'It's Antonia.' She remembered too late that she was supposed to be Catherine. Fortunately he didn't.

'Supposing I *had* come to you looking for a job. What would you tell me?'

'First thing I'd tell you is to read your brochure. HooRay Holidays accepts no responsibility for girls who miss their flights home. Well, it doesn't say girls of course. Not allowed to, are we? Passengers. Passengerpersons, ha! Next thing, I'd point out that foreigners aren't allowed to work here without a work permit and they're like gold dust.' He looked her over. 'On the other hand . . . in your case . . .'

'In my case what?'

'There's a big new leisure complex going up on the island. Won't be like anything here. It's going to have class. Definitely not the HooRay mob. Jackie O and Lady Di will be more like it. They'll want staff with class there to go with the clientele, so no Laranan peasants, not on view anyway. I might be able to swing it, introduce you to somebody. Thinking of making it worth my while?'

She pushed her chair back. 'I'm going now.'

'Hold on, hold on, don't take offence, take a gate. What kind of work do you do anyway?'

'Secretarial.'

'All right, all right, that's all I meant, give me a hand with my paperwork some time and I'll take you out to the island. *Quid pro quo*. Blimey. You can't open your mouth these days. What did you think I meant?'

'Nothing. I'll see you later, Ray, thanks for the drink.' She was tired suddenly, blessedly tired, and wanted to enjoy the feeling lying on her bed. The drink had been strong and the taste of the cigarette was still with her. She had to wait outside the bar while a huge refuse van crawled by, filling the street. Some of the other men in the bar called to her. She ignored them. She was wondering why they would pay money to look at a topless waitress when in the daytime everybody lay about topless anyway.

It was time for Chris and Anne to leave. Antonia offered to go to

151

the airport with them, to help them with their luggage. They wouldn't hear of it. 'You'll see the airport again soon enough,' they said. 'How much longer is it, five days? Lucky you.' She hoped they hadn't found her a bore.

She paced the beach endlessly, thinking about them. They were nice people and they deserved to be happy. She hoped Chris would like his new job and that Anne would have lots more babies. If she wanted them.

'Excuse me, have you seen a blue beach towel and a bag anywhere?'

She'd heard that before. Was she hearing it now?

Still half-naked, the girl Suzi picked her way from family to family, sobbing. Someone gave her money. Antonia waited at a distance. Suzi was discreet and clever. She walked a long way before trying it again.

Antonia seethed till she couldn't contain herself. She loved to earn money, really earn it, given the chance. To buy something she wanted with a five-pound note, or several, and think, *I earned that. I'm entitled to it.*

'Doing well out of this, are you?' She grabbed so-called Suzi's skinny shoulder.

'Who the hell are you?' Suzi spat.

'I've been watching you. You're a bloody con-man. Woman. Why don't you go home and get a job? You're not here with your parents any more than I am, and why don't you use your real name?'

A man with tangled hair and dead eyes emerged from a crowd. His hair only increased Antonia's fury. *Why don't you comb your hair? Doesn't cost anything to comb your hair, does it?* 'You all right, Suzi?' said the man. Suzi shook off Antonia's hand and went with him, pointing and laughing. Even Suzi wasn't alone.

Antonia met another girl giving out tickets for the gypsy dancing. At least it was a job. Antonia asked about it. She said it was quite easy to get, you just went to the place and picked up a pile of the tickets and gave them out, writing your name on the back. (Her name was Jessica.) Then if the people you'd given the tickets to actually went to the gypsy dancing, you got a commission out of what they spent on drinks. Otherwise you didn't get paid at all. Jessica hadn't received any commission yet.

Antonia was budgeting for two drinks a day and she'd already had today's; but she calculated that she wouldn't need any on her last day, she'd be too busy, so she could afford a half bottle of wine with her dinner. She swallowed it in gulps like fruit juice. She was shocked at herself and a little frightened; she knew you could become an alcoholic while hardly noticing it, even if you were young. As soon as she was sure of herself as a nonsmoker she might think about giving up drinking, or cutting down, not that she'd have much choice once she was back with the dole and London prices.

It was a wonder after that little lapse with Ray, that she hadn't smoked. The one with Ray didn't really count, she hadn't smoked it down to the end.

A white-haired woman came over to her table and boomed: 'I was just saying to my husband, "Look at that poor little girl over there with no one to talk to. I'll go and keep her company."'

'Yes?'

The woman pulled up a chair. 'Wouldn't any of your friends come on holiday with you, dear? That's not very nice, is it?'

'Actually,' Antonia said, 'I'm not on holiday.'

'I see.'

'It's my job. I have to travel a lot. On my own.'

'And what is this job, dear?'

'I'm not allowed to say.'

The woman wouldn't take the hint so Antonia left. She heard the woman reporting to her husband. 'She says she's not on holiday. She has to travel alone. She says it's her job.' Antonia decided to go to the gypsy dancing.

CHAPTER EIGHTEEN

Gypsy Dancing

She took off her shoes and walked barefoot on the cool beach beside the road. Mules drew couples past her in carriages, jingling and glowing in the gathering night. She wore her denim office dress and wished she had her silver catsuit.

By the time she realized she wasn't carrying her shoes, had left them where she took them off, it was too late and too dark to go back. She wondered why she had to spoil everything. She tried not to remember what the shoes had cost.

She handed in her ticket and entered the crowded little club. She wondered what system they had for recording what drinks people bought so that commission could be paid to people like Jessica.

The music of a German band hit her like a cuff round the ear. The band consisted of huge grown men in socks, pretending to be goat boys on a mountain top. One had a trumpet, one a trombone. A third sat at something that looked like a computerized piano and emitted the loudest sounds of the lot. She found an empty table and sat down. At her side loomed a broad-chested waiter in a dinner suit.

'I don't want anything just now,' she told him, but his expression made it clear that this would not do, so she ordered a tequila sunrise. She didn't want to hear what it cost: she held out all the money she had left and the waiter took half of it. 'Gypsy dancers?' she enquired clearly. He said something that might have meant 'Later' or 'Tomorrow' or even 'Yesterday.' *Oh well, I'm here now,* she thought, and tapped her bare feet on the gritty floor.

The place shook with thumps of music and people danced in the narrow spaces between the tables, crashing into hers and overturning her drink. They smiled their apologies, but when the waiter came with a cloth and insisted that she buy another drink to sit with, they didn't offer to pay and she had to. At least Jessica would be making a lot.

She focussed her eyes on the surface of the table. The waiter hadn't wiped it properly, it was sticky and wet. She dipped her finger in the stickiness and licked it. It was sweet. Disgusted eyes stared at her through the darkness. She scowled back. 'I paid for it after all.'

The table was coming closer and closer to her face. Her spine felt as if there were something wrong with it, it sagged. Her hair fell forward into the sticky puddle. Her head was moving in slow dizzy circles, she was wiping up the mess with her hair. She laid her head down in it. The music beat up through the table legs and into her ear. She rested, closing her eyes, waiting to be thrown out.

She must have passed out and been abandoned because the place was suddenly in darkness, hissing silence. Her head brushed against something hard. It was her drink. It tilted and slopped but she rescued it in time.

But, she thought, what if I hadn't?

What if I had to order another drink and I drank it, and the waiter waited to be paid and I couldn't pay? What could they do? Hand me over to the police? According to Ray they'd beat me up and deport me but they still wouldn't have been paid for their drink, would they?

It's easy to live as if money doesn't matter when your meals and bed are all paid for but what if I never earn money again?

What if I'm all alone here and I've missed the gypsy dancing? What if I don't exist? I can hardly see myself.

Dim lights came on. Everyone was still there. She must only have slept for a minute or two. The darkness had been for clearing up between acts, the silence was the silence of anticipation.

Guitar music chattered and whirled. The musicians were intense-faced men in dark clothes. They made no attempt to step forward into the wide oval of white spotlight which lit up the women dancers like an enormous sunbeam.

Each woman had a flower behind her ear, matching the colour that predominated in her woven skirt: yellow, scarlet, mauve. Each wore a shawl with long black tassels, and shiny shoes that clacked on the floor as they danced. They were perfect, precise, efficient. They had wide white smiles.

There was polite applause after each dance.

Then one of the women stepped forward and spoke in three languages. When she got to English it was: 'I am happy to present to you the new member of our dancing troupe. Maria is fifteen years old and tonight she dance for you for the first time.'

Maria was dressed the same as her older partners except for her flower which was white. She was slightly dumpy and rather nervous. She tried to smile but her lips would do no more than twitch. A strand of hair escaped from the tight glossy bun at the back of her neck. She tucked it in with shaky hands. The musicians were waiting for her. They started to play. She stood still. They stopped and went back to the beginning. She stood still.

The other dancers clapped time. Maria took a few steps. She tripped, she fell.

Quickly the others swooped round her, gathering her up, forcing her to move, trying to make it look as if this were a proper part of the dance. But it was no good. She covered her face and ran.

Another took her place, her white smile unmoving. But Antonia was watching Maria. One of the musicians had his arm round her. He was talking to her gently but he wouldn't let her escape.

At last she danced. Once she got going she danced like a flame in a fire and the applause crackled and roared like a mountain of burning twigs. A flame in a fire, a firefly. Antonia had never seen a firefly, were they real or mythical? A flame could be white, white as the flower that flew in Maria's hair, flew independently of her, it seemed, up, down, weaving in and out of the changing colours, her skirt, her white hands, black shoes, her smile that wouldn't let itself happen at first, so concentrated was her face on doing every step right, her smile that when it came glowed with pure glee.

She glanced towards the musician who had encouraged her. *See?* said the glance. He was concentrating too, on his playing, but his eyes shone love and pride at her.

Was he her lover? She was only fifteen. Her brother, her father? Antonia could hardly wait for the moment to applaud.

Her own body was pulsing with Maria's, her own breath was coming in gasps. There was breath on her neck from the crowd. She sipped her drink, controlling herself. She wanted to drink and drink, and if she'd had a packet of cigarettes she could have gone right through them. She drank. The waiter's eyes were on her. *Not me, you rat. Watch Maria.*

Maria stopped, beaming, breathless, shiny, exhausted. The other dancers and the musicians hugged her. The applause was huge but not enough. It faded away and the fat, spoiled people started to order drinks. The dancers started to leave. Antonia was on her feet, shouting for more, her hands above her head, her feet stamping – people stared – she sat down, still clapping, bashing her spine against the back of the chair. She was making people uneasy but Maria looked back over her shoulder, caught Antonia's eye and reached behind her ear for the flower which she removed and kissed and tossed towards her, and then she was gone.

A man reached out, caught the flower in mid air, raised it to his lips and put it in his lapel.

Antonia was in a frenzy. 'That's mine! She gave it to me.'

The man bowed ironically but kept the flower.

The dancers were gone, there was nothing they could do. Furniture was being re-arranged for the next act.

'It's *my flower.*'

No use. Probably the man didn't even speak English.

Like hell. He knew what he'd done.

The woman he was with detached the flower from his lapel and gave it to Antonia. There was no kindness in the gesture, no sense of justice, just tolerance. 'D'you think I want it now,' she screamed, remembering he had kissed it, 'with his spit on it?' The waiter was pushing determinedly towards her. 'It's all right,' she said, 'I'm going.'

Stones stabbed up into her feet as she lurched like a wounded animal towards the sea. Her sobs were coming out in howls and soft mews. Along the beach, sun-beds were piled neatly under straw sunshades.

She was thinking about her first lover.

Don't say anything yet, he had said. *You're not giving anything away by just listening to me, are you?*

Hush and *hush* and *hush* went the sea.

157

You're young but you're legal. I checked. No, not your birth certificate, how would I –? I saw that card from your dad. To Antonia with love on your sixteenth birthday. Otherwise I wouldn't be –

At the end of the bathing beach, rocks towered like small mountains: dark and gritty, nut-filled chocolate, a children's picture-book landscape.

I want you so much. It's obsessing me, you're obsessing me, you're all I think about. You're doubtful and a little bit afraid – but if I thought you'd really decided to stay a virgin till you marry or till you're twenty-one I wouldn't be saying this to you. I'd grieve over the waste but I wouldn't try to change your mind if I thought you'd really made it up.

There were tunnels in the rock. Smugglers' caves, Five Go to Larana Again. If she bent to look along the tunnels she could see pools or heaving open sea, black and silver.

But I know a passionate woman when I see one, Antonia, even if she is still a child. You're going to find out anyway – why not find out with me? Learn with me? I cherish you, you delight me. You're going to have many lovers, you're a woman made for love. And I'm the man made to be your first lover. I'm offering myself to you for that. Accept me, please.

All this said softly at restaurant tables, between films, in public places where she could smile and bide her time.

And only later said again in private places, when she trusted him, said as he unzipped and kissed and stroked and sighed, *I'll stop when you want me to, don't believe that propaganda that men can't stop. I'm not a schoolboy.*

And by the time he said, *Darling, stop me now or don't stop me at all,* stopping him was the last thing on her mind.

The last thing.

It was like –

– nothing –

Like nothing she'd dreamed. The warmth of it. The sweet safe violence and abandon, like nothing. A grown woman now and a child too, who could cry and be comforted. Teased. Coaxed. Nothing since had been like his sweet campaign of shrewd persuasion, playing her like a fish because she was important to him. Nothing since had been like that moment she chose to give in and found what she could do and drowned in the applause of his love. Was that really how it had been? She wasn't sure, but that was how she remembered it, and she'd found nothing like

158

it since, however hard she'd tried.

She started to half-walk, half-crawl along the low tunnel towards the pool. The water came up to her knees. She would have no way of knowing if it got deeper unless she fell. A sharp rock dug into her back. She flinched, hitting her head. She panicked, she couldn't escape. She couldn't go back. She went on.

The moon was breaking into identical little moons on the pools surface. Each of them floated away on the ripples and disintegrated at the edge of the pool. Like a hundred little typists disappearing into offices.

Not a hundred. One. They're all me, they've all got my face.

Go here, go there. Everybody thinks they've got me pinned down and nobody has. After a week in an office if I'm working well everybody forgets I'm a temp. They think I belong there until one morning I've gone.

Your typist, your wife, your mascot, your quickie. The ship that passed in your night. Your secret love, if only we'd met before –

Safe to say that.

Never liked it, did they, when I told them that just because I was going with them didn't mean I didn't love Paul. Not that they had any plans for the future but they liked to be the ones to decide who was a one-night-stand and who wasn't.

Who's to say we're not all the same? Not whole people, just bits of people. Samantha Yardley. A name on a magazine, a photo on an identity card, a phone call half overheard by Catherine. And Catherine too. The way she is with Frank you'd think he was her first, but that can't be true. She's THIRTY. And Anne too. I've never seen such a happily married couple but what does Chris know about what she gets up to when he's at work. And Ruth –

No, she wouldn't think that about her father's wife, but who was to say it wasn't the same for all women? Everybody knew men were like that (trust her to marry the only one who wasn't) but –

Another moon bearing her face broke on the rocks at her feet, and another, and another. *The reason I can't handle being alone here is that I don't know who I am when I'm not saying Here Today and yes I can do this and yes I'll do that and yes –*

Creatures popped and clicked in the rocks, water swished and bubbled. Music came faintly from the gypsy dancing place. She took off her dress. It lay like a dead thing on the rock. She'd worn it that first day at Forlex. There'd be no one from Forlex to identify it.

There might. Forlex had contracts here, anyone might happen to pass.

She wondered if it was safe to swim. Didn't matter if it was or not, she'd already decided – no she hadn't decided, but someone had. One of those others floating on the water? She'd take them down with her, every one.

The cold water gripped and let go, it wasn't really cold. She opened her eyes. Long tentacles swirled at her; she backed away. Jellyfish? She waited for the sting, what would it be like, a pin prick, a wasp, a cold sore – there was no sting. The tentacles followed her. They were her own hair.

She wasn't ready yet. She moved her arms and legs to stay afloat. Dancing. One day when Maria got over her stage fright she'd be the best dancer in the world. *What would I ever have been best in the world at? Typing. The party's over, one of these machines can do the work of five Antonias. Sex. Wow you're the greatest, Antonia, where did you learn that?*

Practice.

Would there be machines for that too? Wouldn't make much difference, the machines would be for the men, not the women. No one understood what women like her needed sex for and the women never told, bloody liars.

Down, down she went, holding her breath. Did you hold your breath till you passed out or did you breathe in water, was that how you did it and how did it feel?

Something brushed her cheek. It couldn't be her hair this time, it had grabbed her by the hair. A human hand. She had to come up.

'Hey-hey,' he said. 'Far out.' He said it as if it wasn't really an expression of his. As if he was a foreigner, or half-asleep. 'A fucking mermaid.' He still had hold of her but he was talking to himself. 'A fucking mermaid, a mermaid fucking. How do mermaids fuck? With difficulty. Who do mermaids fuck with? Poseidon, the god of the sea.'

'Whoever he is, he better watch out.'

'Eh?'

'Let go!'

'You mean you're not a mermaid?'

160

She kicked her feet above the water so he could see she wasn't. Her head went down. She came up choking. She'd alarmed him now, good. He said less dreamily, 'Why don't you come out and get dried and we'll talk awhile?'

Awhile, she thought in scorn. *This is all I need*. The scorn turned to rage. The rage burned her head at the point where he'd pulled her hair, and froze into a stream of cold pain right down to her feet where it solidified into a lump just not heavy enough to take her down where she wanted to be. *All I need. A good samaritan. A loonie, a moonie, a bloody boy scout.*

CHAPTER NINETEEN

Dead Stars

'C'mon, woman,' he said. 'Live, why not? There's lots to live for.'

She swam about, getting cold. 'Don't call me woman.'

'I used to call everybody *man*. But the girls told me it was sexist.'

'What girls?'

He didn't answer. She trod water. *I've seen you before, I don't know – how many girls do you live with?*

'Death,' he said, 'masks its own beauty.' He sounded like a religious broadcaster.

'What do you mean?'

'Come out and I'll tell you.'

Give me one good reason, she thought. As if he'd heard he said, 'I wasn't kidding when I asked if you were a mermaid. You could've been, you had such harmony swimming there. But there's no harmony in suicide, babe. You'll be a horrible sight.'

'Don't look then.'

'I can't avoid it.'

'Didn't ask you to come by, did I?'

'Maybe you did.'

Now he'd say something about a cry for help. Well he could stuff such thoughts where the monkey stuffs its nuts; she hadn't even known he was there. She still felt as if great weights were hanging from her feet. If only she could just sink. If only she hadn't answered him.

'See those stars,' he said.

'Where?'

'In the sky.'

'What about them?' The current that had kept carrying the little reflected moons to their doom at the edge of the pool was trying to do the same to her. But she wouldn't get within his reach again. She might come out but she wasn't going to be hauled out. Let him give her a good reason to come out if he knew so much, if it was so important.

'Some of them aren't even there. They've burned out in the time it takes for light to reach us and let us see them.' She'd heard of that. It was the sort of snippet Paul loved and she didn't like to think about.

He'd have to do better than that.

'So what?'

'Maybe what's making you sad is like that too. Not really there.'

'How clever.' *Cleverer than he thinks. An appetite for stars, who was it said that? Catherine. Hey, Catherine, they're not really there.* 'Why should I be sad just because I decided to go for a midnight swim? On my own.'

He thought for a long time. 'Okay,' he said chillingly. 'I'm going. But just get out of the water as a favour from one human being to another, hey? You can do what you want when I've gone, just don't lay it on me that I saw you.'

He helped her out. As his strong hands took her weight she recognized him. Not that there was anything about his hands, they didn't feel stung or damaged in any way, it must just have been that he swung her close to his face and she said, 'Oh! You're the jellyfish man!' as a child might say *Oh! You're Father Christmas.* She felt stupid. She returned his stare. He was wearing what looked like white muslin pyjama bottoms tied at the waist with rope, and a T-shirt. She said, 'All right, you've checked. I'm not a mermaid.'

He looked away. 'Got a towel?'

I thought you said you'd go. 'No.'

He pulled off his shirt and threw it to her. She dried her face with it. He'd be waiting for her to return it. She went on dabbing at herself long after she'd done the best she could. He had his back to her.

'You don't really believe in mermaids, do you?'

He laughed. 'I believe in the Larana Tourist Authority. That's just the sort of trick they'd dream up, only I missed the crowds

163

of nerds gawping at you.'

'I just went to the gypsy dancing, it was – ' She stopped and put on her dress. She was sticky with salt and it was difficult. If he was going to tell her the gypsy dancing wasn't genuine she didn't want to hear. She couldn't jump into the water again now because she had her dress on.

'If you'd been here ten years ago you could have seen them in the mountains. You'd've had to travel ten miles over unmade roads but they'd have welcomed you like a brother.'

'Here's your T-shirt.'

'Thanks. Smoke?'

'Suppose so.'

'You don't have to.'

'Don't I?'

'You don't have to do anything.'

'Don't I?'

'Not now.'

Now he was going to give her his philosophy of life. *Freedom's just another word for nothing left to lose*, would it be? Who was that, Bob Dylan? There'd been the odd teacher at her school who'd said things like that and tried to teach current affairs and sex education. They never lasted long.

She put out her hand for a cigarette. 'I'm supposed to have given up but I keep smoking other people's.' She watched him take out a tin and pouch and wanted to bite her tongue off. When people like him said, 'Smoke?' they didn't mean Benson and bloody Hedges. She wouldn't touch pot with a barge pole but that didn't mean she had to act the country cousin, as if she didn't know anything.

'Make yourself a roll-up if you prefer.'

She shook her head, relieved that she didn't like roll-ups. Bitter threads of tobacco coming away in your mouth.

'Why give it up if you like it?' he said.

'Ever heard of lung cancer?'

He chuckled. She'd been at parties where people smoked pot and this had been the kind of thing that put her off: the way they'd laugh at things like cancer and make you feel *you* were the fool for taking it seriously, drift off into private dreams and make you feel you were the one who was out of it.

She'd go in a minute. Meanwhile he laughed again. 'Good joke?' she enquired.

'No . . . just pleasure at the strength of your life force. Fifteen minutes ago you were trying to drown yourself. Now you're worrying about what's going to happen to your lungs when you're an old, old lady.'

'If I had wanted to,' she said, 'you wouldn't have stopped me.'

He nodded agreeably. 'And you wouldn't have done it in a little pool either. You'd have swum far out to sea, far out of your depth – so far that when your life force rebelled and you wanted to change your mind, you wouldn't have been able to. Then you'd have had one moment of knowing what true loneliness is. And that moment would have lasted for all eternity.'

'How do *you* know?' she snapped so that he wouldn't see her shiver.

He stood up and patted her shoulder. 'Let's walk,' he said.

She couldn't tell where they were going. The direction seemed to be inland and they were leaving the lights of the town far behind, but the sea still sounded near. They crossed building sites filled with rubble, dominated by the shadows of flimsy half-built hotels, immobilized cranes. 'You should have seen Larana,' he said, 'before all this.'

'How long have you been coming here for, then?'

'I live here.'

'How?'

'*How?*' He drew deep breaths. 'Like this.'

'I mean what on?'

He looked pained. 'What *on*? On the ground, man.' He reached down and patted it. 'On the good earth.' He picked up a Coke can and threw it away with disgusted force. It clattered and echoed.

'I meant money, what do you do for money?'

'Is money a big thing for you?'

'I haven't got any, if that's what you mean.'

'And is that why you were trying to – is that why you were so unhappy down by the pool, because you haven't got any money?'

'I haven't got any anything.' She stumbled. 'I haven't even got any shoes. But who cares about shoes, man?'

'You'd better have mine.'

They were huge but they stayed on and protected her feet. He walked easily. 'You must have hard feet,' she said, 'and your hands too, how do you do that trick with the jellyfish?'

'I ask them not to sting me.'

'Pull the other one.'

'Okay.' He smiled as if caught out but not really caring. 'There's a special way of holding them, you can avoid the sting. I'll show you one day.' *One day?* 'But I do believe a lot of pain's in the mind and the mind can cure it . . . don't you?'

'Try telling that to someone who's got an incurable disease.'

'*Life's* an incurable disease,' he said, staring at the sky. He was balanced on a rock as he said this, surrounded by sharp points of smaller rocks. The gentlest of pushes . . . she imagined him covered with blood, indignant, and her saying, *Pain's all in the mind.*

'Is that what's troubling you?' he persisted. 'Somebody . . . close to you is ill?'

'Sort of.'

'Disease,' he said. 'Dis-ease. That's all it means. A person not at ease with himself. There's always a reason . . . you worried before about cigarettes making you ill. But there's been research, you know, it may not be the cigarettes that cause the cancer, it may be the tension that leads the person to smoke in the first place.'

'Who do you work for, Peter Stuyvesant?'

'I don't work for anyone.'

'Neither do I.'

'Is that the problem?'

Wasn't going to give up, was he? 'I've been ill,' she said.

'But you're not ill now,' he said. 'What was it?'

'Stomach upset. I got dizzy and fell over and cut my chin, look.'

'I hadn't noticed till you pointed it out.' He ran a finger gently round the scar. 'And now that I'm looking, all I can see is what a sweet face you've got. So you see, something good's come out of it after all.' He kissed the scar and then her mouth, so lightly that if she'd protested he could have denied doing it at all.

It *had* come out of tension and something good *had* come from it. If she hadn't been lonely and miserable, she wouldn't have eaten so much egg mayonnaise. And if she hadn't cut her chin she wouldn't have got talking to Chris and Anne and Eva, and they'd helped her pass a few pleasant days. And she might not have gone to the gypsy dancing and met this gentle stranger

whom she wasn't quite sure she liked yet but who didn't believe
in illnesses and that was a start.

The hippie camp was in a wide bay with pine trees and pale
sand. The sun had started to rise, bleeding a path through the
rocks, touching pools and wet patches with red.

'What's it remind you of?' he asked. 'I can see that it reminds
you of something.'

'Sores,' she said. 'Raw flesh, broken blisters.'

Just try and bring it naturally into the conversation.

'What is it with you?' he said. 'They're jewels.'

She stopped walking. She didn't want to get any closer to the
camp. The tents were ragged and there was a lot of litter. She
imagined couples inside the tents, curled in each other's arms.
She wondered which was his tent. A few people were lying in
the open in sleeping bags, looking like fat maggots. In ones and
twos they were waking up. Some of them swam or washed.
Others urinated into the sea.

'I still don't know what you all live on,' she said stubbornly.
They had to live on something. They couldn't all beg on the
beach or give away tickets for gypsy dancing. She wondered
why her voice sounded so angry and desperate, she'd thought
the walk had calmed her, and a few people's dirty habits didn't
take from this being a beautiful spot or even – she was beginning to think – a beautiful way to live, if it was possible. He
had to show her it was possible. But she was frightened he
wouldn't be able to.

He said indulgently, 'You've seen people selling handicrafts
in the town?'

Of course! 'You make those things here?'

'I import them. I break even. Listen,' he continued urgently,
'that's all you got to do in life. Break even. Remember that, and
things won't get to you so much.'

'I want to tell you something,' she said. 'But I don't know
who you are.'

'Sometimes strangers are the best people to tell secrets to. But
okay, if you want. What do you want to know?'

'I don't know.' *Some sign of how you're going to react.* 'Where
are you from anyway? When I first saw you I thought you
didn't speak English.'

'I didn't feel like speaking English to all those tourists. I guess

I was English once. I try not to think about it.'

'Why, what's wrong with being English?'

'Nothing's *wrong* with it, babe. It just doesn't matter.' He yawned. 'Every war in the world's started with people thinking it matters.'

They were getting away from the point. She'd decided to tell him. She'd never got that far before. How, though? Which words? There were millions of words about it. There were all those magazine articles Paul had dug out: cheating, dishonest articles, starting off all bright and cheerful and it's-not-as-bad-as-you-think and then going on with their ifs and buts and small-minority-of-cases to show that it was every bit as bad as you thought because one of that small minority of cases might be you. (By the time they said that, you'd probably bought the magazine.)

Which words to choose? She could start by asking him if he'd heard of it.

He had. He thought it was hilarious.

'It's our century's metaphor for sin, babe. It's the Vatican's revenge. It's all media hype.'

'But it's real.'

'Sure it's real. It's an *industry*. You can buy T-shirts about it. In America they've got special dating agencies. Video games. How many singles bars can you get round without catching it? Aw come on, loosen up. You don't *believe* that stuff, do you?'

It had never occurred to her that she didn't have to believe it.

CHAPTER TWENTY

It Doesn't Matter
What You Do

Bright sunlight lit up the beach. A smell of cooking came from a camp fire.

'Breakfast?' he said.

She felt shy. 'I don't want to meet anybody.'

'Suits me, woman. I'm a loner myself.'

Here it came. She got ready to move.

'Sausages?' he said. 'Or sausages?'

'Sausages'll be fine.'

He bounded down the slope, greeting people emerging from tents. He spoke with the woman who was cooking. She felt a wave of jealousy, then selfconsciousness as he pointed at her and they looked up at her on her high perch. They waved. Wind crept through her hair, trying to lift it, getting tangled in the salt. *What's he saying about me? A poor girl I rescued from drowning, look after her. I'm splitting.*

He came back with two sausages wrapped in bread. He also brought a blanket with the name of a hotel embroidered on it. He tucked it round her and they ate in silence, watching the hippies gathering their things together, letting down the tents. She asked him why.

'There's talk of a police bust.'

'Why, you're not doing anything wrong.'

'Sure we are, we're lowering the tone of Larana.'

'Where will they go?'

He waved vaguely but didn't answer.

As the hippies trooped off a crowd of local children appeared, picking over the rubbish. 'Isn't that sad,' Antonia said. 'The stuff that gets wasted at my hotel.'

'They're a damn sight happier than the people in the hotels.'

She wondered how he knew.

'Listen,' he said. 'I'm kind of a night person. I sleep during the day.'

'It's all right. I was just going.'

'Hey-hey, hold on. I only want to check out a few things and get my sleep and leave you to enjoy the first day of your life. You ought to meditate, ever done meditation?'

'No. What do you mean, the first day of my life?'

'You nearly died last night. Now everything's a bonus and it doesn't matter what you do.'

If it doesn't matter what I do, I'll ask. 'Will I see you again?'

Did he hesitate? He might just be thinking. 'I'll meet you tonight,' he said.

'Where?'

'How do you feel about that pool now? It's one of my places, but how do *you* feel about it?'

'Feel about it?'

'Would it be a good place to meet me?'

'What time?'

'Midnight's a good time.'

A good time? A long time. 'Okay,' she said.

'Okay.'

He kissed her again, tasting her with his tongue. Then he walked down towards the camp that was slowly breaking up, being packed into rucksacks and carrier bags, being carried off.

Once when Maggie at Here Today had given up smoking, she had urged Antonia to do the same. 'You feel like you could lift up a house,' she'd said.

Antonia only felt she could run a marathon. Bare feet and all. She could run all the way back to the hotel at least.

She flashed past people eating huge English breakfasts at beach cafés. What was English about those breakfasts? No one she knew started the day with four greasy rashers, two eggs, baked beans, chips, toast. Think of the cholesterol.

Cholesterol doesn't count here. That was what they'd be

thinking, nothing counts here, in the sun, on holiday, these things only matter in London on working days in the rain, like PAYE and the Jubilee Line.

Paul used to like fried food for breakfast before I reformed him. There's me worrying about his health and as soon as I get one tiny thing wrong with me, off he goes.

She walked towards her reflection in the wide glass doors of the hotel. What a sight. No, though. She looked rather nice with her tangled hair and bare feet and dry salt stains whitening her dress.

Her office dress. She wondered if she'd ever wear it to an office again.

She was thirsty but she had no money. Gone on two tequila sunrises. Real sunrises would have to do from now on. She looked into the dining-room; breakfast was over so she couldn't even get free coffee. She went to her room and drank a lot of water from the tap.

She looked through her clothes, sorting out the ones in the best condition. She wondered how much she could sell them for. She had Catherine's things too but she wouldn't touch them. She wondered about sending them back to England. Then there was her box of two hundred cigarettes. Should be easy enough to find a smoker to flog those to, at half the duty free price. Just to tide her over.

Paul could rot with worry for all she cared. But with other people it was more difficult.

There were blank pages at the front and back of *The Thorn Birds*. She tore them out. She wrote to her father, telling him that she'd got a job as secretary to the manager of a hotel. She didn't know how long the job would last, but she'd stay in touch.

To Catherine she wrote: 'I haven't found Samantha Yardley yet but I've got a feeling I know what's happened to her. I may run into her. There's something about this place that makes people want to stay on and forget their troubles.'

Maybe she wouldn't post the letters until she'd actually got a job. She couldn't post them. She hadn't got any envelopes. Ridiculous to be in a situation where you couldn't even buy envelopes, and as for stamps – well, she could post the letters without stamps, and her father and Catherine would have to pay the excess.

Or she could put FREEPOST, you never knew what you could get away with. She giggled, and remembered that hotels sometimes supplied headed notepaper and envelopes. She decided to go down to reception and ask.

She had no luck at reception, they didn't know what she was talking about. She wandered around looking for Ray, he must have stationery, though whether he would give her any was another matter.

She couldn't find him. She tried approaching a few English-speaking people in the bar. None of them had envelopes. They were perfectly nice about it. Some offered her drinks instead but she refused. She felt oddly ashamed. She went back to her room. She'd been away approximately twenty minutes.

The door was open and there was a linen trolley outside. Antonia went in. She saw the heavy figure of the maid with an armful of towels, leaning over the table where Antonia had left her letter to Catherine. She was reading it.

'Good morning,' said Antonia firmly.

'Whassallthis then?' said the maid, running her words wearily together as if it was too much effort to say them separately.

'Oh! You're English.'

'Whatchoo writing about me?'

'Eh?'

'Samantha Yardley.' With a bitten finger-tip the maid hit the place on the letter where the name was written. 'Thass *me*.'

'That's you?'

They stared at each other. 'I s'pose I know my own name when I see it,' said Samantha truculently.

PART THREE

CHAPTER TWENTY-ONE

I Didn't Think So

'We can't go on meeting like this,' said Antonia. It had been Catherine's joke, not even funny the first time. She added a laugh.

She was trying to break through her shock and think. But all she could feel was deep rage and disappointment, as if she'd been given something, the thing she wanted most in the world and this baleful lump of a girl had taken it from her. Which was ridiculous. Nothing had changed. She ought to be pleased. She'd come out here to find Samantha Yardley and she'd found her. The one thing that had worried her about staying on – that Catherine had paid for the holiday and she'd promised to pay her back – might no longer apply. Catherine would be so pleased she'd say, 'Never mind about the money.'

'Eh?' said Samantha Yardley.

Eh? The stupid, animal-like grunt hung in the air. Hung with the sweet-sour smell of the sweat of her hard labour. Antonia walked past her, suppressing an urge to push her out of the way. She wasn't in the way but she seemed to fill the room. What was she doing here, why was she a cleaner? Antonia might have wanted to know once. Now she wished Samantha dead, no, not dead, that was a bit much, but nonexistent, unknown, lost. She opened the door to the balcony to freshen the air. That looked a bit obvious so she walked out on to the balcony as if that was what she'd been planning anyway. Over the road, No Muff Too Tuff waved. The sky was suddenly overcast, the air was like the inside of a huge launderette. Perhaps when she went back inside Samantha would have gone.

175

When she went back inside Samantha appeared to have passed out.

She lay on the spare bed, her pile of towels beside her. Her eyes were shut and her mouth open, revealing bad teeth and a bright pink tongue as if she had been eating cheap sweets. Her nylon overall rode up to reveal a black skirt, a slip with a frill of greying lace and fat thighs. Her knees were bruised and squashed from kneeling.

'Are you all right?'

'Yep. Just shutting me eyes.'

'Be my guest then.'

'They're good, these beds, aren't they?' said Samantha, wriggling luxuriantly.

'Do you – staff – have the same?' It was just something to say. 'Do you live in?' *I don't want to know.*

'You must be joking. You've got the good ones, you have. I hope you don't mind me laying on it. I often get a bit of rest in here, you always leave your room so tidy –'

Antonia had to say: 'Except once I didn't.'

Samantha scoffed. 'That's nothing. I've seen a lot worse. Some people, it's like that every morning.' She eyed the pile of clothes Antonia had sorted out and thought she might sell, and the box of cigarettes. 'You throwing that stuff out?'

'Not exactly.'

'Just as well you told me then, I might've taken it. It wouldn't've been my fault, you leaving it like that.'

'Wouldn't fit you.'

'Thanks a million.'

Antonia sighed. 'Sorry. It's the shock. I mean, there I was looking for you and now here you are.'

'Who are you to look for me? Whew, could I use a smoke.'

'It's bad for you. Give it up, it's easy.'

Samantha got up as if she'd leave. Antonia stopped her. 'I'll give them to you, all two hundred. Only please tell me what you're doing here, so I can tell Catherine.'

'What, the Catherine in the letter? Who is this Catherine? His wife I suppose. Can't bloody well satisfy him herself but no one else is allowed near him –'

'Samantha, who are you talking about? Catherine's not married.'

Samantha's eyes shrank cunningly behind her puffy flesh.

'How much do you know?'

This could go on for ever. 'Catherine's a friend of mine. We both work for Bright Girls of Mayfair. Used to. Catherine heard a rumour that you'd been raped.'

'Oh no,' said Samantha sorrowfully. 'That's not true.'

'She looked for you and she couldn't find you.'

'No, he didn't rape me.'

'I didn't think so.'

'You lousy bitch!'

'What's that for?'

'I s'pose you're thinking, who'd want to rape *her*?' Samantha pushed her trolley out through the door, leaving her pile of towels behind.

Antonia picked them up and followed. 'I didn't mean that at all. Look, let me help you with your work and then we can have a smoke together.' Samantha opened the next door with her bunch of keys. 'What do we do, put clean towels in each room?'

'Don't, you're not allowed to.' Samantha snatched the towels. 'And I'm not allowed to talk to guests and I don't want to either.' She stormed into the room and brought out two wet, smelly towels.

'That's disgusting,' said Antonia sympathetically.

'Who are you to talk?' said Samantha.

All right, Antonia thought. *I've done my best. I can go now.* But she didn't. She followed Samantha into the next room and closed the door. She put her hands on Samantha's shoulders. She couldn't remember when she had last touched another girl like this. Or any other way. She made her sit at the end of the unmade bed. She took her hand. It was clammy and she waited for a feeling of disgust but it didn't come. 'Now,' she said softly. 'Tell me.'

'I'm his wife now,' said Samantha.

'Yes?'

'That's why I can't go back to England. I've got to wait here till he comes to take me away. It's bigamy, y'see, it's wrong, well, they'll always say that about love, won't they?'

'Who?'

'He had to come out here, see, to check up on one of the buildings, and he brought me with him, 'cos I was his secretary. And one day we went for a walk up in the mountains and we found this little church with roses round the door and he goes,

177

"You look beautiful as a bride, Samantha," and I go, "I feel happy as a bride," and this priest comes out and he goes, "Did I hear the word bride? Do you want to get married?" and we did.'

'But why did you tell the agency you'd been raped?'

'Otherwise they'd wonder why I'd left and his wife might find out. I didn't name no names.'

'But – don't you think it's a bit irresponsible, I mean –'

'Why?' Samantha was bitter and triumphant. 'Nobody believed me. They didn't, you didn't. Even the police didn't, not really.' She pushed past Antonia and went on with her work, her face scarlet.

Antonia returned to her room. It had started to rain and spots spattered the floor where the veranda door had been left open. In the muggy warmth of the room her salt-filled dress and hair stuck to her. She started to take a warm shower. She turned down the hot tap bit by bit to see how cold she could stand it.

The water was pleasant, enlivening. It roared past her ears, drowning out the sound of the rain, the remembered drone of Samantha's voice, the soft drawls and whispers of the jellyfish man. It clarified a few things. It helped her to put one thought after another like a child learning to walk.

If there hadn't been a rape, why had Samantha gone to the police?

If she hadn't gone to the police, why had she mentioned them?

She'd seemed to regret mentioning them.

Antonia turned up the force of the cold tap. Icy jets spurted into her head.

What should she do now? Find out more about Samantha or attend to her own plans? Just because he wanted to see her tonight, she mustn't start thinking (or letting him think she thought) she had a lover for life. She guessed he was a bit like her – a bit like she used to be – and she must let him know that she understood that by having something definite to tell him.

But she wanted to know more about Samantha. Know who the man was, at least. It might be possible to accomplish both; if she was clever.

The HooRay Holidays notice said that Ray would be in the bar half an hour before lunchtime. She'd like to have a rest before seeing him but she couldn't risk not waking up. She cleaned her teeth, did her nails, towelled and combed her hair

178

and creamed the beginnings of stubble from her legs. She chose a clean skirt and a white top from the pile of things she'd been thinking of selling.

Ray was holding court with some girls whose pale skin suggested they had just arrived. He gave her a knowing smile, as one old hand to another. She smiled back.

She sat forlornly at a table where he could see her. She crossed and uncrossed her legs and smoothed her skirt. She stared into space.

He showed the new girls the way to the dining-room, then he came over.

'Don't worry,' he said. 'It may never happen.'

'Pardon?'

'You look so miserable, you'll get the firm a bad name.'

'I'm not looking miserable, I'm looking for you. I'm supposed to be going home the day after tomorrow and I wanted to talk to you about that job.'

'Job?' he said, looking round as if he feared someone might have heard. 'Job?'

'Yeah, you said if I'd do some paperwork for you you'd take me out to the island and introduce me to someone who might give me a job there.'

'The island's privately owned and foreigners can't get work permits. I told you that distinctly so don't you start getting me into trouble.' He started to go away. She panicked, she was making a mess of this. She must change the subject at once, try another tack.

'Okay, Ray, sorry, I must've misunderstood. I just thought it'd be fun, that's all. I'm bored today.'

'Is that my fault?'

'Yeah. "It is the responsibility of our couriers to ensure that you have as enjoyable a holiday as—"'

He tried not to laugh but did. 'Just my luck. You're from *Holiday Which?*'

'No, really, Ray. Make it stop raining. I'm so bored I almost wish I was back at work.'

'Won't be long and you'll get your wish.'

'I almost feel like offering to help you with your paperwork anyway.'

'Look, I just told you – '

'As a *favour* I meant.'

'I've got a feeling I'm having my leg pulled.'

'Maybe.' She shrugged and looked away miserably. 'I'll go and have lunch then.'

'You're after something, aren't you?'

'Of course. Anyone who ever offers to help out a friend is after something.'

'Anyone who ever offers to do something for nothing is crazy.'

'It wouldn't be for nothing, just nothing from *you*. Nothing that would cost you anything. Look, I've had such a good time here, I thought I'd like to get a job in the travel business when I get home. Only you know how it is with all the unemployment, even a little bit of experience marks you out from the other girls. And I haven't got any experience. And I thought if you could give me a reference, or even just a letter, saying I'd helped you out. I mean, that would count for something, Ray?' She stopped. She might have overdone it a bit. A reference from an overseas courier with a down-market company that no one had ever heard of? But he preened himself; believed; and admitted that there was a spot of typing that he'd been wondering how he'd get done. 'All very well for those pansies in Maida Vale writing brochures and demanding reports,' he said, 'they can't expect me to be the life and soul of the party *and* the desk man, can they?'

'I'll be the desk man,' said Antonia. 'What would you like me to do?'

He led her round the back of the bar into an office no bigger than a cupboard. It had HooRay posters on the walls and a stiff-looking portable typewriter on the desk. To get to the desk it was necessary to step over rows of box files marked 'Bookings', each for one month of the year.

'Now,' said Ray. 'I've been checking out other hotels we might use and these are my reports.' He produced a ring-bound notebook. 'It's all on different pages,' he explained. 'You have to follow the arrows. Might be easier if I dictate to you.'

They started. He read, she typed. She wished she'd had lunch first but she didn't dare leave now. He might change his mind. How was she going to get rid of him?

'I can read other people's handwriting better than they can read it themselves,' she said. 'Why don't you go off and be the life and soul of the party?'

He ignored her. Maybe she'd made it too obvious. Maybe he just liked dictating. As a last resort she tried a coughing fit. 'Whew, the air's dry in here.'

'Want a drink of wa–'

'I'd love a tequila sunrise, thanks, Ray.'

It was a risk, but he could be gone for a glass of water and back in less than a minute. Cocktails took time, provided this wasn't one of these places where they had them ready mixed in a bottle.

She picked out the April bookings box. There were about twenty names on the list. None was Samantha Yardley.

There were plenty of couples though. Mr and Mrs this, Mr and Mrs that. Any one of them might have been Samantha and her lover. Antonia didn't recognize the men's names either. But then, she realized for the first time, there was no reason why the man should be anyone she knew. She'd been assuming – probably because of Catherine's insistence on playing this like a TV thriller – that one of her friends would turn out to be the man. But Forlex was a whole company, she hadn't met everybody.

Time was passing as she thought. Ray might be listening. She lifted the March and May boxes on to her lap, typing with one hand while she flicked through them with the other.

She found nothing. She looked round the office. Another file caught her eye. LATE BOOKINGS. She fell on it and found what she was looking for.

YARDLEY, MISS S, it said. SINGLE ROOM SUPPLEMENT PAID. And in the space for notes, Ray had casually scrawled, 'No show return journey.'

Ice cream mingled with tomato sauce, apple cores and fish bones as Samantha scraped debris from dinner plates into a yellow plastic bowl. Antonia watched from her table. What a long day Samantha worked, plodding back and forth with different kinds of dirt left over from other people enjoying themselves. None of the other staff talked to her, or each other. Too tired probably. Antonia had never noticed her in the dining-room before, but then why should she? Her face was completely unmemorable without a name and a story to attach to it.

181

A story. What was the true story? Antonia had to know and Samantha had to tell her. In a little under three hours Antonia would meet the jellyfish man by the rock pool. She wanted to do this with a serene, settled mind.

She wanted to be able to tell him about a kindness she had done, a cutting of ropes, a break with conventional society.

'When do you go off duty, Samantha?'

'When do you lot finish stuffing yourselves?'

'Do you like working here?'

'Yep. Love it.'

'So you wouldn't be interested in going home?'

Samantha's eyes narrowed with ill-disguised hope and mistrust. 'What do you mean?'

'I've got a ticket for Gatwick for the day after tomorrow. I don't want it. You can have it if you'll do two things. First, take home some luggage belonging to a friend of mine.'

'What is it, contraband?'

Catherine? Contraband? 'Don't be daft. And take her a letter from me and tell her the truth about you. The truth, mind, none of that stuff about coming out here with somebody and getting married because I know you came by yourself.'

'You calling me a liar?'

'Yes.'

'Well.' Samantha's front teeth appeared in a long, discoloured snarl. 'Ffff you, then.' She crashed the plates down on one another and scraped them deafeningly.

CHAPTER TWENTY-TWO

Working It Off

Antonia cut the hem off her denim dress. She unpicked the fabric to make a fringe like the fringes the jellyfish man's friends had on their jeans.

Funny that they'd talked about all those personal things and not exchanged names.

She listened to the night-life of the town. There was no sign of No Muff Too Tuff. Perhaps he'd gone home.

At half-past ten she had another shower, sponging herself all over and shampooing her hair. She towelled it and combed it out. It dried quickly. It felt funny to be putting on the dress which she'd deliberately made ragged and was far from clean. But still, it didn't smell, she made sure of that, and she had a feeling that this was what he'd want her to be wearing. She'd have washed it if she'd had time, but she'd had so much to do today.

Eleven o'clock came and she set off for the pool. It was another warm night. She wore no underclothes under the dress. The soft, salty fabric brushed her body and the fringes tickled her knees.

She reached the pool at a quarter to twelve, crawled easily along the tunnel and waited, dangling her feet in the water and listening to the sounds of the sea creatures and the ripples.

Little moons bounced and danced on the surface of the sea.

The hands of her watch went round and soon it was one o'clock. She stripped off, dropped like a stone into the pool and swam from side to side.

Then she got out, put her dress and her watch back on and returned to the hotel.

She hadn't really expected him to turn up. She could have gone looking for him at the camp, but why give him the satisfaction of not being there? He probably lived in a villa. It was probably all lies. He probably came from somewhere like Pinner. Where he worked in a health food shop. Not in the shop itself, in the office upstairs. He'd be terribly apologetic about asking you to type, but you'd have to do it anyway.

She kept the light off in her room. She went out and sat on the balcony. There were still a lot of people about and the noise echoed up the side of the building more loudly than she had heard it before. No Muff Too Tuff had a new game. He leaned over his railing with a plastic bottle of mineral water in his hand. He took swigs and spat forcefully. The water came out of his mouth as a shiny white globule and descended to the ground in a fine mist. By the time his passing victims looked up, he had dodged out of sight.

Antonia heard a movement behind her. 'Have you still got them cigarettes?' It was Samantha. She looked half-shy, half-aggressive.

'How did you get in?'

'Have a key, don't I?' Samantha sat down like an old woman.

'Charming.'

'I've run out of fags.'

'You can run out of here. Don't you knock ever?'

'You didn't answer. I thought you was out. I thought, if I just picked up them cigarettes – it wouldn't've been stealing, you said I could have them – only now you're here you can give me that ticket too.'

Give, give, give, thought Antonia. She said, 'Ticket?'

'You said you had a ticket to Gatwick.'

'Oh.'

'And you said you'd give it to me. You *said*. And the cigarettes. You haven't got them, have you? You've smoked them, you haven't given it up at all, oh well, doesn't matter. Don't worry about it. Just give me the ticket and I'll leave you in peace.'

Antonia was trying to make her brain work. But she couldn't because she didn't care enough. She felt as she used to feel just after Paul left when she swallowed draughts of cold-cure to make her sleep, only this time there wasn't the relief of sleepiness, just numbness, stupidity, pain.

'The cigarettes are in there somewhere.'

Samantha went back and put the light on.

'Anybody want a FUCK?'

Samantha appeared in the doorway. 'Oh sure, mate. We're bloody well queueing up. Put your wings on and fly over here.'

Next time I have one, he'll have wings, Antonia thought. She said, 'Put the light off, Samantha. We're all lit up like a television.'

'I can't *stand* him. Going on like that all the time.' She put the light off and grumbled. 'I can't find them.'

'Now there's a girl who looks as if she could do with a fuck!'

A woman's voice called back calmly from somewhere: 'I've got one here if I want one, thanks.'

'Wasn't talking to you, you poxy cow.'

Antonia followed Samantha back into the dark room, closing the curtains. They sat down on separate beds.

'Samantha, you know when you used to go to work at Forlex.'

'Yeah. I was a cleaner there too.'

'I thought you were a secretary.'

'I wanted to be but Bright Girls said I'd be better as a cleaner.'

'Well. Working anywhere. *Going* there. You go on the tube and everyone looks the same. I mean, you've got different clothes on and you go to a lot of trouble with yourself and sometimes you look in a mirror and you think, mm, not bad, but you know you're all the same.'

'I was on the tube once,' said Samantha, 'and there was this man and this woman. And the woman goes, "What an *interesting* face." Talking about me, right? "You couldn't guess her age. She could be sixteen, she could be forty. She'll look like that all her life." Nice, eh?'

'Charming.' Antonia paused, knowing she ought to express the sympathy she felt for Samantha overhearing such a terrible thing. But she didn't want to lose her thread.

Outside, the shouting went on.

'An - y - body - wanna - come to a party? Ha ha! Naughty naughty. What did you think I was going to say?'

Samantha ripped back the curtains. 'Party?' she roared. 'I can't hear no music.'

'I'll sing to you if that's the way you like it, baby.'

185

'Don't *answer* him. I'm not *talking* about that. I'm talking about when you feel you're the same as everybody else and then someone comes along who doesn't think you're the same. Someone who sees – what you've known all along. That you're *special*. And it's like standing in the middle of the world being cheered.' Antonia started to pace up and down. 'It's so easy. They come across so tough but it's so *easy* to make them want you, you don't even know you're doing it half the time. And then there's that time . . . between when you know they want you and you let them know you want them too . . . *that* time . . . and when you actually do it. That's the best time. Your body's all . . . question marks. Like a great big question mark, your body is. Because it's not just that place down there where you want them, your whole body's curling and wondering, what's he going to be like? When? How? Because you don't have to worry about that. He'll fix that. He'll see to it. And then there's that moment when he comes into you for the first time and your stomach turns over. There's never anything like that again. And you know that sooner or later it's going to make you feel bad and empty but it's too late and you're glad it is. There's no backing out. You can't back out, once you've said you would.' She took Samantha's hands. 'Is that what happened? You said yes and then you tried to back out?'

'No,' said Samantha. 'I never – '

'You never what?'

'I never said I would.'

You never said you would. But how often did I ever SAY I would? We might do the same things, you and I, but for you it would mean no and for me it would mean yes. And yes is what he wanted to hear. He. Who? 'Who, Samantha?'

His name was Russel. He worked on the third floor at Forlex. He was an artist but because of his wife and three kids he had to be a draughtsman. He'd got into conversation with Samantha one day when she went up on the roof of the building to eat her lunch. No one was really supposed to go up there but Samantha didn't like to be watched while she ate. 'I'm always expecting someone to come over and say, "But that's not on your diet."'

'Was Russel on a diet too?'

'*No.* He liked looking at the view. Wasn't much of one but he saw hidden beauty in urban sprawl.'

'Oh yeah?'

It became a regular date: lunchtimes on the roof. Samantha gave up eating lunches altogether. They had lots to talk about: he was fed up with being a draughtsman, she was fed up with being a cleaner. She was particularly fed up with being the one who had to put flowers on the desks of the secretaries and take them away when they were dead. 'Who ever gives me flowers?'

He gave her some flowers. A small bunch, but still.

She told him about her private dream of saving up enough money to have a holiday in Larana, after seeing all the pictures around the office.

He said he loved her. He said he'd like to paint her naked. He knew a room where they could be alone.

'And?' said Antonia.

'And – well.'

'What happened afterwards?'

'He went back to work.'

'He raped you and went back to work? What did you do?'

'I went back to work too. I thought probably he didn't realize I didn't want – I mean, I always meant to be a virgin in case I got married but not many girls think that nowadays, do they? I mean, he probably thought I was just saying no because, you know.'

Antonia realized she and Samantha were still holding hands. Samantha seemed to realize it in the same moment and they let go of each other.

'In the evening he just went off home, I mean he didn't look for me or anything. I thought he'd look for me. I thought, I can't come back here tomorrow so I rang up the agency and asked if I could have a different job. And they said no so I told them why. And they said I should go to the police. And I thought, I just might. And then I thought, never mind *might*, I damn well will. And this policewoman, she goes, "Raped, eh? When did this happen?" And I go, "In my lunch hour." She goes, "Why didn't you report it before?" I said I was waiting to see if he'd talk to me.

'And she goes, "Well, from what you've told me, it'll be difficult to convince a jury." She said I'd have to get up in court and say everything and even then they might not believe me. "*I* believe you," she goes, lying her head off. "But it's not up to me." And she told me to leave the job and think about it for a few days and then come back and tell her if I wanted to

187

prosecute him.'

Antonia was thinking, *I understand him better than I understand you. I don't like thinking that. I'm not going to say it. If he
knew you didn't want to and did it anyway they ought to lock him up
and throw away the key.*

*But why would you take your clothes off for a man if you didn't
want to do anything else?*

*You can't have believed that stuff about him wanting to paint your
portrait.*

And then she thought, *when someone seems to want you when
you thought no one would, you believe anything.*

She said, 'What happened then?'

'He came round.'

'To your home?'

'Hostel where I was staying. I must've told him what it was
called and he'd phoned round all these charities and places to
find out where it was. I was ever so surprised to see him.'

And pleased. Weren't you?

'He was ever so upset.'

And you were pleased about that too.

'She'd been to see him, that policewoman. She went in plain
clothes and they just had a chat but you could see he was
scared. It wasn't that, though. "If I've done wrong I'll take the
blame, Samantha," he goes, "but I can't bear to think of you
thinking I meant to hurt you."'

Yes, thought Antonia. *And you swallowed it whole.*

'He wanted to know what he could do to make it up to me.
And I thought – well, if you didn't mean anything bad, it
must've been because you really loved me and you couldn't
stop yourself. And I thought of a little test. I said, "Could we go
away for a few days, Russel, and talk it over?"'

*I bet he couldn't believe his luck. Gets you out of the way and gives
him a chance to sweet talk you out of getting him into any more
trouble. And even if you still want to prosecute him, who's going to
believe you when you've just been away together?*

'He goes, "There's nothing I'd like better in the world than to
take you to Larana. But how can I?" And I go, "You could say
you had to check up on one of your buildings." And he goes,
"Yes, but I couldn't take you."'

'So I told him about something I'd seen in one of my
magazines, last-minute special offers, book this week, go next.

188

"All right," he goes, "where is it?" "In the office," I told him. I told him about this girl who kept a sort of lending library of magazines when people had finished with them. He goes, "I'm going to look a right pansy, aren't I, going through the girls' magazines," and I said, "That's all right, my one's got my name on it. Just tear out the page and put it back."'

'So he booked the holiday and sent you here.'

'He was going to send me a telegram to say when he'd arrive. I kept looking at the noticeboard. I expect something came up.'

'Samantha – ' It was all boiling up, to tell Samantha that decent men didn't *do* that, send people on holiday and leave them there even if they were busy. But all she could see were Samantha's big forgiving eyes. 'Samantha, that stuff about you marrying him.'

'That was just – '

I won't make you say it. 'Yeah. So why are you still here?'

'I couldn't go back.'

'Something wrong with your ticket?'

'No, I just couldn't go back, I'd've felt such a fool.'

Yeah. You wait for someone who doesn't turn up. Once you've admitted to yourself that he really isn't coming, the last thing you want is to run into him by chance. You'd feel ashamed in case he thought you were running after him. Ashamed. You.

'What did you do then?'

'When the coach came I stayed in my room and hid. Lunchtime, I went down and had lunch, same as usual. No one said anything. Dinnertime, same thing. Slept in my room that night. The girl came to clean it, same as usual. No one seemed to want it. After about a week some people arrived so I got out, right? I started sleeping on the beach or in the other hotels, you know, in the lounges. Came back here for all my meals. Nobody stopped me. Then one day the manager did. Took me into his office and gave me a huge bill. I said I couldn't pay it. He said he'd hand me over to the police. Or else I could stay and work it off. He took my passport off me and made me sign something saying I'd stolen from the hotel – '

'You must've nearly worked it off by now.'

'Not really, 'cos you have to pay your board, see. And breakages, and drinks and fags, and even when all that's paid for I was still worrying about how I'd buy a ticket, so you having a spare one's ever such a relief.'

189

Antonia went cold. She hadn't got a spare ticket. She only had her own, that was, Catherine's. There'd be a spare seat on the plane, Frank's, but how would Samantha get on?

So how had she –

She'd promised her own ticket to Samantha. Because she herself had had a dream of not going back.

'You'll manage better than me,' said Samantha, reading her mind. 'You won't end up doing dirty work like me.'

What will I end up doing?

'I'm glad I told you,' said Samantha.

'Yeah, it often feels better to tell people.'

'Specially if they're going to give you a ticket.'

'Well, don't be in such a hurry, Samantha, the flight doesn't go till the day after tomorrow.'

Gives me time to think, at least.

'You said that yesterday,' said Samantha. It was twenty past three in the morning.

'All right, tomorrow then,' said Antonia.

CHAPTER TWENTY-THREE

My Fault

'Tonight.' Ray told the indignant little crowd round the noticeboard. 'The flight's tonight.'

'It's *tomorrow*,' the HooRay holidaymakers insisted, waving their folders of travel documents. 'You can't just chop a day off the end of our holiday like –'

'I'm not,' said Ray smugly. 'Your flight *was* going tomorrow night at 11 pm. Now it's going tomorrow morning at 1 am.'

'But that's tonight.'

'I'm not talking about nights, mate. I'm talking about days and it's all the same day.'

'I shall demand a refund.'

'You do that. Got the address?'

'I shall report you to ABTA.'

'We're not in ABTA.'

He walked past Antonia who stood stunned. He chucked her under the chin. 'Nice to see one person who's not shouting at me. What shall I give you as a reward?'

'It's lucky I was passing, isn't it?'

He quoted: '"It is the responsibility of holidaymakers to consult the noticeboard regularly for changes of schedule." Have you been consulting the noticeboard regularly? I think not.'

'I might have got left behind.'

'I thought that was what you wanted.'

It had been. And what now? The change of flight meant two things. One, less time to think. Less time to wander about full of the hope and the fear that she'd turn a corner and see the jellyfish man. And he'd explain. And it would be a convincing explanation. (Anything was a convincing explanation if you wanted to be convinced.) And then there'd be the waiting for him to take off again. The other thing it meant was the possibility of avoiding Samantha and disappearing without her knowledge.

Could she do that?

What else could she do? Staying here alone and penniless had been a dream, a stupid romantic notion. With no one to help her she'd end up in Samantha's vacant shoes, scraping chips into a bucket of ice cream, and that if she was lucky, otherwise begging on the beach, getting beaten up, worse, and meanwhile Samantha would be back in London with Catherine's luggage which she'd probably steal. She'd make up some explanation for herself that said it was all right, that was Samantha all over: if she wanted something she had to have it. Samantha wouldn't bother to contact Catherine. And since Antonia couldn't afford stamps to write and explain, Catherine would now have two missing girls to worry about instead of one.

It was out of the question. Antonia would just have to go home and resume her life. Perhaps she'd send money to Samantha. She'd have to find a job first. Crawl to Mrs Hook? Take a word-processing course? Paid for with what? She'd have to find somewhere to live, too. Paid for with what? Never mind. She had to go *home*, that was all. She couldn't think straight in this place.

All that remained to decide was whether or not to tell Samantha.

Not to tell her would be a lousy trick.

To tell her would be impossible. To look into those resentful puffy eyes, to read the whole story again in them: the story of her need for love, her need to believe in it. To see her squat, weary limbs and imagine them bent over dirty floors or trailing around after sick-soaked towels and damp sheets –

It was Samantha's own fault of course. Not the – rape? seduction? love affair? – Antonia didn't mean that. That man was to blame. But staying on at the hotel? Samantha must have known she couldn't get away with that.

She must have known that you can't help yourself to something just because you want it.

Everyone has to know that.

'Do you want to or not?' said Ray.

'What?'

'I've asked you three times. Forget it.'

'What?'

'Go out to the island. I've got to be up all night putting you lot on to your plane so I've just given myself the afternoon off in lieu.'

She stared at him. He was *asking her out.*

How sweet, she thought. *How quaint.*

And it was one way of avoiding Samantha.

'Talkative,' said Ray.

Antonia lay back in the boat in her bikini, watching him row. His action was skilful, rhythmic and strong. Her eyes flinched from the gleam of the water, flat, oily, golden-blue, uncut by waves. She looked back and watched the beach recede. Only the staunchest of sunbathers were out this afternoon, glistening under sunshades, hiding from the heat that they had come for.

'I said you're very talkative today.'

Why couldn't he keep quiet?

'Sorry, Ray. I've got something on my mind.'

'Course you have, darling. You girls have got such soft hearts. You never learn.' She tensed. He couldn't have seen her with the jellyfish man. It had been dark night. 'And if Uncle Ray can cheer you up by taking you out to the island – well, you be as miserable as you want.'

'What do you mean, soft hearts?'

'Don't tell me you've been on your own here for two weeks and you haven't fallen in love with anybody.' He pronounced it *lerve.* 'That's why you thought you wanted to stay, isn't it, and now he's let you down. I've heard it all before. I know, I know. I haven't heard it before the way it was with *you,* but I've heard it pretty similar. You ought to learn to use men the way men use you. Have a good time, then say goodbye. Don't you realize they meet the *planes,* these local Romeos?'

She closed her eyes. There was a pause in the swish of the oars, the motion of the boat changed. She tensed, waiting for him to touch her. But all he did was pat her hand. 'Not that I mind cheering you up,' he said. 'It's one of my less onerous duties.' He took away his hand and started rowing again. 'Don't mind me, I'm just the ferryman.' He started to sing. 'Yo - ho -

heave - ho. Your shoulders are red, don't you think you should cover up?'

His words seemed to make sunburn blisters pop up all over her back, but she said, 'I'm fine.' She didn't want to miss a minute of sun so she left her clothes where they were, folded up under the seat with Ray's HooRay jacket.

She wondered what he meant by 'cheering *you* up'. Just her? Or dozens before her, long streams.

He was kind, though. It was surprising. In his clumsy, prickly way, Ray was kind.

'I'll take my turn rowing if you want,' she said.

He scoffed. 'Ever rowed?'

'We used to go on Crystal Palace Pond.'

'Just you lie back and enjoy it,' he said. 'After all, this time tomorrow – ' he shipped his oars and mimed typing. 'Tap - tap - tap. Remind me to give you that reference.'

Kind, so kind. Maybe she'd tell him about Samantha, he might be able to help. Actually he ought to know already. It was his responsibility to look after people, not just write No Show on their booking form and forget about them. On the other hand, he might be on the hotel manager's side. And if he discovered that Samantha was planning to escape before she'd worked off what she owed, there'd be more trouble.

Everything was so difficult. She'd think about it.

She'd think about everything.

The boat spun. She cried out and grabbed the sides. There were whirling eddies all around, holes in the sea. Ray pulled strongly, his face concentrated but calm. Soon they were steady again. 'What was that?' she said, her heart still thumping.

'They call it "the hand of the witch". I should've been ready for it, it's always about here . . . when it happens. Freak current. Heard of the Bermuda Triangle? You don't want amateur oarsmen out here.'

Antonia shrugged. 'We're still in one piece.'

'Sure. Know where you are?'

There was nothing but sky and empty rocks and sea. 'Are we lost?'

'Not really. There's just this one stretch where you can't see where you've come from or where you're going. That's why they drowned her here, so she couldn't get back and haunt them. But she sticks up a finger now and then . . . vulgar, I call

194

it. Watch out forrard and when you see the island say, "Land ho!"'

'Land ho!' she shouted after a while.

'Land ho? Land ho?' He turned to confirm that the line of sand and trees she'd seen was real. 'Land ho, me hearties.' He sped up his rowing. 'Let's pull for the shore.'

'Let me have a go, Ray,' she said, starting to crawl towards him. 'We're nearly there.'

'Go back, you'll upset the balance.'

'Don't be such a spoilsport. I'm depressed. I want to *do* something.'

He gave her the oars and they changed seats. 'Go on then,' he said. 'You know how to do it, after your vast experience.'

Antonia dipped the oars into the sea. The water pulled the blades in deeper and the boat started to rotate. Ray yawned. 'If you lose an oar,' he said, 'you swim out and get it yourself. You can forget chivalry.'

'Oh, I couldn't forget chivalry. Not with you, Ray. Please, teach me to row.'

'You plant your little bottom in the middle of the seat for a start.' She obeyed. 'Now – brace your feet against these ridges here – oh, you can't. Your legs are too short.'

'Sorry.'

'You'll have to brace against me.' She pressed her bare feet against his thick-soled trainers. 'Now, dip the oars just under the surface of the water – you're wasting effort if you go deeper – and pull.' He put his hands over hers on the oars and kept them there long after she'd got the idea. 'You'll be rowing for Oxford next year,' he said. 'They're using girls now, aren't they?'

'Next year,' she said. 'I wonder where I'll be next year.' He mimed typing again. 'Perhaps,' she said.

'Perhaps you'll be in the travel business. It's best to have something steady. We all think about doing the vagrancy bit, but it's just a stage to go through.'

'Yeah. This time next year we might all be dead.'

'Keeps you going, does it? Being so cheerful?'

'The world might blow up.'

'Not this bit.'

'Why?'

'Stands to reason. Why waste a bomb on an island with

195

nothing on it?'

'I thought you said there was a hotel on it.'

'There will be,' said Ray. The boat touched sand with a shushing noise. He leapt out and hauled it up the beach with her still in it. 'The locals used to call this the rainbow beach,' he said.

'What locals?'

'There used to be a village.'

'What happened to it?'

'See why it's called the rainbow beach?'

First there was the sea, greeny-blue like pictures in a holiday brochure. Then there was a fringe of foam, scarcely moving. Then there was a line of pink. Antonia investigated: the pink came from shells, laid in a row by the tide. Some had little creatures inside them. Behind the pink was a lace of green seaweed. And then there were palm trees and pine trees rooted in soil like sugar, different sugars, white and gold and dark brown with flecks of demerara. The air among the trees was silky cool. Birds called to each other in alarm and curiosity.

'Nice to see you smile,' said Ray.

'Thanks for bringing me here.'

'It's a pleasure.' He sighed. 'Most of the clients don't like me.'

She looked at him sidelong. 'You are a bit rude –'

'Suppose I am. It gets you down, though. You get lonely.'

'What, with all those people?'

'Because of all those people.'

Again she considered telling him about Samantha. If she could convince him that there was a spare seat on the aeroplane, already paid for, it was no skin off his nose who sat in it, was it? He was capable of feeling sorry for people. He had to feel sorry for Samantha.

'Stand you up, did he?' Ray asked.

She didn't feel like talking about herself but it was a way into the subject of Samantha. 'I bet you'd never do that, would you, Ray? Promise to meet someone and then change your mind and not turn up. And the way it happened with me was nothing compared with a friend of –'

'Two lonely people on an island,' he said, kissing her.

As if from far away she registered that he liked her, she liked him and his tongue and lips were expert. But there was no thrill. She wasn't in the mood. She wanted to talk about

196

Samantha.

She didn't want to hurt his feelings though. She pushed him away gently. He accepted this, then tried again. 'Come on,' he said. 'He stood you up. Won't I do? What did you agree to come for?'

'I was lonely, I wanted some company.'

'Aren't I company?'

'Yes, but – ' She couldn't find any words that didn't sound like a bad joke or something from a girls' advice page. *I'd like to know you better first. I don't do it on the first date.*

'Come on, Antonia or Catherine or whatever you call yourself.'

She stared, frightened. 'What do you mean?'

'There's no Antonia on my list. According to my list there's a Catherine Lambert – *Ms* Catherine Lambert – and a Frank Spivey in your room. Funny, I thought.'

'What are you going to do about it?'

'Nothing much. *Someone's* paid for your room, so there's no offence committed. Might be a spot of bother at the airport, though, if the wrong name's on the ticket. You're not supposed to chop and change off your own bat. If someone drops out, there's cancellation fees to be paid.'

He took off all his clothes. He had an erection. Antonia clenched her fists and ran a few steps away: 'Please, I'm not in the mood.'

'I suppose I can go swimming without your permission,' he said huffily, going into the water. *That ought to cool him off*, she thought with relief. *I suppose he's entitled to be annoyed.*

Why is he?

He was a good swimmer. 'Come in, it's lovely,' he called. She shook her head. 'Why?' he called. 'Not in the mood?'

'That's right.' She smiled; he seemed quite affable now.

'All right. Sulk then.' He dived like a duck, his little white bottom winking in the sun. He came up again and made a great display of looking down at his body. 'You're quite safe now. I don't seem to be in the mood either.'

He came out of the water and sat beside her. 'No chance of you drying my back, I suppose?'

'No.'

'Blimey. Not in the mood for this, not in the mood for that.'

'I'm in the mood for seeing this hotel of yours. If there is one.'

197

'Should've said,' he retorted. 'We're at the wrong end of the island for that.' He glared at her in her bikini and his penis started to twitch and fatten. 'Look, you little tease. If you're *not in the mood*, put some clothes on for heaven's sake.' He fetched her things from the boat and threw them at her, hard. She stood up to dodge and eyed him coolly, furiously, her hands on her hips. 'Go on,' he said, 'put them on or I'll put them on you.'

She took a deep breath. She said quietly, 'Yeah?' Then her voice became a grating roar. 'You and whose army?'

He raised his eyebrows and laughed. 'Anyone ever tell you you're lovely when you're angry? No? Probably because you're not.'

She stopped dodging him. She advanced on him, pointing her finger. 'They wouldn't know. Because I've never been angry before. How is it – you tell me this, Ray! You tell me this! If I want a bloke and he wants me and something goes wrong, it's *my fault*! And if I want him and he doesn't want me it's *still* my fault! But if you want me and I don't want you, guess whose fault it is! *Mine!*'

'All right, all right, calm down. You're getting hysterical.' He seized her wrists.

She broke free. 'That's right!' she screamed.

'How d'you think you're going to get to the airport, on foot?'

'No!' She ran shrieking towards the sea. 'I'm going to swim. *In* my bikini. And if you don't like the sight of me, *don't look*!'

She swam far out in the buoyant water. She kept putting her feet down to check the depth. At first it was shallow, then there was a ledge. She couldn't feel the bottom. She was frightened but she went on and on.

'Come back, you stupid little cunt! I didn't mean it, of course I'm going to take you back.' She supposed that was an apology. He sounded almost as scared as she was. She turned round, swimming wearily until she could put her feet down. Ray was coming to meet her, looking sheepish. He dived and swam close, under the water. She felt his hair on her thigh as he nosed her like a big fish. She lost her balance and her knee made sharp contact with his face. Suddenly the clear water was red with blood.

She tried to run away. He was on his feet. 'You little bitch –'

'I'm sorry, I'm sorry, it was an accident, it's only a nosebleed,

198

nosebleeds always look worse than – ' He was going white. 'You'd better get out of the water,' she said, 'You look as if you're going to faint.'

'I'm not going to faint,' he said. He raised his hand flat and cuffed her on her ear. He had taken a full swing, the full length of his reach, and she was deafened, stunned. She fell back and the water closed over her head, shrieking and bubbling in her ears. She found a foothold and tried to stand up but his hand was pressing down on her head. Her chest thumped. She pounded at him and he lost his balance. She came up for air and their eyes met: his were narrow and furious above the blood. He grabbed her wrist and twisted her arm behind her back. He was bending her lower and lower, the water was coming up to meet her face.

'Don't kill me, oh please don't, oh don't, Ray – ' she sobbed, taking in mouthfuls of water, struggling. He released her. 'Don't kill me, Ray, don't, don't – '

He spat blood into the water and swam off. 'Kill you? I don't even want to fuck you.' She leaned over and vomited, retching and retching till there was nothing left. She picked up her clothes and ran into the wood.

CHAPTER TWENTY-FOUR

Temp of the Year

Lizards scattered as she ran. When breathlessness slowed her she could see their beady eyes blinking at her from beneath stones and leaves.

The woods gave way to a round, scrub-covered hill. She looked back. Ray had not followed her. She started to climb the hill. The soil was no longer like sugar. It was gritty and sharp and she kept having to stop and brush it from between her toes where it cut her.

Her throat burned and sweat poured into her eyes. Soon she was high enough to see back over the woods and on to the beach. Ray was lying beside the boat, his head tilted back.

He had said the hotel was at the other end of the island. But he hadn't said how big the island was. It could mean twenty miles of these hills. Isolated trees offered meagre shade. She planned her route from one tree to the next, pausing to rest under each one.

She reached the top of the hill. She could see the whole island. It wasn't large. At one end were Ray and his boat. At the other end was a building site.

It was like a great wound, as if some monster had taken a bite out of the land. And the hotel – what must be the beginnings of a hotel – was like bone protruding from the wound. It was grey and solid, five storeys high. The storeys seemed to be balanced on the flimsiest of sticks, only some of which had been surrounded by concrete. There were window-shaped holes in the walls, and a few balconies jutted out. There was nobody about. Earth-movers, cranes, cement-mixers and heaps of rubble shimmered in the heat. On the coast beyond a rough harbour had been constructed. A wide-bottomed freighter rode at anchor, and there was a small motor-boat that looked like a ferry. The water was a different colour this side of the island: very dirty, very deep.

She approached the building site through what seemed to be the remains of an old-style village. She'd seen postcards in Larana: *Typical traditional dwelling.* The white stone cottages had tiny windows like eyes squinting against the sun. There were pig sties and chicken houses but no animals. There were overgrown kitchen gardens, and laden trees with fruit rotting at their feet. The sun gleamed on the nearby heaps of rubble, picking out chunks from the white stone houses that had been demolished.

She walked along what might once have been a path. It was overwhelmed by debris from the newer, wider road from the harbour, patterned with thick deep tyre tracks. Oil and sunlight made sickly rainbow patterns on the surface of a stream. Birdsong and her own footsteps were the only sounds.

She knocked on the door of one of the houses.

There was no reply. She knocked again and pushed the door. The air was heavy with the smell of human breath and sweat, and the sound of men snoring. They hung in hammocks nailed to the walls or lay on mattresses. Every inch of space was occupied, either by sleeping men or their little boxes of belongings. Religious images and family photographs had been nailed and taped to the walls.

She could see no taps or sinks in the house, even if she could have got to them without disturbing the men. One of the men turned over in his sleep, his hammock swinging dangerously. She fled.

She found a pump and wondered how it worked. She fiddled with the handle, leaned on it, and it gave under her weight. There was a gurgling sound deep in the earth. After a few more pushes, clear water emerged from the spout. She let the water play on her face, and drank. When she looked up again a man had come out of the house and was watching her.

She was frightened. Then she thought, *I've come here to be safe, there's no point in being frightened.*

'Lovely water,' she said, miming. 'I was so hot.'

He lit a cigarette butt and smiled at her, brown-toothed. He

201

said something in return that she did not understand.

Another man appeared, a foreman in a hard hat and overalls. He ignored Antonia, strode into the house, blew a whistle and shouted. The men came out into the sunlight, groaning, spitting and grumbling. They took turns at the pump, washing their faces. They gathered in a half circle and looked at her.

'Antonia,' she said hesitantly, pointing to herself. She'd read that once: if you're ever in a dangerous situation with a strange man, tell him your name.

The foreman urged the men to work. One of them pointed at her, said something about Larana and looked quizzical.

She nodded. 'Yes.' She pointed at the harbour and the ferry. She said, 'To Larana?' They nodded, yes.

She pointed to herself and then the ferry again, they consulted among themselves, they laughed and nodded, yes.

She spread her hands and pointed to where her watch would have been if she'd been wearing one and asked, 'When?'

They indicated, two.

'Two hours?' She'd still be in time for the plane, then.

They mimed going to sleep and waking up twice. Two days. Or two shifts at least. The foreman was calling other men to work. They waved to her as she walked away. At least she knew where to find water now. The air was getting cooler. The sun was going down.

'ADTODIA! AD - TOD - IA!' She was back near the beach, although she didn't know what she was going to do there. Ray was looking for her. His voice was full of the sound of the blood in his nose. She hid in the wood. Its noises were different now that it was evening. The birds were quieter, the emerging night creatures were gruff. They croaked and rustled. *Thirteen evenings I've been in Larana*, she thought, *and I've never taken notice of how quickly it gets dark.*

' – sorry I lost by tebper. You've dud for by dose good ad proper, so we're quits – dajerous to row id the dark – cub od love, eh?'

She stayed quite still. He was apologizing and you should always accept an apology. He came into view looking worried, dabbing at his nose with a handkerchief. He looked this way and that. He looked straight at her. She remembered the feel of his hand on her head, pushing her down into the water. She started to shake.

He hadn't seen her. He walked right past her and on towards the hill, still calling. Antonia ran to the boat.

It was beached only a few feet from the water's edge but pushing it took all her strength. The effort made her whimper. She bit her tongue to keep herself quiet. As the boat started to move it made a crunching sound and blocked its own way by building up little piles of sugary sand. She had to keep crawling round to clear them away. She was breathing fast. At last the water took the weight of the boat. She climbed in over the stern, stepping on Ray's jacket and covering it with sand. She started to repeat Ray's rowing instructions.

'Brace your feet. Nothing to brace them against. Sit in the middle and pull evenly. Not too deep, wasted effort. You did it before, you can do it again, just pretend it's Crystal Palace Pond. Oh God, oh God, oh *God*.'

With any luck the light would hold. She couldn't see Larana yet but she could still see the island. For most of the trip she'd be able to see either Larana or the island so if the worst came to the worst she could always find her way somewhere. If not to Larana, back to the island and Ray –

What would he do? What was he doing now? He might be trying to swim after her. He might pop up beside the boat and grab an oar. He might drown.

She rested, rubbing her arms and rotating her shoulders. The island was a pale line in the darkness. Larana was not in sight.

He'll drown. I'll be a murderer. What do they do to murderers here? What if they still have capital punishment? Stop this.

A breeze whipped up little waves. The boat rode them easily.

He tried to murder me. How will I make them believe he tried to murder me? Now I sound like Samantha. She groaned with tiredness. *Samantha. I'd forgotten Samantha. I said I'd give her my ticket. That means I'll have to stay. I don't want to stay. I hate it here. Larana, the island. The whole of Larana must once have been like that island, before – I can't stay. Ray will get a lift back on the ferry. He speaks the language. They won't make him wait two days. He might even get back tonight.*

Now she'd reached the place where she couldn't see Larana yet and couldn't see the island any more either. *Halfway* she thought, *it must be halfway.* Her hands stung and she examined plump white blisters on the insides of her thumbs. It would be torture if they burst. But she must go on rowing, she shouldn't have stopped here, now, not even to look at the blisters, this was the one place she mustn't stop because she couldn't see where she was and the only chance was to keep going straight – straight – which way was straight?

And the hand of the witch. That was somewhere here. They tipped her into the sea here so she couldn't come back and haunt them –
She doesn't always do it.
She doesn't always do it.

She rowed through sea as flat as ice. She felt wind on her face but it seemed not to touch the water, not where she was. There were waves all around her but they parted to let her through. Or so it seemed. There was water in the bottom of the boat so she must have passed through some roughness but she hadn't noticed. She looked over her shoulder at a strip of light. With Larana in sight the waves got to her again. The boat bucked and rolled but the lights were getting nearer. She collapsed, exhausted. She pulled in the oars and lay back in the boat. *It doesn't matter*, she thought, *it doesn't matter what happens.* Stars came out in the still sky. When she sat up again, Larana was close. Individual buildings were clear in the darkness. A current was carrying her in.

Samantha said accusingly, 'I've been looking for you. Thought you'd nipped off home without telling me. What about that ticket?' She wheedled. 'You are going to give it to me, aren't you? I'm all packed.'

'I can't give it to you.'

'What?'

'I have to get out of here.'

'You lousy – '

'*Don't start.* I'm going to try and take you home without a ticket.'

'Oh no,' said Samantha. 'They check at the airport. And I haven't got a passport either – '

'Why not? You must have one.'

'I *told* you, the manager's got it and he won't give it to me till the end of the season.'

'You'll have to steal one,' said Antonia.

'*Steal one?*'

'Try and find someone who looks like you. Don't worry about it, they never look properly. And while you're at it I need a white skirt. Clean, size ten. And enough money for a taxi to the airport.'

'Taxi? I thought they sent a coach.'

'You're going in the coach, I need a taxi. Oh look, don't argue, Samantha. I've got enough to think about.'

'I don't steal,' said Samantha, as if she thought she'd been caught in a trap.

'You do now. You've got keys to all the rooms, right? Get on with it. If you want to get home tonight you're going to have to do as you're told.' Antonia spoke with more roughness and ruthlessness than she felt; there were so many risks . . . she watched hope and then dog-like trust spread over Samantha's face. *She trusts me. I'm telling her to steal money, clothes and passports from people's rooms. So now I'm responsible for that too. What am I turning into?*

'You're barmy,' said Samantha. 'No you're not. You're like those blokes who went in and rescued those other blokes from that embassy. You know, those Arabs. Do as you're told and we'll get you out. I watched it on television.'

'Oh, that was just the SAS,' said Antonia. 'I'm temp of the year.'

CHAPTER TWENTY-FIVE

A Bit Big

'It's a bit big,' said Samantha. Antonia gritted her teeth at this statement of the obvious. The shoulders of Ray's jacket hung down her arms and the sleeves concealed her hands.

It was nearly ten o'clock. As agreed, Samantha had brought her luggage and her pickings from the other rooms to Antonia's, having helped as usual with the evening meal to avoid arousing suspicion.

Antonia tucked up the cuffs. 'Any good at sewing?' She meant it as a joke; even if Samantha turned out to be a master tailor there was no time for that. But Samantha looked forlorn. 'I'm no good at anything.'

'Don't start. You got the skirt, didn't you? You're good at stealing.' It was freshly pressed and fitted perfectly. But it was an ordinary enough skirt, it couldn't be anyone's favourite garment, could it? Not one that it would ruin your holiday to lose? She took it off, and the jacket, and folded them carefully into her shoulder bag with a pair of high-heeled shoes. She put on tights, jeans, her own white blouse and sandals. 'Listen carefully, Samantha. I'm a temp. You're a tourist.' Samantha nodded as if she didn't really believe anything. Antonia went on, 'I'm going to get a taxi out to the airport now. You got the money? Good. I'm going out there as myself. When I get there I've got to suss out what the HooRay staff actually do at the check-in desk before I join them. You keep out of sight here till the HooRay bus comes. You'll have to do something about all this luggage.'

'What do you mean?'

'Three suitcases – yours, mine and Catherine's. No point in drawing attention to yourself. You'll have to leave one behind. Yours.' Samantha looked as if she might cry. 'Look. Put as much of your stuff as you can into the other two and *leave the rest behind*. Why should Catherine and I lose our stuff? When the coach comes, put your head down and get on. Don't talk to anybody. Buy a paper and read it.'

'What if that courier bloke stops me?'

'He won't.'

'But – '

'I'm telling you, he won't. Now – '

'"Don't argue"?' Samantha grinned.

'Right. I'm going to give you the ticket. Don't lose it or I'll kill you. When you get to the airport, look for me behind the HooRay desk.'

'What if you're not there?'

'*I will be behind the HooRay desk*. There'll be other people working there too, so make sure when you get to the front of the queue that you give the ticket to me and nobody else so I can give you two boarding-cards. And you give me the passport too. You did get a passport? Samantha? You did manage to get a passport while you were getting the skirt and the money, didn't you?'

'She hadn't got it in her room, the girl I got the skirt off. She's probably got a safe-deposit box.'

'But the one you got the money from, they can't have had a safe-deposit box, can they? Otherwise their money would've been in it.'

'It was blokes. Can't use a bloke's passport, can I? Why can't I use yours? You said they don't look closely.'

'Samantha.' Antonia gripped her fleshy arm. 'Hasn't it sunk in that *I am travelling too*? You really want jam on it, don't you? I'm travelling on my own passport. By myself if necessary. Got that?' Samantha nodded. Antonia tried to think of something to help her. 'Is there a list of people who have safe-deposit boxes?' Samantha said there was. 'Well, wake up then, try one of the others,' said Antonia. 'They'll have their passports in their rooms.'

At least the airport was crowded. Six flights an hour were arriving and departing. Still wearing her own clothes, her

207

HooRay uniform in her bag, Antonia tried to push to the front of the queue to see how passengers were being checked in for a flight to Luton. They protested.

'*Do* you mind?'

'Who are you pushing?'

'Some people.'

'Absolutely ridiculous.'

She couldn't get near. But she noticed that the HooRay staff were all wearing identity badges with their photographs on them.

She went to the ladies and locked herself into a cubicle. She put on Ray's jacket and tucked up the cuffs. She put on the skirt and high-heeled shoes. She straightened the skirt, packed her clothes into her shoulder bag and dabbed powder all over the red blotches of alarm that were appearing on her face. She opened the cubicle door and peeped out. The ladies was empty. She looked at herself in the full-length mirror, did her hair, straightened her shoulders and returned to the check-in area, wondering if she'd get away with not having an identity card.

'There's one. Miss! Miss! Over here! HooRay Holidays?' A woman passenger had spotted her and was clicking her fingers, a plump, angry woman in a tight shiny cotton dress. She was pushing another woman along with her. The second woman carried three full Shoppers' Paradise bags, a holdall, a large sunshade and a multicoloured, waist-high stuffed donkey with a cheerful expression. The second woman broke away from the first; the first grabbed her again. 'Oh no you don't. There's an official here, she'll sort you out and tell you I'm right.'

'What's the trouble?' asked Antonia faintly.

'It's not fair on everybody else. You tell her.'

'What?'

'One piece of hand luggage per person. That's what it says in the book. Ennit? There's lots more stuff I could've brought but I couldn't get it into my suitcase and I went by what it said in the book. Not like *her*. She kept all her rubbish back when she checked in and now she's going to take all that on to the plane.' The culprit looked sheepish. 'Fine thing if everybody did that. There wouldn't be any room for passengers.'

The two women waited for Antonia's verdict. She looked round wildly. A tall streak of a woman in a HooRay jacket and white skirt, an anxiety rash blazing on her neck, was scything through the crowd towards them. As she came within hearing, Antonia flashed a dazzling smile at the warring passengers and told the angry one: 'As long as she understands she'll be surcharged at the other end.' She looked sadly at the culprit and added, 'It might be quite a lot of money, I'm afraid.'

The accuser was triumphant: 'Hear that? You'll be surcharged a lot of money. And serve you right, blooming selfish . . .'

Whizzing by, the HooRay lady dropped a pleased wink at Antonia. The two others strode off in opposite directions, their noses in the air. The HooRay lady disappeared into the toilet.

Seconds later she was out again, still running. With a scooping motion of her hand she indicated that Antonia should follow her to the desk. 'Nice one,' she said briskly. 'Damn trouble-makers, as if we haven't got enough to do . . .' The crowds parted to let them through. There was one girl at the desk, making very heavy weather of processing passengers.

'Is Ray about?' said Antonia quickly. 'He's got my ID.'

'That's what we'd all like to know.'

'I just came out from London today. I'm not due to start till tomorrow but he said you were short-staffed –'

'. . . not kidding, no time to pee . . .'

'But he did say he'd be here, to show me the ropes.'

'We haven't got any ropes, otherwise I'd hang myself. Head office and their bright ideas –'

'I'll go away if I'm more trouble than I'm worth, but I'm sure I'll be able to do something if you'll show me –'

'I didn't mean *you*, love. It's these things. They're supposed to make life easier, not impossible.' Antonia followed her eyes. The other girl was saying, 'Di. Come and have a look at this,' in a tone of resigned exasperation. Di went round the back of the desk and leaned over the shoulder of the girl who was trying to check passengers in with the aid of what was unmistakably a computer.

Suddenly Antonia's blouse was drenched with sweat. She hardly dared look down, she was so sure that she would be dripping on to the floor. Her face must have shown her horror because Di laughed. 'Yes. That's what we think of it too.'

Keyboard, thought Antonia. *Disk drive. Visual display unit. It can't do anything you haven't told it.*

Halfway between laughter and despair, the girl at the

keyboard said. 'According to Mastermind here, this lot aren't on this flight.'

'Of course we are,' said the passengers. 'It's absolutely – '

'You know that,' Di told them. 'I know that. But if the computer says you're not on the flight it won't give you a boarding card. Come on, Mandy. Show me what it's up to now.'

Di stood behind one of Mandy's shoulders and Antonia stood behind the other. *Concentrate, concentrate. If only I'd been on that course –*

If I'd been on the course, I wouldn't be here now.

Mandy pressed CLEAR and the screen went blank. Gold letters came up. FLIGHT HR 7872 LARANA TO LUTON. PASSENGER CHECK IN LIST. DO YOU WISH TO CHECK IN A PASSENGER?

'What does it think I want to do? What does it think I've been trying to do all night?'

WHAT IS THE PASSENGER'S NAME?

'Watch this, Di.' She looked up at the passengers. 'Mr and Mrs Donald Lynch, right, and Alison and Susan?' They nodded.

MR DONALD LYNCH.

NO PASSENGER OF THIS NAME REGISTERED PLEASE INVESTIGATE.

MRS DONALD LYNCH.

NO PASSENGER OF THIS –

'See?' said Mandy.

Di asked the family: 'It is Luton you're going to?' They nodded. She looked at their tickets. 'Oh, look at this, Mandy. It's L-i-n-c-h, not L-y.'

'Course it is,' said the Linches. 'It's on the ticket.'

'Read it wrong, didn't I. Well, I'm tired.' Mandy grumbled as she keyed the names in correctly. The printer clattered and spat out four boarding cards. The queue shuffled forward.

'I could just give this thing a good kick,' said Mandy. 'Can't even spot a simple mistake like that. I mean, if I'd tried to give it a completely different name, all right, fair enough, you'd expect it to get a fit of the sulks . . . Hey, Di, remember the old days when we just wrote the names on a list and ticked them off when they arrived? Who's this?'

'This is . . .'

'Antonia.'

'Antonia. She's just come out from London, to give us a

hand.'

'She must be mad.' The passengers were going through smoothly now. 'Picked up a nice tan in London, Antonia. Nice there now, is it?'

'Yeah, lovely.'

'I expect you've been on a course to learn these things . . .'

'I'm a bit rusty,' she croaked.

'That's all right, so's Mastermind. I do need a break. Can you take over from me when the Gatwick lot get here? I'll finish off the Lutons and you can watch.'

Samantha entered the airport. She looked good. She'd washed her hair and wore a tan skirt, a raincoat and sandals. It occurred to Antonia that that was probably how she'd dressed when she thought she was going to meet her lover. She carried the two suitcases easily as she made her way with the other passengers towards the HooRay desk.

'Here it comes, the charge of the light brigade, ours not to reason why,' said Mandy. 'Okay, Antonia?' She got up and pointed to the chair.

Antonia panicked and said the only thing she could think of. 'Got a Tampax?' Mandy sighed, gave her one and sat down again. Antonia ran to the ladies, catching Samantha's eye and indicating that she should follow.

'What's up?' said Samantha.

'Only got themselves a blooming computer, haven't they?'

Samantha's eyes were like saucers. 'Am I in it?'

'Of course you're not, there's nothing in a computer that someone hasn't put there.'

'D'you know how they work, then?'

'Oh sure. I worked a word processor. Once.'

'You'll be all right then,' said Samantha, with great kindness and faith.

Antonia knew she'd have to get back. 'Whatever you do, don't let anyone except me see your ticket or passport. Just hand them to me and keep quiet.'

'Antonia – '

'What?'

'I didn't manage to get a passport – '

'What?'

'You look like an air hostess in that gear. Couldn't you

211

pretend to be the air hostess?'

'Do - me - a - favour! Ever heard of a temp air hostess? They'll think I'm a hijacker. *God.* I ask you to do one simple thing – now don't cry. *Don't.* It's all right. I've just thought of something. Don't worry, Samantha. Join the queue. Stay as near the back as you can to give me some time. Not actually the back, though. They might notice you're alone. Try and find a man to stand with.'

She went to Arrivals. Couriers from the different companies were checking passengers into coaches. She spotted a blank clipboard on a desk and picked it up. She went over to three lost-looking girls with HooRay labels on their luggage.

'Hi!' she beamed. 'HooRay Holidays? I'm Rae. Hoo are you?'

They stared at her.

'Susie Smith.'

'Anna Gower.'

'Sandra Luff.'

She consulted her clipboard. 'Smith, Gower and . . . Luff. Fine. You're staying at the Esplanada, aren't you?'

'No,' said Anna Gower. 'The Excelsior.'

'The *Excelsior?*' Antonia looked perplexed. 'I thought we had everybody . . . look, I'm terribly sorry, but the coach has gone without you. Never mind. We'll get you a taxi. On the house, of course.' She eyed the other couriers, but they were all preoccupied. She led the girls out of the building and left them waiting while she went over to a taxi and asked in sign language if the driver would take them to the Excelsior. He said he would. 'I've paid him,' she told the girls as they got in. 'Now, if I could just have a look at your passports?' They handed them over. She examined them, made a few marks on her clipboard, said, 'See you at the hotel,' and indicated for the driver to move off.

Anna Gower said, 'Hey, what about our passports?'

Antonia turned away. The taxi hadn't moved. 'We want our passports back.'

'You'll get them at the hotel.'

'We might need them.'

'Oh you and your passport,' said Susie Smith, winking at Antonia. 'It's new, see, her first time abroad. She spent the whole time in the plane looking at herself.'

'I did not,' said Anna Gower, 'but it says in the passport that you shouldn't let anyone have it in a foreign country.'

Other people were looking for taxis. The driver drummed his fingers. 'You're quite right,' said Antonia. 'Out you get, the three of you.'

'What?'

'It's a simple registration procedure. There's a long queue and we usually do it for our clients, but of course if you're not happy –'

The girls laughed and protested. Susie Smith put her hand over Anna Gower's mouth and Sandra Luff cried, 'Of course we're happy,' and Susie Smith said, 'Shut up, Anna, we want to get to bed some time tonight.' The taxi drove off. Antonia thought, *Half an hour to get to the hotel, fifteen minutes to find out they've been tricked. No. Less. The driver'll want his money. They'll have money, won't they? The police won't be called?* She fled once again to the ladies.

She looked at the pictures. Anna Gower's face was too thin. Sandra Luff's hair was much lighter than Samantha's. Susie Smith's was the best likeness, but she had 'mole on left cheek' written under 'Distinguishing marks'.

'That's the first time I've ever seen anything written under distinguishing marks,' Antonia whispered to Samantha as she slipped her the passport in the queue. 'Remember to show your right cheek when you go through passport control.'

'I can draw myself a mole. I've got a felt tip,' said Samantha with dignity.

Antonia returned to the computer. Mandy was still working it. 'Where did *you* get to?'

'Came on early,' said Antonia with a little laugh. 'Better early than never, eh?'

Mandy checked in two men, glancing at their tickets and passports, keying in their names. Out came two boarding cards from the printer. Di supervised the weighing of the men's luggage and its transfer on to a conveyor belt by two local porters.

Antonia tried to edge Mandy out of her seat. 'I'll have a go now,' she said.

'Ticket and passport, please. It's all right, I'm in the swing of it now. You can help Di.' Another group of passengers went through. Samantha was getting nearer. Antonia said, 'It's ever so bad for your eyes, to work those things for hours and hours . . .'

'Telling me.' Mandy squinted at the name on a ticket. '*What's this?* K–i–s–j–n–?'

Antonia snatched it and read out the rest of the name. '–s–k–y. There you are.' She tore pages out of the ticket as she had watched Mandy do and handed it back to the passenger. The printer issued the boarding-cards. 'Tell you what, Mandy. I'll read them out to you.'

Samantha's turn came. She handed Antonia Catherine's ticket and Susie Smith's passport. Mandy started to look up. 'Miss Catherine Lambert,' said Antonia quickly and loudly. 'And Mr Frank Spivey. Got that? That's L–a–m–b–e–r–t.'

Mandy keyed the letters in. The machine hesitated. Then the letters came up, gold on the green screen.

NO PASSENGER OF THIS NAME REGISTERED PLEASE INVESTIGATE.

CHAPTER TWENTY-SIX

Samantha

Samantha stuck out her hand for the boarding-cards that would get her and Antonia on to the plane and home. Clever old Antonia, knowing how to work a computer.

But there were no cards and Antonia was looking as if the computer had pointed a gun at her.

And the real HooRay girl was saying, 'Let's have a look at the ticket.' Samantha was too indignant to be alarmed when Antonia meekly handed it over, doing the one thing she'd told Samantha she must not do. At least Antonia kept hold of the passports.

'Look at this,' said the HooRay girl. Samantha wondered if she should run for it. 'It's *Ms*, not Miss.' The HooRay girl glared so hard that Samantha was on the point of saying it wasn't her fault. The HooRay girl said, 'They only do it to cover up for not being married.'

Samantha thought of all the other things like that that people had said about her in all the different places where she'd lived.

Samantha snores. She says she can't help it but she goes like a lawn mower.

She's accident prone. She's always got a plaster or a bandage on, or her arm in a sling.

She laughs at jokes before they're finished.

Let her miss her turn at cooking, it's safer in the long run.

'That's not true,' she said. Antonia glared at her, *shut up*, and reached over the HooRay girl's shoulder to type in the name like an expert. She must have got it right, they both seemed quite satisfied with what came up on the screen, and Antonia said quickly, 'The other name's Mr Frank Spivey, that's S–p–i–'

'–v–e–y. Got it. Smoking or non-smoking?'

'Non-smoking,' said Antonia.

'Smoking,' said Samantha, but she wasn't heard.

Out came the boarding-cards. Samantha clutched them.

'Passengers for flight HR 7865 to Gatwick should proceed to the departure lounge for embarkation. This is the last call.'

Passengers standing behind Samantha thought this absolutely ridiculous. They wanted to know how it could be the last call when they hadn't checked in.

Samantha didn't wait to hear the answer. She made for the ladies. She stood in front of the mirror with her felt tip pen in one hand and Susie Smith's passport in the other.

'That's the wrong cheek,' said Antonia wearily, coming up behind her. 'Mole on left cheek. *Left* cheek. See? That's what it says, or can't you read?'

Can't even read.

'In the photograph it's on *this* cheek.'

'Yes, but you're looking in the mirror – oh, never *mind*.' Samantha fetched a bit of toilet paper, ran water on to it and started to scrub. One thing about working at the Excelsior, if people had grumbled at her at least she hadn't understood them.

Antonia dodged into one of the cubicles. In seconds she was out again, transformed from her HooRay uniform into an ordinary traveller. She dropped the HooRay jacket into a rubbish bin and covered it with screwed up paper. She carried the white skirt folded in her hands. She was pale and preoccupied.

'Do you remember the room number of the girl you borrowed this from?'

Borrowed? She'd said to nick it. 'We better hurry. That was the last call for the plane.'

'I'd like to send it back to her.'

After all that? To worry about a skirt?

Antonia leaned against the wall and closed her eyes. 'I suppose the management could pin it on a noticeboard marked "lost property".'

After all that? After nothing. They hadn't escaped yet.

As if suddenly realizing the same thing, Antonia snapped her eyes open. 'Come *on*.' As if Samantha were the one who'd been causing all the delays.

But then that was Antonia, Samantha was coming to realize. All over you one minute, biting your head off the next.

With all the rush, the passport control official wasn't even opening people's passports. He gave Samantha an odd look, though. 'Yeah, I do look funny, don't I,' she said. 'Got ink on my face.'

Samantha would have liked the window seat but Antonia took it. She could still see, though. The lights of Larana spread out like magic. Then there was nothing but the black sea with the occasional twinkle of a ship. Soon clouds came round the plane and they were flying through a storm. They dipped and lurched. It was the second flight of Samantha's whole life. She glanced at Antonia to see if she was afraid.

Antonia was staring at the seat in front of her, mouth slightly open, eyes glazed. She hadn't spoken since shouting at Samantha in the ladies. Was she frightened? The plane plunged and soared, everyone went 'Ooh!' and started singing 'She'll be coming round the mountain'. Samantha joined in. She knew she had the sort of singing voice that annoyed people but if everyone took up the chorus her voice might not be noticed.

Still Antonia stared straight ahead. Was she asleep with her eyes open? Samantha stopped singing; then, to test whether Antonia was awake, she whispered playfully: 'What did you go and put us in non-smoking for?'

'No one's allowed to smoke at the moment so what difference does it make?'

The no smoking sign was still on, of course it was, she should have noticed, then she wouldn't have said such a stupid thing. She decided to ask why. People who were angry with you often calmed down a bit if you asked them things, it made them feel clever, Samantha supposed.

'Why? I mean, just as a matter of interest, I don't want to, but I wonder why, with everyone being a bit nervous and everything.'

Slowly Antonia turned her head and looked at Samantha. She looked as if she'd forgotten she was there and wasn't exactly delighted to find she was. 'I expect,' she said, as if talking to a child, 'with it being so bumpy, they're worried about people

217

dropping lighted cigarettes and setting the plane on fire.'

Charming.

Antonia started to laugh.

Now what? Shock, Samantha decided. Yes, that was it, shock. Antonia gasped and roared. Samantha had seen it in films: people getting all keyed up to do something dangerous and then, when it was over, going to pieces. She remembered giggling in class and teachers saying, 'Share the joke, Samantha. No one enjoys a good joke more than I do.' Then they'd send you out of the room.

'What's so funny?'

'I was just thinking, what if the pilot's a temp too . . .'

Oh very funny.

'I was just thinking, we could set up in business, A & S holidays we could call it. I'll arrange the free flights, you and the jellyfish man can do the free accommodation –'

The jellyfish man?

Humour her, that was the best thing.

'How did you get them to believe you were one of them? I mean, they must know who they work with –'

Antonia snorted into a handkerchief. Tears were squeezing out of the corners of her eyes. She could hardly speak: 'I told – them – I knew – they were – short-staffed –'

'Bit risky, wasn't it?'

'Everyone always thinks they're short-staffed! There isn't an office in the *world* that doesn't think it's short-staffed! You know what, I could go *anywhere*, I could be a spy or a private detective or anything, just walk into offices saying, "I'm a temp, you sent for me, I hear you're short-staffed," and they'd say, "Yes, sure, sit down, type this." After all, we all look the same –'

It wasn't *that* funny. Samantha decided to calm her down. 'What are you going to do when you get back?' Antonia stopped laughing and closed her face up tight. Samantha wanted to bite her tongue off. Wasn't very tactful, was it. Antonia wasn't being rescued, for her it was the end of just another holiday; she'd probably have to go straight back to work, perhaps even today. She wouldn't necessarily want to be thinking about it.

Antonia turned the question back. 'What are *you*?'

Samantha realized that with all the excitement she hadn't been thinking about it either. She had this vision of Russel meeting her at Gatwick, explaining what a terrible mistake it had all been, and taking her off somewhere. How could he? He didn't even know she was coming. Maybe if she rang him up, he'd come in his car. She'd have to give him a chance to explain, that was only fair. You couldn't go around thinking the worst of people without giving them a chance to explain.

She had a feeling Antonia wouldn't see it that way, though. She'd have to find a way to get rid of her, once they arrived.

'I'll go home,' she said.

'That hostel? What's it like?'

'It's all right.' It hurt to hear it called a hostel even though it was. 'There's lots of people there.' She tried to make that sound friendly, instead of people talking and moving about all night and the sleeping-in social worker shouting, 'Be quiet, or else. I'll give you one last chance.' At least she'd had her own tiny room in the staff quarters at the Excelsior.

'Can anyone stay there?'

'You have to be under twenty-one. It's mostly people who've come out of care and haven't got anywhere to go yet.'

Antonia stared. 'Is that what you did?'

If Antonia hadn't asked, Samantha had been all set to tell her about leaving the home and coming to London, only now that she'd guessed Samantha didn't feel like talking about it. 'I'll be getting a flat soon.'

'How?' said Antonia eagerly. 'Do you know of any cheap ones?'

People at Overnight were always saying, 'I'll be getting a flat soon,' and they didn't make it sound too difficult. Still, no sense in increasing the competition.

'Looking forward to getting back to work, eh, Antonia?'

'Could we just be quiet?'

Samantha shrugged to show that she didn't care whether Antonia talked to her or not. What was she so angry about? All right, she'd told her that lie about getting married to Russel in that little church with flowers round the door, but she'd told the truth since then. And even that lie had seemed true at the time; it was a dream she'd been having, where had it come from? It must have come from somewhere . . . she screwed up her eyes to remember. He must have mentioned marriage. In fact, she was sure he had, he was going to divorce his wife for her, and that was why he hadn't been able to get to Larana to meet her, trouble with the divorce. And then of course he couldn't have written. Well, you can't write to your fiancée while your divorce is going through, can you? It was all a misunderstanding. Samantha sighed with relief. Like that time in the office, that was a misunderstanding too. And it wasn't so bad, being made love to, even like that. After all, it wasn't supposed to be good for the girl the first time, was it? At least she could say she'd done it.

The storm calmed and the stewardess brought round boxes of food. Samantha cut into a stale roll with a plastic knife and filled it with the wet slice of ham. Antonia said, 'Have mine too, if you want.' Samantha finished her roll, peeled the foil lid of her portion of salad cream and spread it on a lettuce leaf. She took a mouthful and spat it out.

'For God's sake,' said Antonia.

'Sorry, it's horrible. Remember that lovely mayonnaise at the hotel?'

'It made me throw up, I thought you'd remember that.'

'Sorry.' Samantha picked up a cake. 'And thanks.'

'What for?'

'Rescuing me.'

'Oh, for heaven's sake – ' Now Antonia was the one who looked sorry.

The announcement said to fasten seat belts and get ready for landing. Antonia was asleep. Samantha reached gently over and did up her buckle.

They landed with a bump and a roar. Antonia woke up with a little scream. Samantha patted her hand. 'It's all right, we're here.' The sun was coming up but it wasn't the warm, magnificent sun of Larana, just a few lemonade-coloured beams glinting through the grey. 'We're home, Antonia.'

They disembarked. Not until they were standing in the queue at immigration with the man carefully examining other people's passports did they realize and look at each other in horror.

'Are you thinking what I'm thinking?' said Antonia.

'I'll never get in on that girl's passport.'

'I was going to work all that out on the plane. But I went to sleep. What if they send you back?'

What if they send me back? Samantha reached into her bag

and brought out Susie Smith's passport, hiding it with her hand as she slipped it into Antonia's.

'What are you doing?'

'Ssh, hide it, it's probably a crime to travel on someone else's passport. Specially if you stole it in the first place.'

'But what are you going to do?'

Antonia needn't think she was the only person who could work things out. 'Go through by yourself, you don't know me.' Samantha ducked out of the queue, starting to cry. Funny how easy it was to cry. 'I can't find my passport,' she wailed.

'What's your name?' said Antonia, catching on. 'When did you have it last?' She peered around on the floor.

'Go on. Go *through*. What can they do if I say I've lost it? They can see I'm English.'

'What about the luggage?'

'You take your case. I'll pick up Catherine's after I've sorted this lot out.'

'I think I'll take them both,' said Antonia. Didn't trust her even now. Oh well, that was usual.

'There's stuff of mine in both the cases.'

'All right, phone me up at home – ' Antonia swallowed. 'Phone Catherine up at her home, here's the number, and arrange to come and get it. Catherine's going to want to talk to you anyway.'

I want to talk to you in my office, Samantha.

There was no more time to talk. Antonia went through passport control. Samantha waited for the queue to diminish before tearfully approaching the desk. She said she knew she'd had the passport when she got off the plane – didn't want them going back and searching it, checking passenger lists. Someone must have stolen it inside the airport building. 'Will they send me to prison?' she sobbed. Everyone was sorry for her and treated her well. They put her in an office to wait. Someone was coming on duty at ten o'clock who would be able to deal with her. They brought her a cup of tea and an egg sandwich. Obviously she didn't look the illegal immigrant type.

She asked a hurrying secretary, 'Could I phone my dad? He'll be worried about me.'

'Course you can, love. Got any money? Never mind, use the office phone. Keep it short though, eh? Otherwise I'll get into trouble.'

She phoned Forlex and asked for Russel. It felt funny to say his name like that, over the phone. She was put through to his department and the secretary asked who wanted him.

She had a rush of nerves and thought of using another name, his wife's name, but that would be untrusting. 'Just say it's Samantha.' The secretary went away and Samantha heard voices, his voice, she'd know that laugh anywhere. But of course it couldn't have been his voice because the secretary came back and said, 'Sorry, he doesn't work here any more.'

Well, that was disappointing, but it was good if Russel had got himself a new job. 'Can you give me his new number?'

'Sorry. I can't.'

Probably wasn't allowed to. Samantha hung up, not too perturbed. She'd find a way of tricking the secretary into revealing where he'd gone; she obviously wasn't much good as a secretary. Secretaries were supposed to know who worked in a place and who didn't, not go off to fetch them and find they'd left. And in those open plan offices you could see at a glance who was in and who wasn't. A really stupid secretary, Samantha decided, and rude too: she'd hung up.

CHAPTER TWENTY-SEVEN

Catherine

Catherine was already up when the operator called, asking if she would accept a transfer charge call from Gatwick. She'd been drafting a press release about the strike at Bright Girls. Finding a compromise between what was true and what newspapers could reasonably be expected to print needed a sharp, early-morning mind and no interruption; she hadn't been expecting Antonia back till tomorrow. But once she'd heard what had happened she was swiftly on her way to Victoria with money in her purse to pay for Antonia's rail ticket.

Not that Catherine really knew what had happened – Antonia had been somewhat less than coherent. She'd been up all night. And it sounded as if it had been quite a night.

The important thing was that she'd found Samantha and brought her back. And Samantha was in one piece, with a tale to tell. There *had* been a rape. Catherine forced herself to feel fully her regret and outrage and sympathy before relaxing a little into satisfaction at having been vindicated for her dogged pursuit of the matter. There had been a rape. Not the sort of rape that would send a man to prison, not the sort of rape that would even come to court. But the sort of rape that the victim had called by its name at the time, whatever her confusion and distress had led her to say and do afterwards. Not, as a policeman might say, a routine rape, and not eligible for a routine remedy. But something could be done to unnerve the man, to give meagre satisfaction to the victim.

'I hear,' the TV researcher had said, 'that you're leading a campaign of office girls against rape, Miss Lambert.'

223

Standing at the barrier, Catherine wondered, not for the first time, how long she would go on being surprised about these things. Other women weren't; she must be very naïve. Or perhaps being in love with Frank was leading her to soften up on men. She'd have to watch that, she didn't want to fall into the my-man's-an-exception syndrome. (Even though Frank was.) But look. You didn't get to be a TV researcher by being pig ignorant. And this man hadn't rung up to be offensive, on the contrary, he needed her help. So how was it that out of a possible score of three demerits for sexist language in one sentence, he had scored three: leading, girls and Miss? Four if you counted the audible quotation marks around the word 'rape'.

She had explained these points.

'And it's not just about rape,' she had added. 'Sexual harassment and working conditions generally.'

'Would you be able to find us someone who'd suffered, er, sexual harassment in an office, to talk about it on the programme?'

She was disappointed when Antonia arrived alone and alarmed to hear that Samantha had been detained for not having a passport. She had no idea what happened to people who arrived without passports. First things first, though: Antonia was dead on her feet, speechless and depressed. Of course she was depressed, poor thing. Her problems in her marriage hadn't gone away with two weeks in the sun and a mission accomplished. Leading her like a child on to the tube, Catherine respected her silence, breaking it only to mention the plan she had worked out with Frank (who was fine, thanks, still strung up on pulleys and busily radicalizing the hospital staff), that Antonia could take over his bedsitter because when he came out of hospital he and Catherine planned to live together for a trial period. On reflection, Catherine wished she hadn't mentioned this as a reason; tactless to remind Antonia that some people had lovers and some were alone, but Antonia just said, 'Thanks, Catherine.'

Catherine took her home, stopping on the way to buy bacon, eggs and fresh rolls, but Antonia wasn't hungry. She wanted to sleep. For a week, she said. Catherine said that was fine, got out some clean sheets and put them on the bed. Antonia sat in a chair, watching her. 'Come on,' said Catherine gently, helping her off with her clothes. Antonia climbed into bed. She made no sound but her body seemed to whimper with exhaustion and gratitude and loneliness as Catherine tucked her in.

Catherine phoned the Home Office. She said she was a novelist and needed to know what would happen if someone arrived in the country having lost their passport *en route*. The woman at the other end said there would be no serious problem as long as the person was British. (*And white.*) They'd have to make a few enquiries, check that she was who she said she was. But it wasn't an offence to lose your passport, what on earth did Catherine think Home Office officials were?

Antonia slept on. Catherine busied herself quietly with little jobs around the flat. She wanted to visit Frank at the hospital this afternoon but she wouldn't disturb her guest: if necessary she'd just go and leave a note. She wished Antonia would wake up of her own accord though; Catherine wanted to know how and when she was going to meet Samantha. She was longing to phone the TV researcher back to tell him she had somebody for him who had not only been raped in an office but had been spirited abroad as an encore, and abandoned there. Harassment didn't come much more harassing than that.

She happened to be near the phone when it rang; she was tempted to allow it a couple more rings so that Antonia would wake; but that wouldn't be kind. She picked it up. Call box. She heard money pushed in, then there was nothing, then a dialling tone. Catherine panicked. She knew exactly who it was. It was Samantha. She'd lost her last coin. And now she was going to disappear again.

'Reverse the charges,' Catherine moaned. 'Go on, wherever you are. I'll accept it.'

She realized she was still holding the receiver, had been holding it for some time. She banged it down (*oh God, now I've broken the phone*). It rang again.

'Yes? Yes? Hello, this is Catherine Lambert speaking.' There was a long silence after the pips but somebody was definitely there. Hoping not to sound intimidating, Catherine said, 'Is that you, Samantha?'

'Speaking.'

She was real, then. Catherine caught her breath with

excitement, then sank back into anti-climax. 'Welcome home,' she said. It sounded sentimental, melodramatic, but what else could she say?

'I wondered if I could come and pick up my luggage.'

Luggage? *Luggage?* That was all she had to say, she wanted to come and pick up her luggage?

'Of course . . .'

They made arrangements. The banality of it was stifling. Of course Samantha had had a rough night, a rough time. And gratitude was an uncomfortable emotion, a person with low self-esteem might have difficulty expressing it. And Catherine didn't want gratitude. The only thanks she wanted was some expression of . . . spirit.

Was that too much to ask?

'How do you feel about going on television to talk about your experience?'

'On television?'

'Imagine his face when he turns on his set and there's you telling millions of people what he did.'

'What, say his name? So everyone will know what he did?'

That was more like it. Catherine laughed. 'If you say his name, you say it.'

'Would I get paid?'

Had Catherine heard right?

Of course Samantha was right to demand payment, Catherine herself should have raised the matter with the researcher, but did Samantha have to be so crude?

'I'll see to it,' said Catherine shortly.

Antonia stood there, yawning.

'Hello.'

'Hello.'

'How are you feeling?'

'Hungry.'

Frank could wait for once. Catherine cooked bacon and eggs.

'English breakfast,' said Antonia, tucking in.

'Oh, very English. At half-past two in the afternoon. Feel like talking?'

'What about?'

What about? Patiently, Catherine explained that she'd like a few details of how it had all happened, and Antonia obliged.

226

There was a trace more colour in her cheeks than when she'd arrived, but her voice was husky and her eyes still without lights. She talked as she might talk of a day in a particularly troublesome office.

Am I hearing this? Catherine thought. Antonia seemed to take no delight, find no triumph in the tale. *Then I marooned a rat on an island. Then we stole a skirt.* (No, borrowed. Antonia was going to send it back, first thing.) *Then I conned a couple of passports. Now I'm home. Now what?*

Now what? That would be what was bothering Antonia. Catherine repeated her offer concerning Frank's bedsitter.

And again Antonia said, 'Thanks, Catherine.' She didn't seem to be enjoying this at all. She said she'd like to come with Catherine to visit Frank if that was all right. She didn't want to be alone in the flat, thinking of all the things in the past twenty-four hours that might have gone wrong.

'I like it,' chortled Frank, his pulleys creaking. 'I love it! Tell me again!'

Antonia looked from Frank to Catherine and back again as if they were nursery school children and she a teacher running rapidly out of patience with repeat readings of *Peter Rabbit*. 'What do you want me to tell you again for?'

'Because it's brilliant. The way you understood the system so well you could use it against itself.'

'Is that what I did?'

'It's like something out of the Silent Three,' said Catherine.

'Or Modesty Blaise,' said Frank.

'Wonderwoman, please,' said Catherine.

'All right,' said Antonia. 'How *do* you get to be a private detective?'

'They never seem to say in novels,' said Catherine. 'It's always something that's happened before the book starts.'

'I'm not talking about *books*. In real life.' Antonia looked demandingly from one to the other. They were the teachers now, and she the child. For the first time, it seemed to Catherine, real life had returned to her face, but what was she *talking* about?

'I've heard,' said Frank, 'that private detectives are often people who've been thrown out of the police force after getting caught beating up suspects or taking bribes.'

'*Getting caught* being the operative phrase,' said Catherine. 'Antonia, you're not really thinking of becoming a private –'

'Becoming one? She's one already.' Frank was laughing again. 'Daring sea voyages – computer fraud – missing persons –'

'She'd do better to join the Salvation Army if she's interested in missing persons.'

But there was no stopping Frank now. 'That's what you do, Toni –'

'Antonia.'

'Antonia. Join the police – '

'What qualifications do I need?'

'Literacy helps, I think,' said Catherine sourly. 'But it's not essential.'

'Don't take any notice of her, she's a left-wing trouble-maker. Join the police. Learn everything you have to know at their expense. Driving. Self-defence. Computers, fingerprints, all that. Then leave and set up on your own. That's what accountants do –'

'Accountants?'

'What?'

'Sure. A few years in the Inland Revenue learning all the tricks, then they go private and teach 'em to their rich clients.'

'Well, I'm surprised at you, Frank,' Catherine snapped. 'You're a trade unionist in England in the 1980s and you're encouraging a perfectly nice young woman to join the police.'

'Only to rip them off.'

Antonia interrupted: 'If your flat got burgled, who would you call?'

No answer to that, of course. As Catherine looked into Antonia's eyes she decided they were a little feverish. Antonia was still pretty phased out – sleep deprivation, disorientation, jet lag, fear, all were classic ways to drive a person temporarily mad. This would turn out to be just another of her impulses. She'd think of a more sensible career to pursue. In the meantime it would cost Catherine nothing to be kind. And honest. 'I'd call the police,' she admitted, 'unless of course there was a good women's detective agency I could go to.'

CHAPTER TWENTY-EIGHT

Antonia

Catherine fussed with disgust round Frank's bedsitter when she took Antonia there to settle her in. 'Honestly,' she said, 'fancy leaving it like this to go on holiday.' Antonia was amused. Catherine was acting like a wife embarrassed by her husband's personal habits. The place wasn't that bad. A couple of hours would set it to rights and even if it had appeared spotless she would have had to give it a good clean of her own before she could settle in comfortably.

Catherine wiped a few surfaces and took the sheets off the bed. Antonia teased her: 'Look at you, clearing up after him.'

'It's not for him. It's for you.'

'Well stop it.' Antonia's amusement was turning to fear. Catherine had been alone too long suddenly to live happily with a man who wasn't as tidy as she was. A few weeks after he came out of hospital they'd break up and Frank would want his room back. This would be the first of a series of bedsitters Antonia would occupy while their owners went on holiday, were ill, had love affairs. The rooms would get worse and worse until she ended up in a doss house.

'I'll give you a hand to make it livable – '

'Don't bother, Catherine.'

Catherine and Frank would not break up. They were madly in love, anyone could see that. It was only a matter of adjusting. Frank would have to get domesticated and Catherine would have to be less fussy.

Adjust, that was what you had to do when you lived with someone. If you lived alone, you didn't have to adjust, you could please yourself.

That's it. I can please myself.

'I'll see you later then, Catherine,' she said firmly. They'd arranged to be together in Catherine's flat to watch Samantha on television and have a few drinks and a meal.

Alone, she explored the bedsitter properly. One thing it didn't lack was writing paper. Boxes and boxes of Croxley Script. She was sure Frank wouldn't mind if she took a sheet and used his typewriter.

'Dear Mrs Hook, I expect you'll be surprised to hear from me after all this time . . .'

What do I say next?

'*I now have experience with computers . . .*'

I'll do the washing and think about it.

She took her suitcase down to the launderette. She opened the case and smelled the rich smells of the Mediterranean. She watched her washing go round. When she took her things out they were all covered with blue fluff and bits of thread. Her denim dress was the culprit, coming to pieces where she'd cut the hem. She ditched it, took the rest of the stuff home and spent hours picking bits of blue from the rest of her clothes. It was fiddly work and the skin on her hands still pricked and stung from the rubbing of the oars, but she did it with savage pleasure, getting rid of that stupid pretence that she could give up everything and live in rags on a beach. She looked for a Hoover but couldn't find one. So she set to work on the carpet with a dustpan and stiff brush so that at least she could walk barefoot over it without feeling it was full of crumbs.

I expect you'll be surprised to hear from me after all this time.

All this time? All this time nothing, she'd only been gone two weeks. It took longer than that to stop being angry with someone who'd hurt you, disappointed you, let you down, and in the meantime anything could happen: you could get a new temp of the year, a new wife.

From her window she could watch workers trickle and swarm down into the underground at half-past five. Her longing to be with them, one of them, was like a sharp ache in her gut, but her need to smoke, as she might have once, was quite dead. (*Give up smoking, you can give up anything.*) But, oh, to have a job again, a nice little job, not too much to do, not too little, appreciative boss, good crowd of people who you could have a laugh with; a job lasting about three weeks, a week to learn it, a week to settle, a week to think about moving on . . .

Not that the commuters looked particularly happy to be working, but you didn't, not when you took it for granted. (Catherine had lent her money and made her promise to sign on for social security, but that was a stop-gap, she couldn't live like that.) Some of the commuters looked miserable but they might just be tired or have something on their minds.

What if she went up to one of them and said, 'Excuse me, have you got a problem I could help you with? I'm a private detective.' (Were you allowed to say that? Or was it like calling yourself a doctor, you had to have qualifications, pass exams, or you could be done for fraud?)

Someone might have had something stolen.

Someone might have gone missing.

Someone might want his wife watched in case she'd been unfaithful.

(There'd be none of that. She'd be choosy about which cases she took.)

They'd think she was mad.

No, no, that would be a ridiculous way of going about it. She'd advertise, much better. *Girl in London*, places like that. *Antonia Lyons: Private Investigator*. (Investigator was better than Detective. Vaguer.) The magazine might even send someone to do an interview.

Missing Persons a Speciality.
As Advertised on TV.

When she went round to Catherine's she was surprised to find Samantha there. Antonia had thought she'd be at the TV studio. But they'd recorded the programme earlier in the day.

Catherine seemed intensely nervous as the programme progressed towards Samantha's bit. Samantha didn't seem too bothered one way or the other. She just ate and ate. But when she came on she was transformed. Her hair shone, her make-up was perfect. She neither whined nor hesitated as she told her story. It was her own voice, she wasn't putting anything on, but it was low and calm and sadly angry. Antonia knew that if it had been her she'd have been a gibbering idiot. Or she'd have made a fool of herself trying to sound smarter than she was. But

231

Samantha was – what was the word?

'Professional!' said Catherine, well pleased. 'You looked really professional, Samantha.'

But 'Rotten pigs' was all Samantha would mutter, through a mouthful of brown bread and bean shoots.

'Why?'

'They left out all the bits where I said his name.'

'Why?'

'They said I couldn't if it wasn't proved in court. I said, why not, it's true. They said even so. I said his name anyway, but –'

'They edited it out? Typical,' Catherine soothed. 'Never mind, good for you for trying.'

'D'you think Russel saw the programme?' said Antonia.

'Did he ever. I sent him an anonymous letter telling him to watch. Lousy swine.' Antonia was pleased to see Samantha full of hate for the man; she'd begun to wonder. And Catherine seemed pleased too. Samantha went on: 'I wanted him to be watching with his wife and kids when his name came up. Even that'd be too good for him.'

'We could still try for a prosecution,' said Catherine. 'I'll help all I can, though I doubt –'

'No. Not worth the bother, is it?'

Catherine said, 'Quite honestly, I think your best revenge now would be to get on with your life and forget all about him.'

'Yeah,' said Samantha. 'Yeah, that's what I'll do.' And then she revealed her plans.

At first Antonia thought she hadn't heard right. Catherine had just said, 'Did they pay you?' and Samantha had replied, 'Did they ever. They wanted to send me a cheque but I said cash or I don't go on.'

And then Samantha had said, 'That and a week's social security and I can get one of them bucket shop flights back to Larana.'

'Back to – '

'Back to – ?'

Samantha had worked it all out. She was going to need a job, wasn't she? And she wouldn't be able to get anything except cleaning, would she? Possibly not even that. But she already had a job as a cleaner which she must have been daft to walk out on but she might be able to get it back, or another one, similar.

'I mean, why be a cleaner in London when you can be a cleaner in the sunshine and go on the beach in your time off?'

Catherine looked as if she would spit bullets. But she couldn't think of any good arguments against what Samantha had said.

'We *must* be able to think of something better than a cleaner for you to be.'

'Such as what for instance? Cleaning's all right.'

'After we – after Antonia went to all that trouble to rescue you.'

'It doesn't matter,' said Antonia.

It was a bright, chilly morning. Was the summer over? It was still August. She went into Red Rose Staff Services, did a few tests and registered as a temp.

'Nothing right now, Antonia, but we'll be in touch.'

We'll be in touch, I'll meet you tonight by the rock pool and all your troubles will be over.

No wonder he didn't turn up. I only told him one real thing about myself, as if that was all there was to know. I've been assuming he didn't come because he was disgusted, he might just have been bored.

Wait till I've got a few more solved cases to talk about, they won't care what else I've got and even if they do I won't, I'll be a VIP.

An aeroplane cut through the high blue sky, a silver dot with a trail of white. Samantha was a cleaner.

Catherine wouldn't accept it, couldn't believe that Samantha accepted it, that she'd be a cleaner to the end of her days. In the sun, though. A cleaner in the sun.

A cleaner in the sun.

An appetite for stars.

Of course Catherine accepted it. She'd fretted and tutted and seen Samantha off at the airport. Catherine talked herself into muddles occasionally but she was no fool. She knew you couldn't go round rescuing people who didn't want to be rescued, helping them over roads they didn't want to cross. Antonia would remember that when she was a private detective.

She walked twice past the police station and went into a hamburger place for a coffee.

She toyed with a few fantasies.

A hooded gunman bursts in and holds up the girl at the till. Antonia fells him with a rugby tackle and a few Kung Fu blows.

A divorced mother's children are kidnapped by their father who takes them to a foreign country. Soon Antonia is on a plane.

The computer breaks down in a secret government department. No, a hospital. The computer is the only place where the secret formula for a life-saving drug is stored. (*Do hospitals keep things like that on computers? See, you don't know anything.*) Only one person in the world knows how to fix the computer and that person is Antonia.

Ridiculous, she thought.

But if she joined the police, even for a few months to learn things as Frank had suggested, it would be like going back to school, wouldn't it? Uniforms, homework and lessons. Would she be able to stay long enough to learn anything useful? She was used to moving on after three weeks.

Her advertisements would look better, though, if they said, *former police officer.*

Wouldn't hurt to go in and ask, would it? She needn't give her name.

They might ask, though, and she couldn't give a false name, not to the police. They'd have ways of knowing.

Still, even if she gave her own name, it didn't hurt to ask for information. Asking for information didn't commit you to anything. Couldn't force her to join, could they? She walked quickly up the steps of the police station. A brown-eyed young policeman looked her over. 'What can I do for you, love?'

'A friend of mine wants some information about joining the police, you know, leaflets and details and . . .' her voice tailed off, sounding stupid.

The policeman smiled into her eyes. 'Does he, now? How old is he?'

'It's for me,' she retorted, standing her ground, staring stonily back at him.

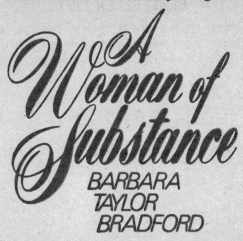